The Helicopter Pilot

- A Novel -

DISCARD
HAMILTON PUBLIC LIBRARY

By Darcy Hoover

This is a work of fiction. Any names or characters, businesses or places, events or incidents, are fictitious. Any resemblance to actual persons, living or dead, or actual events is purely coincidental.

Copyright © 2018 by Darcy Hoover

All rights reserved. No portion of this book may be reproduced in any form without permission.

Cover by Darcy Hoover

For my good friend Juan Lemus,

I reflect on cappuccinos along the Moroccan coast, riding ornery camels through desert dunes, and sussing out dubious bars in South American jungles. You are sorely missed.

Chapter 1

It is Edward's first time in Africa. He navigates the secure echoes and cool air-conditioned cement of the terminal alongside his fellow passengers. Like cattle led to slaughter, herded down narrow corridors without option, tired eyes attempt to locate signage to ratify their progress and the multiple turns, yet after an age, they enter the clamour of the arrivals hall. Edward fills out the arrival form with sweaty hands and dull pencil, then joins the queue at a wall of formidable cubicles and serious men. His heart races and at last, it is his turn and he is through. He envisioned demands for bribes and cumbersome questions but there were none. He finds the luggage trolly and is pleasantly surprised that his bags survived the journey of tight connections, yet another fortuitous headache anticipated for naught. At long last, he stands at the doors to the outside. With feigned confidence, he steps briskly out into the open, and is promptly enveloped by the warm, moist air of the East African evening.

Met with soft yellow light and a sporadic pelt of taps on bare aluminum that resonates through and above the din of voices,

Edward takes a slow breath. It has begun to rain. His eyes dart nervously amongst the busy throng, taking care not to catch any eye. His mind strains to absorb the sea of dark skin and bright colourful fabrics, foreign and exotic to his inexperienced point of view. He yearns to blend, however unrealistic. Hence he feeds his trepidation in his quest for predators, almost disheartened with their absence. He is sure they exist, hidden amongst the kaleidoscopic colours. He realizes his judgement is underdeveloped, and for this, he will take great care. His fear lingers just below the surface, more of being taken for a fool than any physical danger, but there's that too. Edward smiles, *Here he is, the explorer.* A dream fulfilled, or at least, a distant hope achieved via providence. No one else would agree to the assignment, therefor here he stands; Edward in Africa, the man who relented. Edward's chest tightens yet again; the tightness that has plagued him since he agreed to this remote posting. He consciously releases the tension. Vexed with anxiety, he endeavours to gain mastery over it, and feels more the man.

His field of vision is stolen by a cheerful black face, and he involuntarily steps back. His heart thumps loudly in the back of his ears.

"Hello Sir," boomed a deep voice.

Momentarily stupefied, Edward recovers his bearing. A well-dressed and overweight African, skin damp with sweat, stands before him expectantly. He appears pleasant enough. Edward notes aggressive young men clamouring for fares as passengers spill from the terminal.

"Thank you, but I have a driver," said Edward.

"I am your driver Sir."

Edward raises his eyebrow and recalls the warnings; people driven off and robbed, even killed, chopped up by witch doctors and sold piecemeal on the black market for magic, or waking in a tub of ice with fresh stitches and a missing kidney. He recalls deflecting his colleges taunts of risk with jokes and bravado. Now he flounders. His stomach churns.

"Sir, I take your bag?"

On the edge of panic, Edward grips his luggage tightly.

"You are?" He croaks.

The answer to this query will assure the identity of his driver. Then Edward realizes he doesn't know the answer to his own question. Having read and reread the arrival instructions a hundred times on the plane, visible strain grows across his face as he struggles to locate the name somewhere in the recesses of his mind. Conceding failure, Edward releases his death grip on his luggage and digs frantically through his backpack, and eventually holds up the paperwork with satisfaction. He adjusts his glasses and reads to himself.

"Are you Abdul?"

He realizes too late that this sweaty fellow could be anyone agreeing to anything. His heart pounds at the realization of his mistake.

"Yes, *Blother*, I am Abdul, let us go, the drive to the hotel is very far."

Desperate for the induced calm of only moments before, Edward tries again to gain the advantage. Abdul watches patiently. Edward stuffs the paper roughly into his back pocket, yet struggles with the nonchalance, for he desperately wants to fold the paper neatly and file it away in the proper compartment of his backpack.

He breathes deeply and regains his composure. "Which hotel was it again Abdul?"

Abdul looks at this strange emotional man with interest.

"Which hotel you want *Blother?*"

Edward's composure visibly weakens yet again. He catches himself.

"Which hotel have I been booked into? I forget," he lied.

"Where do you want to stay *Blother*? I can take you anywhere you want, no problem."

Edward stares at Abdul's cheerful face, yet finds no malice. He takes a deep breath and resigns himself to whatever fate has in store. He is tired.

"Abdul, I already have a hotel. Take me there please."

"Holiday Inn?"

"Yes! Yes! Holiday Inn!" exclaims Edward. Not in country for even an hour and he has already proven himself resourceful and capable. His chest puffs as the heat of his fear drains away as if it never was.

"Let's go to your car Abdul."

Reflected reds and blues of the evening's lights dance in raindrops on the window but fail to hide the industrial chaos. From the rear seat of Abdul's car, Edward watches squares of light from high factory windows whip past behind silhouettes of power lines, poles and transformers. Mayhem, raised fists and incessant horns from far too many vehicles sparing within an infrastructure long outgrown confounds Edward. He sneers at the audacity of the Chinese motorcycles as they zip effortlessly amongst the heavy traffic, the troubadours with unstrapped helmets donned backwards, while others sport children's bicycle helmets or safety helmets from construction sites. One fellow looks ridiculous with a traffic cone on his head. The fearless riders sport dirty heavy winter coats, which Edward cannot fathom in this muggy equatorial heat, and worn backwards, the hood hangs useless and lifeless on the chest. He stares incredulously at the loads balanced on brazen motorcycles, with women in colourful kangas laden with grocery bags and babies while other small children cling for dear life, or with cargo of multiple queen-sized mattresses and large flat screen TVs attached with cheap yellow nylon rope.

Edward turns inward to avoid witnessing an accident and notes the huge bottle of Monte Carlo cologne attached to Abdul's dashboard. If Abdul had used any, it does little to stem the raw body odour that assaults the nostrils. Edward does not consider that the offensive scents may be his own. They drive and drive while Swahili rap blasts from Abdul's car radio, incoherent and distorted, as one song blends into the next and erases time. Jarred fiercely over endless potholes with impotent suspension, it outstrips Edward's illusion of how things should be, and fatigued, he fights and loses the battle with his weighted eyelids and drifts into slumber.

Edward awakes with a start as bared teeth hover over him. The possibility of a robbery underway drifts into his wakened consciousness but the teeth belong to a smile that suffocates the thought. As his slumber ebbs, he realizes they've arrived. The happy uniformed concierge holds the car door open for him expectantly. Quickly recovered, Edward jumps from the vehicle's tainted air into the well-lit hotel entranceway and takes a deep breath of the heavy air. He watches the concierge struggle to extract his luggage from the boot. Since he had not yet obtained any foreign currency, Edward figures in lieu of a tip, he'll be extraordinarily polite.

"Thank you," beams a cordial Edward as he aggressively wrests his luggage from the concierge. "I've got it, thank you!"

Awkward and red faced Edward extracts his remaining suitcase with a grunt.

Abdul shakes his head as he disappears into his small Toyota. With the stuttered grind of an injured starter, followed by a hiccup and a cough and a proud puff of black smoke, gears are found and Abdul disappears into the heavy stream of noise, fumes and metal.

Edward strives to play the experienced ex-pat as he casually surveys the Holiday Inn lobby. There are African businessmen engaged on cell phones, a vacation-dressed Caucasian couple waits on someone, and a rugged fellow chats with two youthful local ladies. He waits for another large African in a colourful robe to complete his business, and then saunters up to the dark wood of the desk. Certainly this *International jet-setter man-of-the-world* business isn't as scary as he had been led to believe.

The check-in is uneventful for they expected him, and Edward even attains local currency at a reasonable rate. The bellboy offers escort to his room, but is dismissed with a shake of head and false smile. Edward manhandles his luggage into the small mirror lined elevator and pushes the worn brass number seven.

With a slight delay as the metal cables take up the slack followed by a disconcerting jolt, Edward begins his ascent. He reads the laminated hotel advertisement stuck to the elevator's mirror, praising the virtues of their fine breakfast buffet and their rooftop bar. He struggles with his luggage over the thick carpet, and notes the quaint African motif of the hallway as he finds his numbered door. His room is dated and timeworn and he avoids inhaling the musty scent too deeply. Edward sets his luggage aside and takes stock. Accustomed to the movement of his voyage, he doesn't desire quietude. It is his first night in Africa, hence Edward decides a drink at the rooftop bar is in order. He looks for a safe and doesn't find one, so he stuffs everything of value into his pockets and heads for the roof.

The rooftop bar is surprisingly busy for a Tuesday evening, and with a quick glance Edward realizes that the clientele is predominately of the fairer sex. Obscure flashes of fluorescent light reflect off contemporary fabrics and dance with dark skin and phosphorus teeth amidst the throbbing beat. It is foreign and an effort yet he forages ahead into the murk. Eventually he finds himself a vacant seat and awaits service, content to be seated and somewhat grounded. Edward is out of his element and takes pleasure in this. As his eyes adjust, he realizes that a young lady now stands in front of him.

"Mind if I join you?" she asked.

Edward's eyes open wide, his fear unveiled. He makes an ugly face to display discomfort, his disapproval, his disinterest. Unfortunately she does not take this as rejection and sits beside him on the couch. Edward wishes he had stayed in his room.

"I've not seen you here before," she said. A fairy-like waif, she is young and pretty and appears disconcertingly innocent to Edward. She smiles warmly and Edward melts a little. The waiter arrives, and the young lady speaks with him in Swahili. Despite himself, Edward notices the smooth dark skin of her long lithe legs. She is exquisite and dark, and a slight whiff of her perfume makes him reconsider every decision he has ever made. She puts a warm hand on his thigh.

"You can maybe buy a drink for my friends too?" she asked, with a simultaneous nod towards a happy group a table away, their glasses raised to greet. Edward turns towards the table and smiles at her friends, and realizes the trap has been set.

"Certainly not!" exclaimed Edward. He jumps up too quickly and knocks the table. A wooden menu stand and a flower vase with a single plastic rose fall over. Flustered, Edward stumbles amongst the tables through the darkness and heavy beat. Although the music is loud, he imagines he hears their laughter. He dares no rearward glance as he scrambles to the elevator, returning to the embrace of his room.

Chapter 2

The heaviest sleep, born of exhaustion, carries Edward blissfully into the morning. His shower is tepid. He ran the hot water at length to no avail. Naked and awkward, Edward steps into the weak cool stream with the small hotel soap, his lips pursed tightly to prevent contamination. Afterwards he dries himself with an off-white towel with faded stains and rough on his skin. He digs through his luggage for suitable attire, and dressed, refreshed and ready to face another day, he locks his luggage and heads downstairs.

The breakfast buffet appears inviting, *but this is Africa*, he reminds himself, and who knows what is tainted with norovirus, salmonella, e-coli, typhoid, hepatitis, Ebola or rat feces? Then again, he'll be here for six weeks and he's hungry. He settles on toast.

As Edward eats, he watches his fellow travellers of the Dark Continent, and what wild men they must be, brave and adventurous and hard men, much like himself.

"Are you Edward?" boomed a voice and Edward jumps, spilling tea in his lap.

"Mike," stated the man who towers over Edward. "Guess we're headed in together."

Edward looks up from his wet lap with a grimace and sees a man who obviously commands far more space than he occupies. Edward recognizes that he is in the presence of something solid, an entity immovable and certain. Mike looks at Edward as well, and sees a thin, awkward fellow better suited to sort mail in a post office than to fly helicopters in Africa. Edward's mouth is agape, with a look of confusion, and stares at the man before him. Mike snorts.

"I'm the guy who sorted all your security crap. The boss gave me your photos so I could pass them along to the base security staff. But that was last tour, I figured you'd have gone in by now."

Edward doesn't understand, yet feels a need to satisfy Mike's curiosity.

"I had personal commitments."

"Aha, sweet. Full six week tour?"

"Yes."

"Then I guess we're stuck together Ed."

"Edward," he corrects.

"Ed-Ward," Mike said. "Right."

Mike pulls out a chair and seats himself at Edward's table.

"So Ed, first time in Africa I gather?"

"Yes, how can you tell?"

"Manager got a kick out of all the stupid questions you were asking."

Mike smiles and Edward is unsure whether he should feel offended. He tries to recall which of his questions might be construed as stupid. He had asked many questions. He still wonders when Mike interrupts.

"I saw you last night in the lobby, but I was busy."

Edward remembers the rugged fellow chatting with the two girls.

"Sisters," said Mike. He winks. "You didn't take to Kidawa too well, did you Ed?"

"Ed-ward. Who is Kidawa?"

"The sexy little number I sent to your table last night." Seeing the absent look of confusion on Edward's face, Mike added, "In the bar dude. You'd think I'd sent a rattlesnake the way you bolted." Mike laughed. "She's a sweetie."

Once again, Edward wonders if he is being insulted. He is equally uncertain whether he likes or dislikes Mike.

"So we're heading down to the base in about an hour. You'll like it Ed."

"Ed-ward. Is it safe?"

With a straight face Mike added, "A fresh lad like you, they'll have you stewing in a pot before sundown."

An hour later Mike's hotel room phone rings. He walks over and picks it up.

At the other end Edward waits for a response, then realizes there won't be one. "I don't think I'll make the trip, I have a bad stomach."

Mike rolls his eyes, drops the phone receiver to his side and looks out the window. After a long moment, he moves the receiver back to his ear.

"How the hell do you think the stock holders are going to make any money if their pilots can't show up for work Ed? Suck it up and throw a spare pair of gitches in your carry-on. See you downstairs." He hangs up.

Mike looks over from the front desk when Edward stumbles out of the elevator, clumsy and awkward with too much luggage. The same bellboy from the evening before moves to help, then reconsiders. The concierge gives him a stern look, so he saunters over grudgingly. Edward refuses him. Edward leaves his luggage by the front door and shuffles to the desk. He's pale and drawn, and makes a show of his discomfort. Mike watches Edward's opus in amusement while the lady behind the front desk prints his receipt. She then neatly folds the paper, inserts it with flare into an envelope, and hands it to Mike, accompanied with a wink. Mike returns the wink with sly grin.

As Mike walks by Edward, slumped on the lobby couch, he said, "Get cracking Ed, Abdul will be here any second." He then continues outside with a worn backpack over his shoulder.

"Edward," Edward corrects. "Where's your luggage?"

"This is it," Mike answered, already half way out the door.

Edward completes his checkout, and accepts the receipt with a solemn face, and takes the time to place it neatly in the proper compartment of his backpack. The receptionist does not smile. Feeling damp, sweaty and nervous, with a disconcerting burbling in the depths of his guts, Edward reluctantly throws his backpack over his shoulder, collects his heap of luggage and heads to the car. He is somewhat relieved to travel with someone who knows his way around, however unpleasant he may be.

Despite the enveloping warmth of the evening prior, Edward is unprepared for the onslaught of humidity and heat that greets him as he walks from the Holiday Inn's air-conditioned lobby out into the open air. Cool rivulets run down his back as he breaks out in sweat. Edward inhales deeply and stolidly bears the scorched air that fills his lungs. While his eyes adjust to the glare, he cannot find beauty in any of it. There is only unpainted cement bleached in sunlight, with dust and garbage strewn about. The Holiday Inn driveway is at the juxtaposition of two busy streets, which merge only feet away. The horns blare, accompanied by a dizzying amount of movement, aggression and obvious desire to occupy the same space, the victor determined only by a coward's relent. It fills Edward with dread. Tires squeal and a car swerves sharply into the Holiday Inn driveway and Edward cringes with the fierceness of it. Abdul stomps on his brakes and the front end of his car dives with the sudden loss of momentum and the cologne on his dash sloshes wildly in its large glass jar.

   Abdul remotely pops open the trunk then rolls out with his perpetual smile, then takes the hand of the concierge in his own and they kiss each others cheek. Abdul treats the concierge as a long lost brother. Edward surmises that Abdul treats everyone in this manner. Edward continues to manhandle his luggage to the rear of the car when suddenly Mike intercedes. He quickly grabs the handle of the largest bag, and with a single fluid movement the behemoth is up and over the trunk's edge. Mike quickly positions it in Abdul's capricious trunk to make room for the other bags. With more deft grace the second and third bags are stored for the voyage as well.
   Before Edward can thank him, Mike smiles. "Hate to see you soil yourself before we leave the hotel!" Mike winks. "And besides, I have to sit next to you. Smells bad enough in there

already." He gives the concierge a solid handshake, and slips into the right seat. Edward struggles with the left door latch then wiggles in. Abdul is soon behind the wheel and with everyone settled in, the starter whines, the Toyota coughs, gears grind, and Abdul eases the nose gently into the mechanical stream.

"Thank you Mike."
"No worries Ed."
"Edward," Edward corrected.

In stop and go traffic, they lurch forward as the engine roars to satisfy the demand of Abdul's heavy foot, then immediately the seatbelt digs into Edward's lower abdomen as Abdul fills the desired gap. Each tap of Abdul's brake pedal causes the Toyota's nose to plunge and Edward's sphincter to clench. It is untenable, and aggressive beyond anything Edward has ever experienced. It's a battle of who possesses the greatest desire to move forward, and Abdul's desire is great. Edward smiles apologetically at the other drivers and passengers, who pass inches from his window. They stare back blankly.

Mike pats Abdul warmly on the shoulder, "That's it Abdul, work your magic!" Mike laughs deeply, and it resonates throughout the interior of the car.

The traffic does eventually ease, and consequentially the vehicles settle into their rightful hierarchy, dependant on the pugnacity of their drivers. The traffic begins to open and breath and Edward doesn't need to fight the urges of his bowels so diligently, yet hard clunks as the suspension bottoms out over the numerous potholes causes him to wince. Edward watches the busy hustle of an urban East Africa. Fellow commuters stare down at him with vacant eyes through the dusty windows of overcrowded *Matatus*, passenger vans that remind Edward of *Scooby Doo's Mystery Machine*, the public transport of choice as the three-wheeled *Tuk Tuks* have recently been outlawed within the city limits. The *Matatus* course freely amongst the heavy traffic like trout in a stream. There is always one fellow who hangs from the open door and hails pedestrians for fares as they cut across multiple lanes in complete disregard, with brightly coloured themes and slogans painted on every available space of every van. These range from *God is Great* to *Snipers Rule* or *Spanish Guitar* with a hand painted facsimile of Hendrix, or *On God We Trust* with a painting of a Magnum .44, or the reasonable *Be Hopeful*. Edward asks Abdul about a *Wasi Wasi Wenu* painted in large letters across the rear of one van, and Abdul explains that it is Swahili for *Your Worries Are Not My Worries*. Edward spends some time contemplating that.

Behind the intoxicating dance of the *Matatus* the city takes on an ephemeral quality, with peeled paint and crumbled cement of the buildings proper, peppered with mounds of garbage and grazing cattle, giving way to rough hewn buildings of no permanence whatsoever. It's as if there is no future, only the now, a struggle to maintain what is. As they proceed further from the city centre, small primitive shops begin to line the roadside. Seemingly no more than poles cut from nearby trees tied haphazardly together, then covered by sheets of corrugated aluminum, with all manner of plastic container that hang unkempt and chaotic. The tenants sit behind hastily constructed tables that offer wares of cheap Chinese sunglasses, purses, and bottled water. A strong breeze and tomorrow it could all be gone. Rather than portray despair, the image before Edward begs for hope and a strong desire to move forward against all odds. It is humanity's struggle. These are impoverished people, yet they are entrepreneurs with self-made businesses to provide for their families. Edward sees only squalor.

As they drive, even the endless stands of impromptu markets wither in number, replaced by the odd rudimentary enterprise sandwiched between garages of broken cement, goats, rusty barrels and wheel wells, with worn tires stacked high. Edward ceases to focus on the scene laid out before him and allows his mind to drift to the neatly manicured lawns and artistically patterned gardens of his home. The images float by pleasant and calm and he allows himself freedom within his mind's eye, as each memory carries him closer to comfort and home. There is a jolt as another pothole is met with brutal harshness and he's dragged back to Africa and now. As his mind recalibrates, clouds of seagulls fill the heavens and Edward wonders the cause. His eyes cast downward to see why the scavengers have gathered. He finds a sea of garbage that stretches to the horizon with great yellow bulldozers belching smoke amid colossal mountains of mixed colours that fall before their might. Suddenly the air reeks of rot and foul things and Edward shuts his mouth firmly and shallows his breath. He contemplates pulling his shirt over his nose then notes that Mike and Abdul are nonplussed, so he simply limits the movement of air through his lungs. Edward surveys the scene laid out, and he is shocked to see people pick through the refuge, and he thinks he even recognizes makeshift domiciles amongst the great mounds of waste. Abdul begins to overtake a truck that blocks Edward's view and they bounce alongside the rusty red container. There is impatience and frustration as Edward wishes to consolidate what he thought he had seen. As they finally pass the truck, they enter a large roundabout and the car careens around and exits in another direction and it is gone.

Further and further from the heart of the city they travel, through the outskirts and now and again there are flashes of green foliage cast by Edward's window, but mostly the colours are mottled tans and browns of dry bushes and long since dead trees. They soon leave the urbanites, the concentrated populace, the conglomeration of those seeking comfort from proximity to like-minded souls, the air thin and cool as they push into the countryside and climb. The clearway is larger now that they have left the city, with wide red sand shoulders that offer better views of the countryside. Discarded aluminum pie plates skewered on sticks stuck in the sand dance and shimmer in the sunlight. Their dazzle signals a buyer for fuel stands by, should the city-bound truckers wish to sell their excess, now so close to their ports of call, having hauled wares and produce from deep in the interior of the continent.

Climbing, climbing, it becomes more rural, with buildings interspersed here and there. Inspections stations cause long lines of heavy and rugged trucks bearing patient men. The trucks that escape the tedious beadledom spew great clouds of diesel fumes as their engines growl and bark loudly, as they fight against gravity's purchase of their great mass up the long and difficult climb. They pass apocalyptic contraptions that Edward cannot fathom until he has seen his third or fourth. Now he recognizes them as large cab-over semi-trucks minus the cab, the driver in his open chair just above the rattling engine, buffeted by the draft, teeth bared and eyes shielded behind goggles from another era.

After an age on the open roads, Edward relishing the cooling breeze through Abdul's cramped car, they turn off the main highway, and begin to twist and turn on a small two-lane road that winds into a valley. For the first time since his arrival, Edward can see a horizon, and even the Indian Ocean far off in the haze, with an expansive view of lush green and soft rolling hills. Edward was not aware that they had climbed that high above the sea.

There is still garbage scattered roadside as they descend into the lush valley but there is less of it now. As they continue down Edward notes the small houses sprinkled here and there, as chickens, children, and the odd goat scurry. It is not so ugly now, muses Edward. Still he cannot imagine their lives.

The foliage thickens as they continue their descent, and the air grows heavy. Edward searches for some frame of reference to make sense of it all. Are these the jungles of his imagination? He desires the exotic and evaluates this as mundane and not worthy of his emotion. *Does the world grow smaller with exposure?* he wonders sadly.

Abdul eventually pulls into a gas station beside a rusty pump and kills the engine. Mike is the first to hop from the car, followed by Abdul, and with feigned agony, Edward. The place looks quite rough but Edward is desperately uncomfortable.

Edward called to Mike, "Would they have a toilet?"

Mike looks around. "Not to your standard I'm sure. Listen Ed, if I were you I'd just hang it out in the woods, this garage will have a hole in the floor at best."

As Edward considers his options, Mike reaches into Abdul's car's rear seat and takes a rag from the floor and tosses it to Edward.

"I doubt there'd be paper in there anyway, there's never any paper, and there certainly isn't any in the woods. Just make sure you leave it wherever you do decide to go. I don't want it back," Mike laughed.

The attendant saunters out slowly and Abdul engages in abrupt and rancorous conversation. The attendant smiles and laughs and retorts with equal vigour. It sounds cheerful and familiar. Edward turns towards the woods, looks back at the gas station, then back at the woods.

"Get going Ed, we won't be long."

Edward frowns and heads across the road and into the forest.

Mike calls after him, "Watch your step, go slowly, and just far enough that I can't see your lily white ass. I don't want to have to come find you."

Edward turns and considers for a moment, then disappears into the green foliage. Mike hears laughter and turns to see a large lady peeling potatoes in the doorway of a hut beside the garage. When Mike looks at her, she shakes her head and laughs louder.

"Hate to have some snake bite him in the balls," said Mike.

Her eyes go wide and she giggles so hard she can't control herself. She wipes her eyes with her apron and waves a hand at Mike in admonition to stop, her mass jiggling with joy. She disappears into the hut. Mike hears her say something loud in Swahili and there is laughter from within the hut. There is commotion followed by numerous smiling faces that peek out the door. Mike laughs.

Edward eventually stumbles out of the forest with a stupid grin on his face, and everyone breaks out in more spirited laughter.

"Come on, we're almost there" called Mike, and within moments they are all in the car and back on the road.

By and by, they abandon the cozy shelter of the hills. Presently they stretch out across the open scrubland of red sand interrupted with bushes of dark knurled branches and thorns, the earth stabbed here and there with huge baobabs that claw for the heavens.

To Edward it all looks barren and desolate. The rough domiciles of the hill country are left behind, but people live and thrive here too, life as it has been for eons, long before Edward. He is surprised, in this barren landscape, to witness a solitary man who stands alone amongst the thorn bushes, a tall and majestic Masai, dressed in rough hand-hewn fabrics. These simple herdsmen tend their goats, yet lions have fell to these hard and resolute men. For this skill they are revered and given wide berth when they venture into the villages. After an hour or so the road begins to rise and fall with gentle meanderings around hillocks and small streams and there are only smatterings of green foliage now. They pass tall towers of sand, as high and even higher than the brush, where industrious insects mutate the landscape for their own purpose. Now and again, there are men in orange jumpsuits tending pathetic stands of corn while guards lounge in the shade. Traffic begins anew of heavy trucks, decrepit Land Rovers with loads of burlap sacks piled high on their racks, cars of unfamiliar brands and small Chinese motorcycles.

A cacophonic snarl rises over the engine noise of Abdul's car, now familiar and disregarded. The change catches Edward's ear, growing and differential, and the car grows dark as they are momentarily shaded from the bright African sun. Edward looks up as a Beechcraft 1900 passes low overhead and disappears. The noise changes tenor and fades and is gone.

"That's the airport off to the right but we'll head into town and drop you at the hotel," said Mike.

Small communities set amongst the palm trees and brush appear here and nether, with small domiciles walled with branches of equal length tied in a line and packed with mud and grass, sporting roofs of dried grass or at times the more affluent don silvery aluminum sheeting. There is a school yard of dirt and uniformed youngsters that run to and fro and chase balls and yell or whisper secrets and all burst with happiness. Shops begin to appear, similar to the city shops, only farther back from the road. Older women in colourful cotton robes and headdresses sweep dust and chaff from the road's pavement and shirtless and lean teenagers lounge on small red motorcycles looking cool in mirrored sunglasses and tough scowls. Banana, mango and cashew stands nest amongst the gaudy and garish cellular shops as rural morphs into urban.

Edward smacks his head on the ceiling as Abdul harshly exits the road into a sand lot and is about to complain when a larger lurch causes a disconcerting metal-to-metal clank and launches him against his seatbelt. Yet another stiff jolt pummels the car violently and Edward fears for the enamel of his teeth. The front end of the car then dives as Abdul stands on the brakes and Edward's upper body is thrust firmly against the front seat. His seat belt digs deep. Abdul lies on his horn, which wails loudly and does its duty yet Abdul does not relent. Edward looks forward to see the fuss and notes they have stopped at a solid dark green and rusty metal gate. He grits his teeth to the incessant barrage of horn.

An opening appears in the centre of the green gate and Abdul allows his horn to die as if it had finally released the last breath of its copious lungs, for it changes pitch and struggles pathetically before it lies to rest. A sad and apathetic face with bloodshot eyes appears and scrutinizes the disruption, and with a sneer, the face and opening disappear.

There is a clank and grating of metal on stone as the gate creeps opens. They drive into the compound. They have arrived.

Chapter 3

Edward surveys the scene from Abdul's car. He spots an older gentleman in a chef's smock exit a small hut, and bored waitresses check their nails. There are numerous others, uniformed and not, bystanders and hotel staff with unknown purpose. They are smiles and curiosity.

Edward crawls from Abdul's car weary of travel and dizzy with motion sickness. The mayhem of the next few moments overwhelm him as everyone jostles for position to greet the new addition. Edward is horrified to find his hand taken in someone else's, sweaty and warm and firm, and no doubt oozing of germs. He looks down at his returned hand, then an ugly grimace distorts his face. The introductions are lost to Edward even as they leave their bearer's mouth. Instructions and guidance for the hotel's amenities are given but Edward's mind is occupied with contagion. He wants space and time to temper his acclimation to this new environment. He wants to wash his hand.

Henceforth Mike rescues him. "Come on Ed, someone will bring your bags up."

The metal frame of the glass door squeals against the cement step as it is wrested open, grating on Edward's fatigued nerves. They step into the small whitewashed hotel amid weak incandescent lighting and musty scents. Old bicycles and empty pails and mops clutter the foyer. They squeeze past and navigate the narrow linoleum steps. Their feet grind in freshly tracked sand. As Edward climbs his heart sinks into despair, for he accepts that this will be his home for the indiscernible future. They take a hallway off the third floor landing and it's darker now with empty hanging sockets. They arrive at a dark wood door and the porter-cum-landlord draws a handful of unmarked keys from his pocket and fumbles with each. Edward can fathom no fixed order, certain some keys are tried more than once. Eventually there is a satisfying clunk of the deadbolt as the brass tumbler finds its way, and Edward steps into a room far worse than he could have imagined. Lost in forlorn thoughts of self-pity, Edward is pushed forward by the lads dragging his luggage into the room. He fights back a tear.

"Not bad, eh Ed?" offered the perpetually jovial Mike. "I'll leave you to get yourself sorted. Supper is downstairs in the courtyard at seven. Wear lots of mozzie juice, they're bad right now." He turns and leaves Edward to his fate.

Edward surveys the single room with bed and desk, with another door that leads to the bathroom. The floor is covered with the same linoleum as the steps and hallway. The walls are freshly painted yet large holes remain that disappear into blackness wherever wires enter the room, and there is bubbling and discolouration from moisture behind the walls. A gecko scrambles across the upper wall opposite. The bed is large and wide and low, and the threadbare sheets ill fitting. There are metal grates on the outside of the windows. They look insecure, held by rusty bolts in crumbling cement. The windows themselves don't appear flush or properly aligned with open gaps in most corners. Edward tries to force the gaps closed. Now he understands the need for the mosquito netting thrown up over a metal rectangular contraption suspended from the ceiling. The bed frame, door, dresser, desk and chair all appear to be of the same dark local wood, hand-hewn and imperfect.

He steps into his bathroom to see pipe stemming from far too large a hole, and shudders at what the darkness beyond may hold. The shower-head appears to be plastic, covered with white powdery mold. The drain is clogged with hair and thick strands from an old mop. He sees open air along a misaligned window high above the toilet, the sill littered with dead flies and a can of bug spray. The sink hangs askew from the wall and its cracked enamel is unevenly stained in brown. The shower lacks any curtain or divider. It is all open and exposed, raw and unpleasant. At long last he vigorously washes his hands. He breathes deeply to release the stress built up in his chest and he re-enters his bedroom.

There is loud scratching as crows struggle to find purchase on the aluminum roof, just above his room. The acoustics of the building amplify the noise and add a metallic twinge. Just then the obscene wail of a child gives Edward start. It is somehow unnatural and incessant and he searches for it's source.

Through his dirty window he watches a herd of goats feed on the hotel's garbage thrown indiscriminately over the compound wall. Having never heard goats before, Edward is unnerved by their human sounding bleat. Coupled with the amplified cawing and scratching of the crows resonating throughout the hotel, Edward fears for his sanity.

By and by the afternoon passes as Edward unpacks and sorts his gear, his empty luggage set aside high on the cabinet tops, the dresser drawers neatly organized. Back home, Edward deliberated at length over his accoutrements. Here in Africa, he is unsure of those choices. However, despite a strong desire to be elsewhere, despite his regret and remorse and vow to never come again, he has resolved himself to his fate and surroundings, for the next six weeks at least. Edward checks the time and the supper hour has arrived, so he sprays on copious amounts of DEET, his eyes and mouth shut firmly as he squeezes the spray cap and the vile concoction mists over the exposed skin of the back of his neck and head and hands. He wears long pants and a long sleeved shirt buttoned to the neck, with as little skin exposed as possible to stem the purchase of airborne death, and satisfied, he heads downstairs to the courtyard. Edward cringes as the high-pitched squeal of the metal doorframe against cement marks its protest yet again, and he steps into the courtyard. It is dark now, and full of parked white Toyota SUVs and the song of cicadas. Consequently he sees lights and hears voices from the open-air restaurant, so he saunters over, apprehensive yet striving to convey confidence.
It is time to meet everyone. The *restaurant* consists of a roof over a concrete pad, open to the African night. Two walls are hung with privacy bamboo blinds, and the area is adorned with cheap plastic chairs and plastic tables covered with gaudy plastic tablecloths. Fans suspended from the ceiling whir and vociferously beat the air, markedly unbalanced and unsteady. Edward inhales and steps inside.
   It takes a moment for anyone to notice Edward, and he stands and waits awkwardly.

"Here he is!" exclaimed Mike, happy and slightly polluted in a faded t-shirt, cargo shorts and barefoot. Two or three empty beer bottles sit on the table in front of him, with another half empty and sweating in his hand. Most turn to appraise the latest addition to the crew.

Only the manager stands to greet him. "Welcome Edward. Hope you had a swell trip. Ah, there's a toilet and sink and I believe some soap to wash up over there to the left, and the food is laid out there." He subsequently motions with his hand. "Just grab a plate and help yourself. If you want a soda or a beer, they're in the fridge, just sign the sheet and make sure you clear your bill at least weekly."

Edward looks around the tables and no one offers much more than a cursory glance, and perhaps a nod. Edward grabs a plate and receives stew and rice from the waitresses that stand behind the food table. He heads over and sits beside Mike, already engaged in conversation. An older fellow seated across from Edward nods in greeting.

"Chet," he stated. "How was the trip?"

"Very interesting."

"I can imagine, the first trip in always is. Welcome to paradise."

"Thank you, " laughed Edward. He then wondered if he had just insulted this friendly fellow.

The conversations are light and wary, with awkwardness and uncertainty, as if everyone is unsure of whom to trust. Edward looks around the dining area, and the waitresses behind the row of food smile at him. He smiles back politely. Chet sits across from him, thoroughly engrossed with his meal, as a funnel cloud of mosquitoes circle above him like vultures over a corpse. Edward looks at the others but only Chet has collected a cloud. The mosquitoes don't appear to bother him.

"Are you wearing DEET?" asked Edward.

"No, can't stand the stuff."

"What about the mosquitos?"

"Don't bother me much."

"But what about malaria?"

Chet shrugs.

"You're taking the Malarone?" asked Edward.

"No, I don't. I don't think anyone bothers, really. Too hard on the kidneys, and it masks the symptoms. Better to know right away that you've got it then treat it."

"That's not what the Doctors say."

"Yeah, well."

"I thought we had to take it."

Chet shrugs again and digs back into his meal.

Edward takes a few bites of his stew and surveys the room, adjusting to this new community. The manager is engaged in conversation with some local chaps and the elderly chef. A few of the guys eat distractedly and watch football on the large flat screen TV suspended against one wall, with multiple wires connecting everything to a cheap component stereo, all locked into a roughly welded metal enclosure with a large combination lock.

The chef gets up and heads for the kitchen, and the base manger looks around then calls across to Mike, "Hey Mike, how was the time off?"

"Too short."

Edward laughs too loudly, and is immediately embarrassed that he is the only one. His face flushes as he perceives that his laughter is obsequious, and that his desire to be accepted appears obvious and contrived. He notes a few raised eyebrows and shrinks a little.

"Did you get hunting?" continued the manager.

"Sure did. Got a freezer full of moose meat."

"Right on!"

"You hunt?" asked Edward to regain lost ground with the men, disapproval strongly conveyed in his scowl.

"Yeah," answered Mike. He does not notice Edward's contentious tone or facial expression, or perhaps doesn't care. "Out in camp with my brothers. We go every fall."

"You killed a moose?" asked Edward.

"Yeah, young female, the best meat mate."

"That's horrible!"

Mike turns towards Edward with renewed interest. "What's horrible about it Ed?"

"Here we go," said the guy on Edward's left and he gets up and takes his plate over to where he can watch the TV.

"It's barbarous!" stated Edward.

"You don't eat meat Ed?"

"Yes, but that's not it, I don't approve of hunting. It's deplorable."

"Ah, another soft-hearted urbanite. I suppose you only eat meat that's died of natural causes?"

"Don't be daft, I get my meat from a grocery," Edward responded nervously.

"Something still has to die to feed you Ed, even if it is sanitized for your delicate sensibilities in a neat little Styrofoam package. Someone else has just done the killing for you."

"Well, it's not the same."

"How so?"

Edward forms his thoughts before he replies. It takes awhile. "Those are farmed animals, not wild creatures."

"Ah, I see. So in your world, the life of a farmed animal is worth less than a wild animal?"

Edward frowns. "I guess so, they are bred specifically for our consumption, for food."

"So morally its better to kill a farmed animal that's been confined and fed all manner of drugs and vitamins, that's never known freedom?"

"Yeah," murmured Edward. He is frustrated, certain of his moral high ground yet unsure how to convey it.

"You know those wild animals die too Ed, of old age, predators, cold wet winters, or even loss of habitat from you self-righteous urbanites building new subdivisions. They are a renewable resource, you know. You new-age guys are all about natural sustainability, isn't that all the rage right now? What's more natural than hunting for your own food?"

Edward struggles for a rebuttal. "Well, I wish those poor animals had guns to shoot back at you, then it'd be fair."

"Somebody told you life was fair Ed?"

Edward thinks on it.

"I don't expect you to understand, you've been raised with the skewed mindset you've been raised with, and I get that, but try to understand." Mike lowers his voice. "There is something deep inside yourself to be found stalking through the woods and hunting for wary game. Humans have been hunting for their food for eons. Hunting is in our nature, despite what popular culture has been forcing down our throats for the past forty years or so. There's a deep connection to our ancestors, with the old ways, and to be honest, there is nothing as satisfying as

33

providing for your family by your own hand. That's food I'm proud to put on my table."

"But how can you enjoy killing something?"

"Ah, the killing is the sad part, it's the hunting I like. When you pull the trigger, the fun is over. Especially with a thousand pound moose!"

Mike senses Edward's confusion, and he smiles and stands up. "Don't worry yourself Ed, some can't help themselves but having opinions about things they know nothing about. I'll see you tomorrow morning." He turns and walks away.

Edward looks to Chet. Sensing a comrade, he tries to regain some status. "You believe that? He hunts?"

"You should protest."

"What?"

"Isn't that what you sort of folk like to do? Try to get everyone aligned with your way of thinking? Force your ideals on others because you figure you know better than the rest of us?"

Edward frowns and turns to watch Mike leave. He expects him to turn towards the hotel as he exits the restaurant. Edward's eyes open wide as Mike heads for the gate and disappears outside.

"Where is he going?" he asked.

"Out on the prowl I suppose," offered Chet.

"I thought we had to stay in the compound?"

"Well, you can tell him then."

Edward looks over at the manager who doesn't appear to be the slightest bit concerned.

"And he leaves the compound and goes out into town?"

"Yeah, I guess we aren't supposed to, but nobody cares. The oil companies have a shit load of rules for us but most don't bother with them."

"It's the rules!"

Chet looks at him for a good while.

"Well, you best be following them then. See you tomorrow." He gets up from the table and heads for the hotel, his cloud of mosquitoes in pursuit.

Edward wakes late at night to the clang of the gate. He sneaks over to his window and peaks past the curtain, and watches Mike saunters in with a local girl under his arm. They chat with the night guard then disappear into the hotel. There are footsteps on the stairs, giggles and hushes and the jangle of keys. A door opens and closes followed by the brass clank of a deadbolt. Edward goes back to bed.

Chapter 4

Breakfast the next morning consists of cheese omelette or pancakes, toast, a selection of assorted jams, freshly squeezed mango juice and instant coffee, all laid out as supper had been the evening before. The pilots are decked out in white uniform shirts with gold thread Captain's bars and black trousers. Some wear dress shoes, some wear boots, some wear running shoes, and all are black. One heavy set Russian fellow wears black sandals over black socks. Apart from goats baying opposite the breeze block wall, the only chatter is amongst the drivers standing in wait by their four-wheeled steeds. Then as one pilot stands, all stand and head for the SUVs. The drivers joke with their fares as they open the doors, and the pilots pile indiscriminately into the various Toyotas. Edward notes Mike's ride is full, so he jumps in with Chet. The engineers had gone in earlier to prep the helicopters for the day's flights. The SUVs are full of mosquitoes and hands wave about and smack against windows and curses flow.

On the drive to the airport Edward leans to Chet and asks softly, "I saw someone bring a girl back to the hotel last night."

Chet shrugs while watching the scenery drift by.

"I thought we weren't allowed guests in the hotel?"

"You really like those rules, don't you?"

Edward frowns and stares out the window as well. They drive out of town and back into the countryside, through the scenery Edward had passed yesterday. Eventually they turn onto a small dirt road and navigate the potholes while rusty signs advertise the local airport. They slow further and turn into an open sand pit opposite a chain link fence that separates the hangars within from the open brush land. It is set far from the main terminal of the small rural airport, barely visible on the horizon.

"Stick with me Edward, I'll show you around," said the manager as they arrive.

"I can do it boss," offers Chet. "I'm not flying until ten, and I know how busy you are," he said with sarcasm and a wink.

The manager smiles and does not rise to the slight. "Thanks Chet."

Chet takes Edward to the security gate and signs him in, then ambles towards the large fabric covered open-ended hangar. Portable prefab cabins line both walls while others stand beyond the hangar's shade. They first enter the pilot's cabin and drop off their day bags. It's busy and crowded and Chet advises Edward that they'll return after the first wave of flights departs. They cross the hangar to meet the engineers in their main office. The engineers barely acknowledge their passing save one gruff "another fucking pilot" spoken just loud enough.

Edward is shown the stores room of spare parts and nuts and bolts and the cabinets for combustibles and cleaning products. The safety stations are highlighted with easily read signage

37

with first aid kits in white plastic cases beside emergency eye wash stations. He is acquainted with the auxiliary power units and where they are charged, and the portable fuel bowser should the main fuel truck break down. He is then led into the passenger check-in area and the safety briefing room. It is mayhem and disorganization with confused and overwrought passengers laden with excess luggage as local security staff wave beeping wands and issue stern warnings, so they continue through and into the flight follower's office. There is more hustle and bustle with rustling paperwork handed over heads, as phones ring and ancient printers clack away. Stressed voices yell to be heard over the racket, so they ease out and skip the introductions for the time being.

"That's pretty much it Mate, you'll get a feel for it after the dust settles. It's typically a bit mad during the first round of flights of the day, especially after the weekend. I should probably take you over to Dave's office, he's the base's training pilot and he'll have things to sort out with you." Chet then leads Edward to a cabin off by itself in the sun. He knocks loudly and waits. There is no response and Edward leans forward to knock again. Chet shakes his head.

"Best to wait Mate."

Edward looks around at the hive of activity; aircraft towed out of the hangar and out onto the ramp, as pilots and engineers hustle in all directions. Edward desperately wishes to be a part of it.

"Come on in," called Dave.

Chet gives Edward a nod and turns and walks away. Edward apprehensively opens the door and steps inside.

"Have a seat," offered Dave. "I was just reviewing your files."

Edward sits.

"You've got time on type, thank goodness. You wouldn't believe some of the guys they send us out here. So I figure a line indoctrination flight or two and I'll sign you off to fly the line. I'll get the manager to schedule us for tomorrow. I've got a copy of the local area exam here for you. All the answers can be found in either of these two manuals." He pushes two large and worn binders across the desk.

"That should take you most of the morning. After lunch I'll take you through flight planning, and we'll go over the aircraft. Any questions?"

Edward looks at the exam and flips through the pages.

"Good enough," said Dave. "You can work on the desk there behind me," motioning to the back of the cubical. "Move a few boxes to make yourself some room."

Edward heads to the other desk, littered with oil cases and crates of water. He struggles with the binders and exam under his arm as he removes the clutter from the desk. Edward shrieks at a sinister snake on the table. The manuals fly and he trips and falls backwards over a small garbage can. He frantically scrambles backwards as he kicks and scatters debris in his wake. Dave turns to watch the commotion.

"Fuck sakes, I forgot about that stupid thing. Sorry Edward." Dave walks over and picks up the plastic snake. "Somebody's idea of a joke. They got me too, though not as bad as they got you," he laughed. He throws the toy into a box and returns to his desk.

"Better keep your eyes open through, they caught a black mamba while cleaning the air conditioner in the flight following office last week. Deadly bastards."

Dave sits and focuses on his laptop.

39

Edward slowly gets up and collects the manuals, rights the trash bin and further organizes the desk for his use. While his heart still thumps and his hands shake from adrenaline, he eventually tackles the test. The first question regards radio communication frequencies and Edward scours through the thick binders in search of answers. His hands shake.

Edward sits at the desk surrounded in clutter, the air dank of mould and oil and diesel fuel as flies seek freedom and thud relentlessly against panes of glass. Edward works while the base breathes, with barking diesel generators, the whine of turbines chasing struggling starters, the air smacked with composite blades of aerodynamic marvel, followed by a long period of idling choppers as passengers load and pilots run checklists. The training cabin shudders as the pilots finally pull pitch to taxi and once on the coral gravel runway, the pilots lift into the air and push the nose over and climb into the African skies. The noise grows faint and all is quiet again. As the morning progresses, helicopters sporadically return from the offshore, as a few had departed early and the distances to their rigs short, while others had been destined for platforms far out beyond the shore, well out into the Indian Ocean, well past the deep greens of the spectacular coral reefs, and out into the deep heaving blue. Those helicopters bound for distant rigs return much later in the morning while others depart for their second and even third trips of the day. The helicopters return at intervals known to those who scrutinize their flights on satellite tracking screens, shown as blue lines of automated position reports, superimposed over symbols for land masses, exploration rigs and itinerant ships. The flight followers tend to the helicopters' progress for safety and planning of further taskings, to prepare for subsequent flights if so required. A distant buzz grows clearer and louder, and soon there is movement and yelling as crews prep for another arrival, while the helicopters announce their ingress over the buzz of flies thudding against the window. All their enterprise is interspersed with the odd noisy and cumbersome itinerant fixed wing aircraft that come and go from parts unknown. The birds eventually find their way home with different loads of passengers than had departed, souls destined for all the corners of the globe, with cargo holds of luggage and samples of their endeavours meant for further study and hopefully, the discovery of resources of untold wealth for those that wear suits and profit from such things. Dave doesn't move from his laptop throughout it all. The morning passes despite their lack of interaction with it, and with his task finally rendered complete, Edward stands and proudly carries his exam over to Dave. Having spent hours working on the written test, Edward is dismayed as he watches Dave hastily run through it, with quick checkmarks here and there. Dave then scratches *100%* and signs his name and tosses the papers into a bin on his desk, the entire process not taking twenty-seconds.

Dave looks at his watch and said, "Lets get some lunch and then we'll go through flight planning."

Edward nods subservient and fawning as he follows Dave out the door and over to the engineer's office. They walk right in without a knock.

"What the fuck do you want?" bellows Tor, one of the engineers, his accent Scandinavian and thick. He is all Viking and a man of contentious ilk.

"Fuck you," Dave responded and they both laugh. "Where's my lunch you Norse twit?"

Tor completely ignores the remark and concentrates on the pile of paperwork before him. Dave looks through the numerous plastic bags on the desk, checking the names scrawled indecipherably in pen on each bag. He soon finds the one he seeks and looks inside and swears, "Goddamn it, I ordered chicken."

Tor laughs.

"We were supposed to order lunch?" asked Edward.

"Nobody told you?"

"No."

"Well, here's half of mine, a damn egg sandwich." Dave hands half of his sandwich to Edward. Edward takes it apprehensively, concerned with germs, as it had come from Dave's unwashed hand.

"There's a sheet on the table at breakfast where you fill in what you want for lunch. Make sure you fill it out next time. They'll mess the order up but at least you'll have something."

Dave takes a large bite out of the remaining half of his sandwich. Edward wants to sit and relax while eating and finds this all somewhat crass. Still, he follows suit, and unconsciously makes a face.

"Don't like it?" asked Dave.

Thinking it unwise to offend Dave with his concern for shared germs, Edward responded, "It's all right." Edward's stomach protests with a slight heave.

Fed far too quickly for Edward's taste, they immediately head off to the pilot's cabin and flight planning. Edward chews his mouthful of egg sandwich as Dave holds the door open. Edward swallows and grimaces at the unpleasantness of the whole affair, then wipes his hands on his pants as he steps inside.

He sits in a plastic chair in front of one of the computers. While he waits for it to come to life Dave states; "Somebody will have already printed the weather for the day, you can find it there." He points to a cork-board nearby on the wall, then he stares blankly at the computer while it whirs and clicks and sorts itself out. Eventually the flight-planning program opens and Dave begins to click quickly with the mouse. Edward does his best to follow along.

"Obviously we depart the airport here, that never changes, and the rigs are on these drop down menus in these fields." Dave demonstrates and selects the appropriate boxes of the program. "You'll get the schedule of where you're headed in the morning when you first arrive. Just follow the Captain's lead, and you'll get the hang of it soon enough."

"I'm a Captain," protested Edward.

"Are you now?" taunts Dave. "You're a Captain when I say you are."

"But I was hired as a Captain."

Dave looks out the window for a while, then looks back to Edward.

"Listen, be prepared to be a First Officer for the time being. Get yourself used to the place and the operation, and we'll look at upgrading you later on. We've got more than enough Captains to cover the roster now."

"I was told I was a Captain."

"That may very well be, but you won't be flying here as a Captain until I release you as such."

"I'm going to call head office." Edward protested.

"Go ahead, but they're going to defer you to me."

Edward thinks about that for a few moments. Another helicopter taxies by and the cabin rattles.

When the noise abates Dave continues with the indoctrination, ignoring Edward's plea for Captaincy. "Give the program a try. Use this morning's weather, plan a trip out to the Sierra Foxtrot Twelve and the return. There's no fuel on the rig so you can click the *no refuel* box and the program will do the rest."

Edward consults the printed weather on the cork-board , and he begins typing the many variables of temperatures and winds and altitudes into the program.

"What do we use for an alternate?" Edward asked.

"You can use back here as the alternate for the leg to the rig."

"And what about the leg back to here?"

"There isn't anything."

"You have no alternates for returning to base?"

"Nope."

"Where would you go if the weather is bad here?"

"This is it buddy, you come back here."

"You need an alternate if you're flying instrument rules."

"We're not flying instrument rules here Edward."

"But the manual says we are supposed to fly instrument rules."

"If you read the manual again, you'll see that it says; *Should*, not *Shall*. There's a difference."

Edward is quiet for a while and thinks it all over. Dave watches him.

"Listen Edward, the weather is always pretty damn good here. The odd rain shower brings the visibility down once in awhile, but it never lasts long. If you ever get caught, just wait it out offshore, or worse case, cloud break over the sea and scud run in."

Edward cringes at the old school procedure. His heart thumps loudly in his chest but he proceeds, finishing off the program's inputs.

"So what's your payload?" asked Dave.

"Well, the program is giving me around one thousand kilos but that has me back here with minimum fuel."

"Perfect Edward, that sounds about right."

"But we don't have an alternate. What if the weather moves in? Shouldn't we carry more fuel?"

Dave looks at Edward for a very long time. Edward knows that he should agree, but it's not his nature. He wants to stand his ground.

"So how would you explain the extra fuel and reduced payload to the customer?" asked Dave.

"It's safer. It's pilot's discretion. I'd want to carry extra fuel for the possibility of bad weather back here."

"Edward, it's your first day on the base. Lets just get you on the line and go from there, okay?"

Edward sighs and nods. Dave demonstrates a few more things that may help operationally around the flight-planning cabin and shows Edward the ICAO forms with multiple carbon copies to be filed with the local civil aviation office.

"I haven't filled one of those out in years!" protested Edward.

"Well, in most of Africa you'll be filling out these forms regularly, all by hand. Pain in the ass but there it is. Normally we send the completed forms over with a driver but we can head over to the tower and say hello."

Edward follows Dave out through the security gate, and waits while Dave finds one of the drivers lounging in the shade of a nearby baobab. Once in the Toyota they thump and bounce out of the sand lot and back onto the dirt road and head up to the terminal area. Off to the side of the old terminal is the control tower with two security guards playing a game of *Bao*, a traditional mancala board game, in the shade of the external staircase. When they recognize Dave, or perhaps in deference to his pilot's uniform, they nod and return to their game. Dave and Edward climb the narrow and unsteady staircase, running their hands carefully along the peeled paint and rust of the rail. Dave ducks his head to clear the short entranceway and steps up into the control tower, with Edward close behind. Inside there is a woman breast-feeding her baby on a couch. She smiles and greets them warmly. A garbled radio call echoes though the control tower through speakers long since blown. The lady rises and makes her way to the radio on a long desk against the window overlooking the runway. It's an ancient radio with dials from one of the World Wars. The lady keys the mic as her suckling child watches the foreigners with interest, and responds to the call. The aircraft radios back and Edward cannot comprehend any of it.

"Jeez," he mutters to Dave, "did you understand any of that?"

Dave shakes his head.

She turns to them and offers tea.

"No, thank you Love, just showing a new pilot around."

She offers a soft *Karibu*, a Swahili *Welcome* , accompanied by a smile so open and friendly that Edward can hardly fathom the warmth behind it.

"Our flight plans come here, and she'll stamp it and give us one copy for our files, then she calls the information into centre."

"Thank you," Dave offered to the lady as they turn to leave and she waves again as they make their way back down the external staircase. The two security guards raise their heads again and after a wave and more smiles Dave and Edward hop into the Toyota and make their way back to base.

"Friendly place, isn't it?" asked Edward.

"The friendliest Edward, the friendliest."

Back at base there is a helicopter off by itself. Most have cowlings open with engineers up on the stands. The men either complete their post flight inspections or prep for another flight. Edward and Dave head straight for the lone bird and pass Tor as he walks past.

"Is *Charlie Uniform* good for showing Edward a few things?"

"Yeah, no problem," responded Tor absently.

Dave swells with pride now, walking up to his *raison d'être*, for all the rest of his duties are merely necessary evils to placate the safety dogma so prevalent in the offshore industry. This beast of metal and rivets and bearings and rods and electronics and a plethora of applied science is what he loves, and it is what he has always loved, since the days of his youth. Noise and oil and grease and mechanical magic lack any semblance of grace. They are purposeful and brutal despite themselves. And what of the men that fly them? He smiles at the thought. He loves helicopters so thoroughly he can barely comprehend those that do not.

"She's a beauty, isn't she?" he asked Edward as they arrive.

"It's a helicopter," responded Edward flatly.

Dave looks at Edward for a long while with a disappointed expression.

"Yeah, just a helicopter, it's just a job, a means to a paycheque," he responded but his sarcasm is lost on Edward.

"Exactly," Edward said.

Dave takes Edward through the aircraft, doing a full walk-around and going over the multifarious equipment nestled here and there. Edward pays unreserved attention but senses Dave's motivation has waned. They eventually sit in the cockpit as near to their central purpose as possible since Edward had first set foot on the continent. Both the pilot and co-pilot controls and primary flight instruments are laid out in exactly the same configuration, so the aircraft can easily be flown from either seat. By convention and time-worn ergonomics, the aircraft is generally flown from the right seat, and this is where Dave has Edward seated so they can run through the cockpit and all the displays and knobs and switches. It's not as if Edward doesn't know, as he is fully trained and experienced on the type. Nevertheless there may be differences, and Dave spends the rest of the afternoon running through far more than Edward's brain can handle.

That evening over supper, scented with DEET, Edward sits across from Chet and his cloud of mosquitoes. Other crew watch a football match on the large screen TV.
"Chet, I'm flying with Dave tomorrow. What's he like?"
"He's all right. He absolutely loves flying. He's an excellent pilot, though he may have a tad too much passion for it in my opinion. I dare say that's why he's so good at it, one of them *naturals*. Never seen someone so adept and at ease with taking to the skies. For most of us, this is just a job, but Dave really, really loves flying. To his credit, he doesn't seem to hold it against those of us that don't take it as seriously as he does."
"You don't love it?"
"It's just a job. Pays the bills."

"And what do you think about Mike?" They both look across at Mike, who brought a stunning local girl to dinner.

"Man, Mike is all right. He loves everything, loves flying, loves Africa, loves the ladies. That cat can really fly too. And Africa was made for Mike," Chet laughs, shaking his head. "That guy thrives on this place. Take Mike out of Africa and he'd probably wither and die."

Chapter 5

The next morning after breakfast, Edward rides into the airport with Dave.

After firing off a few texts, Dave turns towards Edward, "Just relax and pay attention to what's going on and get used to the procedures. Follow me and see how it's done and feel free to ask any questions. That's why we're here. I'll give you a few tasks as things progress."

"You'll be assessing me?"

"Nope, not at all, today is training. We've got three flights so you should get a good feel for the operation. I've got you tomorrow too, and that's when I'll assess if you've paid attention, though we may get it done today too. We'll see how it goes."

"And I'll be a Captain?"

"I seriously doubt we'll get around to that this tour but let's not get ahead of ourselves. Regardless, you'll fly the first two trips, right seat, and try to follow along as I'll get you over to the left seat to run the radios for our third trip. As you well know, the flying is the easy part."

Dave's phone beeps and recaptures his attention. Edward's nerves flutter, and he frets over possible blunders. Though an integral component of the job, he abhors having his skills assessed. *I should be accustomed to it by now*, he thinks, but it's little consolation. The self-induced stress causes a slight light-headedness, and Edward consciously suppresses the early signs of a panic attack.

With the flight planned and the ICAO forms filled out, signed, and delivered to the tower, it's time for flying. Not that any of it was superfluous, only now their central purpose lies before them.

Thankfully Dave had requested a later flight, to depart after the first wave of birds had departed for the offshore, thus lowering the overall stress of the flight, and to have more time to instruct Edward on the finer points of the operation. Clipboard in hand, with the morning's weather, the plan for this trip, available payloads, and a copy of their ICAO form stuck inside, they gather their headsets and sunglasses and whatever other paraphernalia they deem essential for the flight.

They walk across the ramp together. They had been through the aircraft's daily *pilot's inspection* earlier while the helicopter was still within the hangar's shade. Dave and Edward had run through the numerous checks together after confirming the engineers had released the aircraft for service.

They strut, with a swagger born of their mastery of the elements and all things earth bound, and in their minds at least, their prowess of flight, their ethereal skill in manhandling these incorrigible and beastly conglomerations of metal and noise up, up and upwards into the sky, against gravity's own reign, against the gods themselves. The engineers guffaw at the pilots and their elevated self-worth, for they see the forced nonchalance, products of their own delusion, but most of them have been around pilots long enough. The pilots' bravado is lost on their audience; the odd passenger only requires a ride to work. *Goddamned prima donnas*, considers the engineer, watching. *Fucking pilots, but they're good for a laugh.*

   Securely strapped into his seat with personal gear stowed, Dave inspects his watch. He allows for extra time to teach a newbie the ropes.

   They run the appropriate checklists and then nod to the engineer. With consent, Edward hits the starter.

   The auxiliary power cart's diesel engine lags from the massive draw as the starter engages. The first engine's compressor and gas turbine blades accelerate with a high pitched whine, and an intense spark ignites vaporized jet fuel and compressed gases. The resulting interminable combustion is forced through the power turbine which rotates and drives multiple gears and shafts and bearings and all manner of mechanical wonder. Slowly the heavy rotor blades begin to creep across the arc of the front window. As momentum develops and the turbine spins faster and faster, the huge electrical draw wanes as the gas generator, now fed entirely by hot combustion gases, takes over, and the starter drops out.

The rotor blades spin faster now and cut though the air with a thump-thump-thump until the individual slaps gradually blend into a roar. The centrifugal force exerted on the whirling mass raises the drooped blade tips and the high temperatures of the engine abate to levels sustainable and everything settles into equilibrium. Individual chinks of metal against metal meld into caterwauling, blended with the rotor blades' relentless assault on the atmosphere. The buzz of the tail rotor join in, an onslaught to one's senses united as if a mighty beast best left undisturbed has been awoken and there is some tinge of regret.

Accustomed to the noise, the pilots run through a few more system checks and then give a hand signal for number two. The engineer nods and the process begins anew for the second engine albeit quicker now as the heavy rotor head is at speed and there is little load on the engine joining the festivities.

The auxiliary power cart is disconnected and towed away and the two engines are matched up with overhead throttles.

While Dave and Edward complete even more checks, the passengers are loaded and seatbelts checked and doors secured.

A final walk-around is completed by the engineer and another *thumbs-up* is given. They are ready to depart.

Dave calls the tower and gets a response. Edward doesn't understand a word of the garbled static.

"Are we cleared?"

"Yeah, you can pick it up and taxi Alpha to the right then straight to the button of zero-six. We're cleared to line up. There's nobody inbound."

Edward pulls up the collective control on his left side as he simultaneously adjusts the cyclic stick between his knees to assure a smooth pickup. There is a minor lateral drift and Edward checks it with cyclic as he continues to lift, but they are still somewhat askew and the last wheel breaks free of the ground yet slams down again sideways as the aircraft settles around its moment. The error jars the airframe. Edward cringes as he continues into the hover, the nose drifting as he corrects with pedals. Dave doesn't speak, as it's a common enough mistake.

Once airborne and pointed in the correct direction, flying low up the taxiway at a walking pace, Edward apologized, "Sorry about that."

"Don't sweat it, happens to the best of us. I'm sure a few of the passengers shit their pants but don't worry about it."

Edward looks over horrified but Dave smiles.

Lined up, the nose pointed down the long coral-gravel runway, Edward tries his best to maintain a stable hover to impress Dave. He tries too hard. Edward pushes too firmly on the pedals and squeezes the cyclic with forearm strapping rigidity. The aircraft reacts to his tension unfavourably and twitches uncomfortably, and the nose drifts nervously. Edward wants to immediately rotate and fly away but Dave is taking inordinately long to complete the hover checks and to get final departure clearance. Edward tires from his exertion and his exhaustion causes the helicopter to become less frantic.

"Relax Edward," coached Dave. "She knows what to do, just coax her, don't fight her." He calls tower on the radio.

There is a muffled response through the headphones with static and noise and a strong African accent that Edward doesn't catch, but Dave gives Edward the all clear. Relieved, Edward pushes the helicopter's nose over and pulls power. He struggles to keep the nose pointed down the runway as the fluctuations in torque and morphed airflow over the aerodynamic surfaces and whirly bits require nuance and expertise. The helicopter shudders as she escapes her own downwash, then leaves her self-churned brew of turbulence behind. The blades find renewed purchase, biting now into virgin atmosphere. They accelerate and climb into the African sky, commanded by Edward's own hands, sweaty as they are.

Through five hundred feet above ground Dave reaches across and raises the gear and runs the after-takeoff checks. Consulting the onboard navigation computer he calls, "Right to zero seven two Edward, three thousand five hundred feet if you please." Edward complies.

Edward is too engrossed with the task at hand to pay any attention to the scenery below. He fails to notice the red dirt of the roads or the flashes of reflected sun off countless tin roofs, or the numerous pedestrians whose gaze turn skyward as they pass overhead. The green and lush East African foliage, fed by the intermittent and refreshing short rains, pass below as the helicopter nears the shore, followed by beaches of pristine sand and turquoise shallow waters over endless reefs while fishermen cast handmade nets from dugout canoes. The water turns deep blue as they continue offshore.

At cruise, autopilots coupled and straight and level and enroute, Dave demonstrates fuel calculations and progress reports and radio calls to shore. There is other helicopter traffic but no requirement to deconflict. East and Westbound traffic travel at odds and even thousands of feet as dictated by International law. Still they remain vigilant, for complacency is a subtle and deadly foe to airmen.

Eventually, some forty miles from the platform, Dave calls the rig's radio operator, and after some back and forth and some scribbles on the flight log, Dave reads back the information to Edward.

"Winds are pretty steady here, almost the same everyday until the short rains end, then they swing one hundred and eighty degrees for a few months. With these winds, and deck heading, it'll be your landing, you lucky bugger. I'll set up the inbound course on your display." Dave's fingers dance across the flight management computer and Edward's display registers the appropriate track.

Soon the rig appears on the horizon and more checks are completed to prepare for landing. Edward follows the guidance of the flight management system and subsequently they make final approach to the large helipad that hangs off the side of the monstrous structure. Passengers briefed, floats are armed, the gear are dropped and locked.

Edward strives to maintain a constant descent profile, to hit specific height, speed and distance gates spelled out in excruciating detail in their operations manual. The wind is brisk, which facilitates their approach, and as they come over the deck, Edward pulls back on the cyclic to flare off their remaining forward speed, and pulls collective as they settle over the deck. Despite himself, he over-controls again, almost pushing the pedals through the floor with excessive force. Not yet completely stable, he plants the aircraft firmly on the deck with enough lack of grace for Dave to grab for the controls, but too late, for they are down.

"Some room for improvement," is all Dave offered for comment, however sardonically.

Checklists are run again and external lights are turned off. The wheels are soon chocked by helideck crews, accustomed to operating below whirling blades and downwash and the whine of turbines, and Edward brings the throttles back to idle. They have arrived.

Despite the helicopter's advent, massive machinery and driven men continue their endeavours all about them in the never-ending quest for resources. Cranes bunker fuel from large supply vessels anchored alongside and massive drill bits are swapped out and plunged into the seabed floor. Heavily rusted cables pass through immense and greasy pulley systems and dark fumes from multiple diesel engines drift into the atmosphere. The search for oil is a massive undertaking and the helicopters moving crews on and off the rigs for their respective rotations is a tiny cog. The helicopter's comings and goings are disruptive to operations, though a welcome interruption for those headed home. The helicopter crews do their utmost to assure their interference is minimal, for these lads are their bread and butter.

"Do you need to stretch your legs?" Dave asked.

"No, I'm fine," Edward replied. In reality he does not wish to upset the delicate alliance developed with the whirling dervish he controls, nestled into his seat and controls in hand, warmed by his grip and damp with his sweat. The bond is tenuous at best, and he does not wish to compromise it.

Dave hops out onto the deck and watches over the activity. Luggage is unceremoniously retrieved and thrown into a pile. The loaders cringe as they pass through the hot exhaust from the helicopter's turbines. Passengers disembark and are guided below decks by crews in bright yellow Nomex garb and safety boots and goggles and hearing protection and helmets. With the deck quickly cleared, for this dance is orchestrated day in and day out by well rehearsed performers, Dave takes a walk around the aircraft and checks for any sign of oil leak.

Soon another fresh batch of faces walk onto the helideck, much happier than those they had delivered, for these lucky souls are headed home. Cheerful exuberance tampered with a smatter of apprehensive concern, not all these hardy souls love to fly. Dave is cognizant of the fact and takes pride in reassuring those who find this workplace commute the most challenging aspect of their jobs. He strives to instil confidence with competence and professionalism. Edward's performance has failed to impress, for in his unease and lack of finesse, he has surely worried the souls condemned to his manifestations.

Dave also knows, from years upon years of instruction and guiding others, that his personal standard is far above the average, and to expect less. He has been criticized for being overly harsh and demanding, and ever introspective in his quest to improve, he has taken the criticism to heart. He seeks rationale to excuse weakness in others, and hopefully with forced patience, he can guide them to betterment. At times he purports himself a seer, a harbinger of amelioration, and thus he assiduously applies himself to his task. It is Edward's first flight on this operation, and obviously his nerves affect his performance. Dave's thoughts clear now that he's had time to reflect, and with his disapproval diminished, he opens his cockpit door and flashes Edward a reassuring smile. He then eases back into his seat with a grace of having done so countless times before.

"Hey Edward," he said, his headset plugged back into the aircraft's jack, "I'm getting the impression you're stressing a tad. There's no need. Just relax and enjoy the flying and it'll all settle into place. I'm just showing you the ropes. Force yourself to slacken that death grip on the controls, and if you feel like you're pushing the pedals through the floor, you'll sense it in your groin if you pay attention, just force the muscles to relax. Let this old girl show you what she can do. Ease up on that tension and it'll all settle down. I realize that it's easier said than done but give it a try and see how it goes."

Edward nods but does not appreciate the guidance, for he doesn't grasp the compulsion for finesse. They've arrived in one piece, hadn't they? He doesn't desire perfection and can't fathom the desire to hone skills beyond the minimum required. Edward thinks he did just fine. Here they are and he followed procedures and hit the gates as spelled out in the operations manual. He remembers what Chet had said the evening prior, and he agrees that Dave takes all this too seriously.

Thumbs up are passed to the helideck landing officer after all the caution lights for open doors extinguish, and cleared to depart and checks complete, Edward slowly pulls pitch and the helicopter responds with a shudder and a shift on her oleos. The blades attack the air with renewed vigour. Edward adjusts the cyclic as he deems necessary, changing the vector of the spinning mass above their heads, and continues his upward pressure on the collective control. The engines' fuel controls pour additional Jet-A1 into the combustion chamber to maintain the rotor's r.p.m. against the increased drag. The nose lifts first, followed by a second wheel. Edward corrects again, and as the third and final wheel breaks away from the surface it slides sideways and catches the deck again with a solid jolt. He pulls quicker now and they pop into the sky unstable and far too high.

"Let's go," said Dave in the calmest voice he can muster. Even lost in his own stress, Edward notes the dissatisfaction.

The sun climbs into the sky and the shadows shift and mark the passing of the day. As the afternoon progresses, Dave loads Edward with more tasks. While Edward's handling of the aircraft improves, Dave resigns himself to the fact that Edward is not very good. Is he unsafe? This is the very question that Dave is responsible for. *No, he is not*, considered Dave.

Edward is capable, albeit barely. Dave always pines for a kindred spirit, like minded and passionate, or even to meet someone more than himself. It happens from time to time, but most disappoint. Dave strives for perfection in his performance, but is cognizant of it's absurdity. Still, he enjoys the quest for its own sake. In all things Dave is hardest on his own shortcomings, but in others he sees a chance to help them improve. He is well aware of the standard that is required, for it is spelled out by legislation. Checking and maintaining that standard is Dave's vocation, and that standard is somewhat quantifiable, and he must admit that Edward meets this, at the very least.

Dave grows bored and decides to give Edward a little lesson as they cruise through the East African sky on one of the longer legs.

"Flying is all about managing what you've been given to work with," said Dave. "Resource management is key. We have autopilots to free our brains from the tedious concentration required to maintain cruise flight so we can deal with more complex issues. While we have to monitor the autopilot to confirm it's doing its job, for the most part, our brain is free for other tasks." He looks over at Edward and continues. "There are lots of questions to contend with in the cockpit when you make Captain; do you keep flying or let the co-pilot handle the more mundane task of aircraft handling so you can get on with the big picture? Especially when things start going wrong. All that workload has to be properly managed. Checklists and standard operating procedures help with all this, and you should be using them. Should you even try to remember complex procedures that you are never called upon besides once a year in training? You have that procedure spelled out in a checklist that is readily available so you don't need to task your brain with it. You can free up your mind for decision making."

Dave looks over at Edward to see if any of it has sunken in. Edward nods.

"We training pilots had a big presentation on resource management, and we're supposed to pass it down the line." Edward stares into space with his hands on the controls. Dave sighs and turns his attention back to the clipboard on his lap, to complete whatever paperwork he can before they return to base.

The hours tick off and the day wanes. Multiple flights are flown and numerous oil workers are carried across the expanse of ocean that separates them from their trade. It is a day of endless noise and oppressive heat, the pilots exposed for hours on end to the relentless jostle of disturbed aerodynamics. The body grows weary of forces unaligned with gravity's pull.
There are constant demands on their competency, experience and concentration. Their professionalism and resolve are challenged throughout the day, but most pilots crave this battle, one they have long made peace with. Still, there is fatigue and eyes burn from sweat, glare and turbine fumes. It has been a long day.

Back at base, the hectic pace of the day's activity is replaced with quietude, cicadas and a setting sun, but there are still tasks at hand. Engineers and helpers refuel, inspect and tow aircraft back into the hangar. Other helos are washed of black soot and sea salt, and others reside under maintenance stands with cowlings open as scheduled maintenance requirements dictate, or for trouble shooting snags identified by the day's crews.
Crews complete paperwork and prepare for the morrow. Most of the pilots have left, save a few required for maintenance runs

should the engineers require, and Dave and Edward debrief in the Training Pilot cabin.

"So any questions Edward?"

"No, I think I got the gist of it."

"Perfect, I'm glad we were able to get more flights in and complete your line check today. I didn't think we had the time but those extra flights helped. So I've got you all signed off to fly the line. Just scribble your *John Henry* on these forms and I'll forward them to head office. Tomorrow you can fly the line with Chet."

Later that evening with a plate full of food, Edward surveys the faces spread around the dining area and spots Chet. He heads over.

"How was the flying today?" Chet asked as Edward sits.

"It was good, and I'm all signed off."

"Great. You and I tomorrow."

"Yeah."

"How was Dave to fly with? Was he hard on you?"

"He was kind of picky about a few things, but it was all right."

"That's his job."

Mike struts into the dining area and heads for the food table. He yells across the room, "How was the flying Ed?"

Edward blushes at Mike's audacity, and at being the centre of attention. A few turn their heads to watch.

"It was good," Edward croaks.

"Dave get all your calls and procedures finely honed?" Mike bellowed across the room while a waitress ladles a chicken stir-fry onto his plate.

"Goddamned calls and procedures," interrupted a heavy set American pilot in an earthy Southern drawl.

"Wasn't asking you, you hillbilly," laughed Mike.

"Well, I'm answering," the American challenges. "Ya all got this operation run like a damn airline. I feel like I'm flying a 747 across the Atlantic, not a helicopter twenty miles offshore to a rig. All those calls and procedures are a pain in the ass."

"Here, here," responded Mike, as he searches for a place to sit.

"I could fire that bird up and fly back and forth to the rig all day long by myself, without all that bullshit."

"We all could," interjected Dave, who Edward had not seen. "I know the flying here is not overly challenging, but the company wants us to operate like we do everywhere else in the world, with the same two crew standard operating procedures whether you're launching into a full blown blizzard two hundred miles off Canada's East coast, or if you're buzzing out to a rig you can see from shore in blue African skies. Studies show over and over again that solid procedures are safer, and the oil companies have bought into it. The oil companies demand it, our company demands it, and as long as you're collecting a paycheque from these lads, you'll do it the way they want it done."

Edward looks around, relieved to no longer be the focus of interest. He notes that only a few seem to follow the conversation yelled across the room.

Chet leans forward and whispers to Edward, "They have this same argument a couple of times a week."

"I quite like the structure myself," said Edward. He leans back to avoid Chet's cloud of mosquitoes.

"Yeah, the North Sea guys take to the rigid procedures better than the old bush pilots. Those old dogs are more comfortable operating with freer reign."

"What's your background?"

"I'm an old bush pilot, like Mike, and Dave too by the way, but most of these guys are ex-military, or North Sea guys. There are a few of us old souls left. I don't mind all the fancy procedures so much, I've been at the offshore long enough to have the bush driven right out me."

The American continues to berate Dave. "All those stupid calls! Why do I have to have someone calling out all those stupid airspeeds? I can look down and see how fast I'm going."

"If your engine quits, you'll know what flight regime you're in and what procedure to use."

"He's ex-military but hates the procedures," whispered Chet.

"I can tell," agreed Edward.

"If my engine quits?" continued the American, yelling across the room. "If and when an engine were to quit, I'd decide then and there what to do."

"Well, there's been guys that didn't know what to do and made a cock-up of it and hence the procedures," Dave retorted.

"You can't have a specific and spelled out procedure for every goddamned thing that can possibly happen."

"They sure are trying!" laughed Mike. He sits with his food beside Edward and Chet.

"Next thing you know there's going to be a procedure for wiping my ass," said the American.

"If you want to go back to flying in the bush and do whatever the hell you want, that's your choice, but if you want to work here, you'll toe the line."

"Ah, you know I do Buddy, but you North Sea types write up a new twenty page procedure every time one of you fucks something up. It's getting stupid. You've sucked the life out of this profession with your goddamned procedures. You'd do good to get back to being proper pilots who can make a decision. I came to Africa to get away from that bullshit."

"Studies show...."

"Fucking studies. Just fly the fucking aircraft. I'll toe the line and do things your way, because some idiot put you lot in charge, but mark my words, trying to prevent accidents with all these complicated procedures and calls and having to know six different manuals is going to backfire on you. You'll have a bunch of rule minding idiots with no skills. You got to get back to being a pilot and taking responsibility. You guys are just trying to protect your ass from litigation by spelling out everything we do, but trust me, it won't end well. You have the lot of us afraid to do our jobs because we're worried about breaking a stupid rule. There's so many of them, no one can keep track. You've ruined the best job on the planet!" The American stands and marches out of the restaurant.

"And that's usually how the conversation ends," whispered Chet.

After everyone has finished, Mike sits down beside Edward and asked, "I'm headed out for a quick drink, want to join?"

Edward eyes open wide. "Outside the compound?"

"Yeah, don't sweat it little buddy, this place is cool, and everybody knows me. I'll take care of you."

"Thank you, but I'm pretty tired, and flying again tomorrow," he responded truthfully, but venturing outside the compound scared the hell out of him.

"I'll go Mike," called Tor the engineer. Mike nods.

Moses the chef walks by.

"Moses, come join us for a drink, it's on me."

Moses smiles softly, "Thank you Mike, I would like to join you, but the girls are not yet finished the dishes. It would be rude to leave while they are still working, would it not?"

"Yeah, you're probably right. Invite them too, what the hell. Just let us know when they're done and we'll head out." He turns again to Edward. "You're going to miss some fun tonight."

Edward smiles and stands. "I'm off to bed guys, good night."

"Good night Ed," he hears from different voices.

Hopeful the internet will be relatively fast as everyone is still eating, Edward logs in and tries to call his wife. The video won't function so they resolve to chat with voice. Edward tells his wife of the horrid conditions and death lurking in every corner and how hard he works, but his wife seems distant and uninterested. Her voice cuts in and out due to the poor connection and eventually the line goes dead. Edward closes his laptop and goes to bed.

Chapter 6

Edward awakes to the clang of the gate, followed by a hushed female giggle. Edward is exhausted yet struggles to return to sleep. He tosses and turns and try as he might to force his mind to rest, it continues to chase scattered worries that cannot be quelled, as if an entity separate to himself with its own wishes, desires and fears. His lack of dominion over it angers him. As these reflections become the devilish entities to squash, Edward thrashes more violently in a vain attempt to vanquish them. He drifts in and out of slumber and breaks free from the edge of sleep to discover his legs entwined in the threadbare sheets of his bed, and his face sweaty on the bare mattress, stained and revolting. Somehow exhaustion and frustration battle until sleep finally takes hold, however an amplified noise, not unlike a needle dropped on a spinning record, searching for the groove, grasps at his drifting conscious. Then it starts, the piercing call to prayer, for *Fajr* is broadcast to the faithful by a haughty nasal voice through a speaker that clips with the excessive volume and distorts beyond comprehension. The onslaught to his senses does not relent. Eventually its distorted poetic drone is lost on

Edward as he finally dozes off. When his alarm yanks him from a deep and profound sleep, he sheepishly concedes that he slept at all.

At breakfast with the boys, groggy and surly, Edward asks about the early call to prayer that so flagrantly disrespected his sleep.

"There's a mosque across the street. Be thankful you're not on that side of the hotel," said a pilot.

"It's unacceptable, I need my sleep."

"It's been that way long before we got here and will be here long afterwards, I'm sure. Besides, it wasn't your first night here. You didn't hear it before?"

"No."

"So you've slept through it before, you'll sleep through it again."

"I like the call to prayer, gives the place an exotic flare," said Mike as he pours a coffee. Someone groans.

"This hotel is horrendous. Why do you guys put up with it?" asked Edward.

"Well, I doubt we have much say in the matter, and honestly, I don't think there are too many options in town," said another.

"I'm going to refuse to fly if I can't get my rest."

"Do what you got to do."

They eat their breakfast in silence, then raise as one and head for the vehicles for the ride into work.

The day's preparation for flight is the same as the previous day, but Edward asks Chet question after question about altitudes and fuel, and weather, and centre of gravity charts, and flight planning protocols and aircraft maintenance releases.

Chet looks perplexed as he expected Dave to cover all that in training. He patiently explains it to Edward again.

"And shouldn't we have an alternate for returning?"

"No, we don't need one."

"We should carry a lot of extra fuel then, if we don't have an alternate back here, we could run out of options quickly," Edward advised.

"Have you looked out the window Mate? There is no weather. We don't need extra fuel."

"I think we should have extra fuel."

"Well, we aren't carrying any extra fuel. Take this payload to the flight followers so they can sort our passengers."

"I don't think we have enough fuel."

Chet stares at Edward reassessing his opinion of the guy. Once again, he favours the patient and benevolent side of his personality, a constant struggle he rarely wins.

"It's plenty of fuel, I've done this trip often enough, and we'll be back with spades in the tank. Just trust me Edward, watch and learn. After a few days you'll get the hang of it."

Now it's Edward's turn to look at Chet and wonder. It's difficult for him to settle with anything he hasn't decided for himself, but he likes Chet and respects his input. Chet is the Captain, and if things go wrong, Edward reminds himself, it'll be Chet's fault. Still, he'd like more fuel.

"I don't like it at all, and I'll be drafting a letter to the manager about all this when we get back, but okay," Edward said with a snort. "I'll pass along the payload as is." Edward takes the sheet and heads out the door in a huff.

Chet has flown with the same fuels and payloads since the start of the contract. To humour Edward and suppress his naturally impatient self, he nods and smiles.

Edward continues to be argumentative throughout the preflight and start up, and Chet struggles to maintain his composure.

After the departure and level at cruise altitude, Edward begins again. "Do you really think we should be doing Class Two departures out of that runway? If we were in the North Sea...."

Chet interrupts, "Mate, forget about the North Sea. This is Africa. We got this contract because we get shit done. If you want North Sea flying, perhaps that's where you should be."

"I didn't have much choice, they needed someone to fill in here and..."

"Yeah, no shit, and they didn't give you any option."

"Well, I had a choice."

"Sure you did, this or the unemployment line. I tell you what; you are going to find yourself washed out of here if you don't just buckle down and do the job. It's all right to ask questions, but jeez mate, you argue with everything. Just try to go with it, at least a little. This is only your second day. Just wind your neck in. We've been at this for a while you know. Maybe you could learn something."

Edward complains incessantly on the flights, from not getting enough sleep, to the horrid living conditions of the hotel, to the heat and the high risk of disease. He laments about the snakes and rats and lizards and sharks. He whines about the dust and the rain and the lack of English speaking locals. He wonders aloud about the poor internet and the constant power and cellular signal outages. He voices his concerns over the lack of security and the poor aptitude of the drivers, and the lax airport staff, and the fuel status, and the inconsistency of the weather reports. Edward perhaps realizes that he prattles on, but can't hold his tongue. On the third flight, after a departure from the rig and just levelling off for the flight home to base, Edward starts yet again, having stated the same on each of the subsequent flights; "I think we should be Class One off the rig."

"Class One! Jeez Mate, do you know what the Class One weights are? In this heat? We would hardly give them any payload. Have you listened the last three times I explained it?"

"I don't think we should be considering ditching in the event of an engine failure, which at Class Two weights we are. If we lose an engine at these weights, we could very well have to ditch."

"The water is twenty-eight degrees Edward! And the seas are barely at three feet, we've got automatic pop-out floats, we're all wearing life jackets and there are deployable rafts all over this aircraft, everyone onboard gets regular dunker training, and there's a supply vessel alongside the rig with full recovery gear, standing by to come get us should we ditch. When is the last time you ever heard of any engine failing anyway?"

"It could happen."

"Fuck sakes man, really?"

"I think we should be operating at Class One weights and carry alternate fuel."

Chet just stares off at the horizon. He tried, he tells himself. He really did.

Edward continues, "If we were in the North Sea...."

Chet reaches across and pulls Edward's headset plug out from the overhead cabin outlet.

As soon as they land, Edward jumps out of the aircraft, the rotor blades at full speed, then heads across the ramp and into the hangar. The engineer flashes an inquisitive glance but Chet shrugs his shoulders and brings the throttles back to idle and begins the shutdown checklist.

When the passengers and baggage are unloaded and the engines rinsed of salt spray from flights over the ocean, the engines are shut down. As the blades decelerate and eventually stop, Chet releases his seat belt and eases his stiff frame from the cockpit. He over-arches his back to stretch after hours confined to worn and poorly designed seats, and deeply inhales the fresh breeze carried across the grass of the infield. He regards the tree line beyond the runway, of swaying palms and baobabs and so unlike the pines of home. The engineer breaks his moment of reflection.

"How is everything?"

"All serviceable."

"And Edward? Did he have the shits?"

"He's just acclimatizing."

Chet ambles across the ramp to the hangar and greets the various engineers and helpers along the way. The manager stands outside his office, and when he catches Chet's eye he beckons, then turns and walks back into his office. Chet soon follows inside and shuts the door.

"So you pulled his headset, did ya?" asked the manager, already sitting at his desk.

"Yup."

The manager smiles and continues, "And why would you do that?"

"Because he wouldn't shut up."

"I see."

"It was endless Boss, he kept whining and complaining and questioning everything. I couldn't stand it anymore."

"Okay, fair enough. I'll have a word with him."

"Any paperwork on this?"

"Probably but don't sweat it, I'll sort it out. Thanks Chet."

The manager follows Chet out of his office, and Edward stands by the pilot's cabin and scowls at them both. Edward dons a self-satisfied smirk as he glares. Chet shakes his head and continues toward the Toyotas as they prepare to head into town.

"Another word Edward?" said the manager, and Edward's scowl fades. With a look of concern he contemplates how refusal might affect his fate, yet he heads reluctantly towards the manager, and follows him back into his office.

That evening at supper, Edward walks into the restaurant dejected and morose. Nobody notices. Mike wanders in with a gorgeous local girl on his arm and they sit by Edward.

"Hey Ed, meet Aisha."

"Hello Aisha,"

"Hello Edward, it's nice to meet you." She offers her hand. Edward looks with apprehension, as he dislikes touching anyone, especially locals. Eventually he takes her hand, and it's warm and delicate and light. It's a quick shake, and flustered, Edward stares down at his plate. The American had finished eating and comes over.

"Hey pretty girl, how are you doing?"

She smiles brightly and her eyes light up at the compliment.

"What are you doing with this ugly mug?"

"You're calling *me* ugly?" Mike asked with sarcasm and raised eyebrow. It's a conversation they have had before.

"I'm a very good looking man," said the American, wiggling his eyebrows in mock flirtation. "You, my friend, are not. Jeez, but you are ugly!"

Mike is not ugly, nor is the American handsome. The American's opinion doesn't matter in the slightest to Mike, and he quickly gets bored with these conversations.

"So beautiful. Why are you with this guy? Big wallet?" he asked, winking at Aisha.

"Big cock," she responded, and she laughs and grabs Mike's thigh.

"I'm sure she could find someone for you that doesn't mind a small dick," added Mike.

The American laughs but one can see he doesn't appreciate the taunt.

"Nah, I can take care of myself, but thanks."

"Ha, I heard you taking care of yourself last night," someone called from the next table and everyone laughs. The American doesn't appreciate being ridiculed, but he gracefully accepts defeat with a smile and a nod.

"Night guys," he said still laughing, as he heads for the door. "Going to go take care of myself."

The restaurant breaks out in laughter.

Chapter 7

The days meld into a forgettable cumulation of mundane moments and tedious rituals. Edward settles into his tasks and grows less obtuse. Still, the others are wary. They've worked with difficult personalities before, but these are driven men and routine is their rote, and one odd duck is but an annoyance. The others begin to shun Edward after hours, yet they tolerate his presence in the cockpit. He is considered another challenge to overcome. The crews pride themselves on professionalism by performing their jobs well and on time. While flying with Edward, their departures are often delayed, which generates paperwork, and questions, and frustration, but they thrive on challenge. No one seeks frustration, but placed before them, they will endure.

Eventually Edward finds himself off the schedule for the day, as regulations dictate rest amongst so many days worked. Fatigue had been identified as a major contributing factor in accidents, and the regulators have done their part to induce forced rest. It was a hard-fought battle, one that litigation wary customers are on board with. Edward sleeps well past breakfast, despite the onslaught of noise from the early morning call to prayer. He slept through the clunk of deadbolts and slammed doors, through all manner of activity and conversation in the hallways, though the multiple diesel engines that fire to life with a roar and noisy metal gates swung open and closed. Edward eventually stumbles downstairs, well rested and relaxed, and finds the kitchen closed.

He heads to the dining area, where Mike watches television in board shorts and a faded t-shirt, accompanied by two waitresses. Edward joins them for a few moments but the TV show doesn't make sense. The acting is extremely poor quality, and the special effects laughable. With a puff of smoke an actor dives out of frame, as if the witch-doctor caused the disappearance with magic. Mike and the girls laugh.

"You understand it?" asked Edward.

"Not really, but it's funny just the same. I think these soaps are out of Nigeria. The girls will watch them all day if Moses doesn't catch them." He turns away from the television. "I'm just waiting on Aisha and we're headed to the beach for the day, why don't you join us?"

"I don't think so."

"Listen Eddie, do you really want to be that guy that came all the way to Africa and didn't see or do anything?"

Edward doesn't respond.

"Most of these yahoos don't have a clue how to live, they're just here for the coin. Off to the airport and back to the hotel, six weeks straight and then they head home. You spend half your life on these oversea postings, why not enjoy yourself? Live a little. This place has a lot to offer if you look around." He notes Edward's confused face, and adds, "You'll be with me, you'll be completely safe."

"You know what? I think I will go."

"Awesome Ed! Go get yourself some shorts and grab a towel."

Edward soon returns in his swim trunks, far too large for his skinny frame. The oversized shorts accent the thinness of his pasty white legs that jut out like some deformed stork. The waitresses laugh. The dark socks and dress shoes do little to compliment the look.

"You didn't bring any sandals or flip-flops?"

"No."

"We'll get you some."

Aisha arrives, as pretty as ever, with a grace and presence that makes Edward feel small.

"Lets go!" Mike exclaimed as he spots her, and he jumps up and heads out the gate. Edward and Aisha fall in line and follow him as quickly as they can. Aisha giggles, happy.

As he steps outside the gate, Edward stands like a doe in headlights, but there is only sand and trees and Africa. It is Edward's first time outside the compound while not safely hidden behind the smoked windows of a company vehicle. His heart races and his imagination runs far ahead of him, but he sees nothing to fear, despite his preconceived notions, despite his drear concept of this place. It is disappointingly docile and placid. Still, he feels reckless and decadent as he forages ahead.

Baying goats scatter as they pass, annoyed crows caw from the trees and scabrous chickens peck the dirt road. People stop and stare at the procession, which unnerves Edward considerably. They do not approach and Mike and Aisha seem undaunted, so Edward looks to the ground ahead of him and saunters on.

Out on the street proper, Mike whistles and hails a *Bajaj*, the popular Indian tricycled-wheeled *Tuk Tuk* taxi. Four respond simultaneously, and race for the fare. The drivers smile and laugh as they cut each other off dangerously, skidding around corners of loose sand and rough ground, and both Edward and Aisha jump back when the winner skids to a stop before them.

"I thought we weren't supposed to ride in these things?" asked Edward.

"You can walk," offered Mike, settled into the back seat beside Aisha.

"I don't know where we are going."

"Exactly, get in and quit your belly-aching."

The *Bajaj* engine roars in protest of the excessive weight of the three passengers, the feeble suspension fully compressed and rendered useless. Underway, they buck roughly over the sand road that undulates heavily from continuous use and little maintenance. They bounce and laugh, for it's like an amusement park ride, and Edward thoroughly enjoys himself. Mike says something in Swahili to the driver and the driver guffaws and slaps his knee.

"You speak Swahili?" asked Edward.

"Some."

They turn down a side road past heavy set women with rocking hips, their heavily patterned kangas sway to the motion, with plastic bins of dried fish or fresh fruit balanced adeptly atop their heads. Motorcycles, other *Tuk Tuks* and bicycles from the fifties pass along either side and everyone stares unabashedly at the *mzungus* .

They enter a subdivision, with pleasant houses, welcoming and inviting, with gardens and well kept yards, the larger ones proper and set back from the road, with manicured lawns and little clutter to distract. Edward tries to keep track of the twists and turns of their route but he is thoroughly lost as they drift further and further from the safety of the compound. The exposure exhilarates and scares him in equal measure.

They pass herds of skinny cattle and brahma bulls with broad dangerous horns. Bells clang and frayed sisal rope drags forlorn, tended by bare foot boys clad in torn shorts.

Eventually they arrive at a rustic single story hotel with a large sand parking lot that circles an ancient baobab, while Masai guards lounge in its shade amongst mongrels flea bitten and mean tempered.

Mike negotiates with the driver and hands over some local currency, and they spill from the cramped *tuk-tuk*. Edward follows Aisha and Mike through an open door into the hotel's foyer, unlit and darkened further by the jet black colour of the wood. Local carvings of giraffes, elephants and Masai abound but there is no one at the front desk. They continue through into the restaurant, open and exposed to the cool breezes off the Indian Ocean. There is an expansive straw roof specially designed by the Norwegian owner that covers the dining area, with rocks piled artistically into a low wall approximating the circumference of the roof. Edward points out a large rat that runs along one of the beams of the roof but no one pays attention. The tables are bare without a server in sight. As they walk they spot a table with three local girls along the waterfront. The fresh salt tainted air flows through the empty tables and chairs, and provides welcome relief from the oppressive heat. Edward squints and regards the razor sharp horizon that cuts through the azure blue of the sky and the turquoise waters of the Ocean, glittering with sunlight reflected off the wind driven chop.

One of the girls squeals when she notices Aisha, and Aisha scampers to their table. As the girls chat, Mike explains; "This is a pretty popular local hangout, with lots of ex-pats too. We often come here after shift for a drink. They have a restaurant but the food ain't so great. They have a BBQ on Friday night that is pretty descent though."

"Our meals are provided at the compound."

"Yeah, sometimes you need a change in scenery."

"It's money out of your pocket," argued Edward.

"Yeah, you can't take it with you Mate, and it's only a few bucks. The entire beach is public but most of the locals hang out to the left. I prefer a little cove off to the right there." He motions. "There's more privacy and a nice reef if you want to snorkel."

The girls stand to join them, so with Mike at the lead, they depart the shade of the grass roof, the girls casually bringing up the rear. Mike heads for a small opening in the brush and a few of the mongrels, tails wagging, join the parade.

Edward falls behind as he takes care with his step amongst sharp and abrasive coral interspersed with soft fine sand and branches and thorns and piles of broken shells. Eventually they make the beach, wide and white and littered with debris, but gorgeous nevertheless. Local boys play at the far end of this stretch of sand and the dogs charge for them, teeth bared and snarling, and sand kicks up behind them in their zest. The boys look up at their attackers and scream. The boys stumble and clumsy in their fear, they scramble for the long abandoned fish market as the dogs bare down.

"Fuck sakes," exclaimed Mike, and he takes off at a sprint after the dogs.

The kids scramble up the crumbled wall of the market. Older teens along the beach have come up to see the commotion. As the dogs bark at the youths, one teen picks up a rock and nails one dog firmly enough to knock it sideways. The other dogs hesitate now, cowering yet their aggression seethes. Mike breathing heavily now stands between the dogs and the old wall and trembling boys. A few more rocks are thrown and the dogs back off.

"You shouldn't bring your dogs to the beach," admonished one of the older teens.

"They're not my fucking dogs Mate, they followed us from the hotel."

The teen nods and throws another rock at the canines. A dog yelps and backs off. The other dogs look confused. Mike joins the teen, lobbing more stones half heartedly in the general direction of the mongrels, and the mongrels gradually understand that they aren't welcome, and saunter off whence they came.

The teen yells to the kids clung to the wall and they start climbing down. The kids seem angry and the teen speaks with them. While not fully understood by Mike, he gathers that they understand that they were not his dogs. They nod at him as they hit the sand, dropped from their precarious purchase near the top of the wall.

"Hey *Meester*," one greeted in heavily accented English.

"*Mambo!*" greeted Mike.

"*Poa*," responded the lot in unison, giggling.

"*Habari ya ashubi?*" Mike asked and the kids laugh and run off.

Edward arrives, and he asks Mike what was said to the youths.

"I told them that you like black boys."

"Fuck off," Edward laughed. "That's not funny."

The girls arrive now, oblivious to the drama, engrossed in conversation. They continue together down the beach and descend into the cove, out of sight from the others.

The girls look around and begin to undress. Edward notes that Aisha is wearing a bikini under her t-shirt and skirt as she removes them. The other three are down to bras and panties, and they remove those as well. Edward watches flabbergasted as they are soon completely naked on the beach, rummaging through their bags. Their lithe brown bodies, perfectly proportioned and taut, naked and unabashed and completely lacking in shame, forces Edward to discretely adjust his shorts.

"You can stare Mate, they don't care, they're strippers. Fucking hot, aren't they?"

Edward continues to stare, mouth agape.

"They're used to being naked in front of people," Mike added, watching as well.

Still, Aisha is embarrassed for Edward and she admonishes the girls. The girls giggle and with bathing suits recovered from the recesses of their bags, they begin to dress again.

"Are they all strippers?" Edward asked, a slight quiver in his voice.

"Those three are."

"What about Aisha?"

"No, she has her own salon. I think she does all their hair."

"Yeah, I guess you wouldn't date a stripper."

"Why the hell not?" asked Mike, giving Edward his raised eyebrow stare. "They're really cool girls. They're just using their gifts to get ahead. There aren't many opportunities here for women. I give them credit, they're resourceful and pretty switched on. And they're young and beautiful, might as well profit from it."

"It's rather distasteful I think. They're strippers," Edward replied. He makes an ugly face showcasing his disapproval.

"Judgemental little fuck, aren't you? These girls are really sweet, and a blast too, always having fun, and they don't take anything too seriously. I'd rather hang out with strippers than most of the gals back home. These girls see things how they are, not how they want them to be. Brutally practical, and I respect that," he added as they watch the giggling girls ease into the warm waters. "I bet you haven't met any strippers before, have you?"

"Of course not."

"Just roll with it Ed. These girls are sweet." Mike watches the girls and cannot hide the involuntary curl of his upper lip. Aisha notices and gives him a sharp look. Mike laughs and winks at her.

"Wait till you've been away from home for a few weeks and see what you think of them then," he said, still watching as they ease into the sea. "You know I almost married a stripper."

"What happened?"

"Long story. Come on." Mike turns and runs into the shallow water splashing the girls who squeal in delight.

Mike continues past them into deeper water and dives and Edward watches his shape glide below the surface, then there is a kick and splash and he disappears. Edward watches nervously and after an age Mike's head breaks the surface an impossible distance from shore.

Edward peels off his buttoned shirt, his pale body thin and bleached in the harsh hot sun, and grows shy when he notices the girls watching him. He steps tentatively into the Indian

Ocean, and is surprised at the bathwater temperature, the water crystal clear and inviting. He wades out slowly, shuffling his feet to scare off imagined sting rays and sea snakes.

He looks at the girls just beside him and asked, "There aren't any sharks, are there?"

The girls eyes go wide with fear perhaps to mock but he is unsure, then one stripper responded, "There are sharks?" All the girls await his response.

"I'm asking you," Edward stated embarrassed and slightly concerned that he has worried the girls, or worse, that they tease.

"Ain't no shark that would want your skinny carcass," laughed Mike who has popped up behind him. "And besides, the crocs keep the sharks away." He quickly disappears below the surface again.

The girls laugh and start to swim, and Edward continues to wade out deeper, feeling a little silly. He puts his arms high over his head and touches his hands together and forms the shape he was taught as a youth at swimming lessons. He then puts his head down and hunches his back, and looking ridiculous, propels himself forward and slaps his upper body onto the water in an absurd form of shallow dive. He relaxes enough to savour the warm water on his skin as he splashes along. More comfortable after a time, Edward ventures into deeper water. He reaches far and slaps the water and propels himself forward in what might be construed as an overhead crawl, but he quickly gives up and settles into more of a dog paddle. Eventually he heads towards Mike.

"This is actually quite nice," Edward said.

"Not hard to take, is it? Glad you came?"

"Yes, actually, I am."

Edward looks towards the beach and watches as the girls swim and chat. He watches more local children run along the beach then spots the white skin of a Caucasian with blonde hair.

"There's a white kid!"

Mike looks. "What do you mean?"

"There is a white kid running with those boys."

"Yeah, and?"

"Well, do you think that's safe? Where are his parents?"

Mike looks at Edward for a while before responding. "Listen Ed, I know us pale skin folk are definitely in the minority here, but there are lots of families living here; white, Asian, Indian, maybe even some Dutch folk." He laughed.

"Really? White families live here?"

"Definitely man. I see that kid here all the time, I think they live just up the road. His father is a technician for the water works or something."

Edward watches and lets his mind adjust to this new information. He considers that perhaps he needs to readdress some of his preconceived notions of this place. Maybe it isn't so scary.

He swims around again then slaps hard at the water.

"Ouch!" he yelled. "Something stung me!"

"Probably a jellyfish," answered Mike.

"A jellyfish!" Edward looks about himself in the water. "I don't see anything?"

"Sometimes in the rough water their tentacles get torn off and float around. That's what usually gets you."

"Is it dangerous?"

"Nah, just irritating. I don't think they have the real dangerous ones around here. The sting doesn't last long."

Edward, with a concerned scowl, forces himself to relax and tentatively swims around again, when snap, there's another sting like a hot ember against his lips and chin. Edward slaps at his face and tries to flush it with salt water, but the pain spreads across his face. In his pain and fear he forgets to combat his lack of buoyancy and sinks below the surface. He gasps in pain and receives a lungful of seawater and thrashes more. Through the fracas of pain and panic and salt water flooding his mouth and sinus cavity, he senses a firm grasp on his spindly upper arm. There is a firm yank he fears will wretch his arm from the socket, but suddenly it is bright and there is air. He coughs violently and water spills from his lungs and he gasps again while his face burns. He coughs and gasps and between the two his body takes oxygen and his panic subsides a little. He realizes that Mike keeps his head above water while he drags him shoreward and Edward relaxes somewhat. His face burns.

As they near the shore and Mike can stand in the shallows, he hauls Edward up fully so he can get his feet beneath himself. Mike looks concerned at his sputtering friend.

"You okay?"

Edward coughs a few more times and wipes his nose and sputtered, "I think so."

"Well, you're talking so that's a good sign. Gave me a scare. I can't imagine the paperwork if I lost you." He still holds Edward's arm in support, and leads him through the shallows to the beach. The girls follow closely to see the cause of the commotion.

Edward sits on his towel and Mike pushes his head back so he can look at his face.

"Damn, they got you good."

"What got him good?" asked one stripper.

"Jellyfish. Good welt on your lips and a few stings around your lower face. You can see it swell now."

"I heard that you are supposed to pee on a jellyfish sting," Aisha said, concerned.

"I'll pee on him," offered one stripper huskily.

"Ewwww. Nobody is going to pee on me!" protested Edward.

"Well, you can pee on him if you want but if you give it an hour or so the pain will all be gone," laughed Mike.

"I think I'll wait it out," said Edward shyly.

Edward's lip continues to swell. The welts are red and burn. He does his utmost to suffer it quietly, but he shivers from time to time from the effort. Everybody lounges on their towels as the salt dries on their skin in the hot sun and soft breeze off the sea. The girls chatter amongst themselves.

"How ya doing Ed?" asked Mike after a time.

"It still hurts."

"Yeah, it actually looks like the swelling is going down."

"Yes, I guess it's getting better."

"You should take a selfie for your missus, show her the big adventure you're on. You are married, aren't you?"

"Yes, but she'll think I'm stupid for swimming in the ocean. Why didn't you tell me about the jellyfish beforehand?"

"You never know when they're around. Sometimes it looks like you could walk across the water it's so thick with them. They don't sting bad, I got a few here and there too, but never on the face."

"I never should have come," said Edward forlornly, feeling sorry for himself.

Mike looks at Edward for a time. He has little patience for self-pity and he gets up and joins the girls.

As the afternoon advances and the sun creeps across the sky and begins to settle on the horizon, they relax languidly, their skin rough from the sea salt dried in the African sun. Edward watches as the tide turns and draws out the sea. The beach grows ever wider and the shallower reefs break the surface, until the edge of the water is a long walk over uninviting puddles and mottled beige and dead coral. Edward has long been impatient to depart, but it is Mike who stirs first, standing and stretching. The girls take note and strip anew, soon donning the more conservative vestments worn on arrival. As they strip and redress Edward discretely adjusts his shorts again. They pack their gear into their colourful woven bags and with nothing spoken, they all head back for the restaurant of the hotel.

"I'll get the girls an ice cream," Mike announced, and he advises the girls in Swahili and they squeal. As they sit in the empty restaurant it takes a long while to catch the attention of a waitress. Eventually one dispassionate lady saunters towards them.

The girls start a conversation with the waitress in Swahili and they chatter while the men watch disinterested until the girl turns to get the ice cream.

"Hold on there, Sweetheart," Mike said loudly to catch her attention, "I'll have a gin and tonic. What about you Ed?"

"Just a water, please."

"A beer is the same price as a bottle of water."

"Just a water."

"Okay, gin and tonic and a water," said Mike. The waitress does not reply nor acknowledge, she simply turns and leaves.

Mike elbows Edward. "Now you can tell your friends back home you took some strippers for ice cream!"

As they wait, enjoying the shade and refreshing breeze off the ocean, Edward regards the reef, now fully exposed at low tide and barren. The reef extends a few hundred metres and the waves break far off on the horizon. There are women now with plastic pails who scrounge far out and collect what Edward does not know. One stripper does her best to catch Edward's eye but does not succeed.

They hear a motorcycle and Mike looks perplexed.

"What's wrong?" Edward asked.

"I hear a motorcycle but…."

A small Chinese motorcycle rounds the point and bounces roughly over the dips and pockets of the broken coral.

"No way!" Mike laughs, as the bike perseveres over the impossible terrain, the spectacle in perfect view from their perch in the restaurant. The rider bucks along and bounces high above his seat then regains control, legs flailing. All take notice as he progresses across the reef, for somehow he has discovered a rideable route where no one has dared ride a motorcycle before, and he bounces and lurches and continues as if driven by demons and none can fathom it. In time the absurd terrain is navigated in a wide arch. The rider then passes in front of the restaurant and the deep sand of the beach envelopes the motorcycle's wheels. The bike protests and the rider applies more throttle and sand is thrown high into the air and the cyclist waivers yet retains control. The tail end sways wildly. With the beach conquered he attacks a slight mud cliff and successfully rides up and over and into the grass and into the brush and is gone.

"What the hell?" asked Mike of no one in particular, laughing all the while.

Then they hear a second motorcycle and turn to watch yet another struggle around the point. This stead carries a policemen in uniform. He bounces along and struggles as had the other, obviously in hot pursuit. Nothing is said as they watch and eventually this rider makes the beach at the same point and struggles as had his quarry in the deep sand. He conquers the rise and attains the high ground above the cliff and disappears into the same brush as consumed the other.

After the ice cream is consumed and the gin and tonic absorbed, the girls grab the sole *tuk-tuk* in attendance and disappear, their chatter and laughter incessant all the while. Without transport, Mike and Edward begin to walk and travel some distance before Mike succeeds in flagging a *bajaj* to quell Edward's complaints. At the hotel, Mike pays the driver and pounds on the gate.

As they walk through the courtyard they pass a pilot who states, "Water is out again."

"What does he mean? asked Edward.

"Out of water. Happens all the time here unfortunately."

"What does that mean?"

"There's no water in the hotel. No showers, no flushing toilets. Typically lasts a few days. You get the idea?"

"I need a shower."

"Yup," Mike agreed. "So do I. I'm heading over to Moses's place shortly to help his kid move into his first apartment, want to come?"

"But I need a shower."

"You're just going to get dirty again anyway."

Edward rolls his eyes and stomps into the hotel. Mike laughs and heads into Moses's kitchen.

Chapter 8

Next morning Mike walks into breakfast in a foul mood. He spots the manager and stomps towards him.

"What's this stupid memo about nobody being allowed to go to the beach?" he asked.

"Someone got stung by jellyfish and almost drowned yesterday. When head office received the report they went ballistic. You should have heard the damn conference call last night. That memo is from on high Mike, went way over my head."

"Who almost drowned?" asked one of the other pilots.

"Who put a report in?" asked Mike.

"Well," the manager hesitated, "I really can't say, but who all knew about it?" he asked with a smirk on his face.

"Only Edward and……" Mike responded and his voice trails off.

"And there's your answer, but you didn't hear it from me."

"Fuck! Where is the little twerp anyway? Isn't he flying today?"

"Refused to fly because there isn't any water and he can't have his shower," the manager responded cooly.

"And screwed up my day off," complained another pilot. "Not that it matters, I was planning on going to the beach."

At the end of the day the crews return in unison. Edward stands in the courtyard upon their arrival, not unlike a school kid with a secret he cannot wait to share. He looks clean and refreshed. As the crews pile out of the vehicles, shirttails out and disheveled, sweaty and dusty, Edward takes overt joy in being the bearer of good news.

"The water is back on! They got it around two."

They ignore him and walk into the hotel.

The manager stops by Edward, "So I guess we can expect to have you working tomorrow?"

"As long as I get my shower in the morning," Edward answered brightly, oblivious to the ill will. The manager rolls his eyes.

Shortly afterwards, Mike and a few of the pilots spill out of the hotel in swim trunks and carrying towels.

"Don't ask," suggested Mike firmly as he passes.

The manager holds his tongue.

"I think they're going to the beach," said Edward.

The manager rolls his eyes again and walks into the hotel, leaving Edward alone in the courtyard.

A week passes and the incident report is forgotten, as everyone continues to visit the beach whenever they please. Reports to head office are frowned upon if they negatively affect lifestyle on the job, but the guys are now accustomed to Edward's bizarre mannerisms. Long weeks away from home in a difficult environment, their days tasked with high stress, they live, eat and work with the same people day in and day out, which does not favour those who are easily irked by inconsequential things. They all consider themselves professionals and appreciate that crew cohesion is paramount to their well being. There is no place for pettiness here. They have forgiven but have not forgotten, and they keep their distance from Edward whenever possible. The days pass and they get on with their jobs.

Later that week, on their third flight of the day, workers have been transported from the mainland to offshore platforms and back again, and more are outbound to a rig with Edward at the controls. Still festering over his lack of Captaincy status, Edward nevertheless sits right seat and flies. He keeps his questions and criticisms to a minimum, but has to force himself. Chet has noticed Edward's restraint and relaxes a little, as he was unimpressed to discover he had been scheduled with Edward again today. He wonders if perhaps that chat with the manager had set Edward straight. Regardless, Chet is more at ease than he expected to be, and as always, enjoys being airborne.

With the clipboard on his lap, Chet catches up on paperwork, when Edward senses movement on the instrument panel that catches his eye. There is a concurrent oscillation of the airframe that gives him pause, but could be dismissed as a gust of wind. Edward scans the instruments but sees no cause for concern, and decides it doesn't warrant mention. It woke him up somewhat, for his thoughts had drifted from the task at hand, trusting the aircraft's automation to mind his inattentiveness.

He glances at Chet and notes he has stowed the clipboard, and now scans the instruments closely. Edward is embarrassed that he hadn't spoken up.

"A gust of wind I think," Edward offered.

"I think the number two fuel control is acting up."

"What? How can you possibly know that?"

"A feeling."

The airframe oscillates again only more violently. The aircraft yaws hard to starboard and the autopilot banks left to compensate, its task not defined by engine surges but by complex algorithms to maintain track while trimmed. A corresponding change of pitch in the turbine joins the ruckus. Edward immediately grabs for the controls and punches off the autopilot and the aircraft yaws left now and banks right and pitches up and climbs. Edward attempts to compensate and pushes the nose down and steps hard on the right pedal and lowers the collective and over corrects massively, then he quickly reverses his control inputs as centrifugal force pushes him left against his seatbelt.

"I got it," Chet said calmly. He takes the controls and over-rides Edward who is saturated and doesn't register the transfer. He continues to fight with Chet.

"I got it Edward!" Chet yells and this time Edward relinquishes control. The aircraft immediately settles into level and trimmed flight.

"You okay over there?" he calmly asked Edward .

"It was all over the place!" croaked Edward.

"Yeah, but I'd gather that ninety percent of that was self-induced. Why don't you couple up to the auto-pilot and take her again so I can sort this out. Next time it goes, just leave it coupled up. If it goes for rat shit, I'll take over."

Edward frowns at the implied criticism of his skills. He retakes control, and quickly punches the appropriate buttons to re-couple to the autopilots.

"Ladies and Gentlemen," Chet announced calmly over the aircraft's public address system, "we apologize for the rough ride but we are experiencing some technical difficulties and we'll head back to shore. Don't worry yourselves, one engine is acting up a little and…"

The turbine whines again and the aircraft yaws to starboard heavily. Edward, hands loose on the controls, grabs for the autopilot release but remembers Chet's advice and restrains himself. He keeps his hands lightly on the controls but allows the autopilot to settle everything out and they are straight and level in an instant.

"Looks like the number two again, it's leading."

Edward was far too busy to even glance at the engine instruments to help identify the cause, but doesn't possess the confidence to question Chet. In a vain attempt to appear somewhat in control, he responded, "I agree."

Chet looks over at Edward with a dubious look, and added, "How about we turn towards base? I'll call it in."

Edward nods and turns the aircraft while Chet calls into the flight followers, followed by a quick call to air traffic control.
Midway through the turn all hell breaks loose. One engine surges and the other drops to compensate, or is it the other way around? Edward watches in horror as the two engines' gas turbine gauges surge, followed by temperature and power turbine fluctuations, all chasing each other to wild extremes, the result being massive power and torque changes that cause the airframe to yaw wildly. One turbine stalls repeatedly and loud explosive bangs accompany the uncommanded power changes.

Fear grips Edward and with a death grip on the controls he fights against the autopilot.

He hears Chet's impossibly calm voice over the melee, "Bringing the number two back to idle." Edward watches Chet's hands rise to the overhead throttles and panics. He lowers the collective control heavily setting up a massive rate of descent amid riotous forces pulling his body left and right and back again. Panic grips his chest tightly.

As soon as Chet pulls the number two engine to idle, both of his hands move quickly to the controls to take the helm yet again.

"I've got it Ed," he said calmly. This time Edward releases his death grip and with Chet at the controls, the aircraft settles immediately into stable flight. Chet gently corrects for the altitude loss and takes a heading to regain their track to the shore base.

Chet keys his mic and advised the passengers, "My apologies folks, one engine went a little wild on us but it's under control now and won't cause us any further distress. The engine's computer was acting up but I've taken it out of the equation. You can all relax, we'll be back on the ground at base in twenty minutes. I apologize for the inconvenience."

Afterwards he turns towards Edward, "You okay?"

Edward is embarrassed, but despite his lack of competence, he is impressed with Chet's handling of the emergency, and his poise throughout. Adrenaline courses through his veins and he doesn't trust himself to attempt speech, knowing his voice will quiver and expose his fear. Chet realizes that Edward is addled. He gently attempts to bring his co-pilot's mind back into the cockpit.

"Tell you what," Chet continued, "how about you pull out the emergency checklist and run through it for me, I'll keep flying for now."

Edward pulls the binder and after a time finds the proper emergency and calls off items. He calms considerably.

Chet elects to keep the questionable engine at bay and runs the bird onto the runway at speed while maintaining the limits of the good engine. He taxis clear, parks as per the engineer's guidance, and they begin the shutdown checks.

"Going to be quite a bit of paperwork and explaining on this one," complained Chet.

"I suppose you have to report my performance?"

"Yeah, well Edward, I'm sorry but it probably should be on record somewhere. You are inclined to overreact, and the training staff should be made aware. I won't put it in the written report but I'll have to have a one-on-one with Dave. See where he wants to go with it, fulfill my responsibility to the travelling public."

Edward's heart pounds in his chest again. Nausea grows as a panic attack bubbles below the surface. It is worse now then when actually in flight.

"I could tell about you too," Edward stammers.

Chet regards Edward for an inordinate amount of time then takes a deep breath.

"Good luck with that," he responded cooly.

That evening at supper Edward sits by himself. No one acknowledges his presence, but they generally don't. He is nearly finished when Mike and Aisha join him.

"Heard you had some excitement today Eddie," said Mike.

Edward looks up as Mike takes a chair and nods.

"Fuel control?"

Edward nods again.

"I had one a few years back, off the East coast of Canada, almost two hundred miles out. Dead of winter. Black-ass night." He slaps Aisha's bottom as she returns with a soda. She responds with a stern but playful scowl.

Edward doesn't feel for engaging anyone and nods weakly.

"Stop talking work, it bores me," complained Aisha. "I think Edward needs a girlfriend." She raises her eyebrows inquisitively.

This gets Edward's attention.

"No thank you!" he states.

"I know someone who really likes you,'" Aisha continued coyly.

"Yeah, the stripper that offered to pee on you Eddie," laughed Mike. Quite a few heads turn towards them. The statement was loud and heard throughout the restaurant. Edward blushes heavily and shrinks in his seat.

"Leave him alone you brat!" Aisha scolds, and she puts her hand over Edward's to comfort him. He quickly snaps his hand back.

"Are you married?" Aisha asked softly.

"Yes," Edward answered.

"I'm guessing she picked you up," taunted Mike.

"That's not nice Micheal," admonished Aisha.

"Well, he doesn't exactly come across as the aggressive type. I'm thinking your misses set her sights on you, didn't she Eddie?"

Aisha rolls her eyes. Edward thinks back to the beginning of his relationship with his wife and Mike is correct, but he isn't about to admit it. He lies.

"Not at all, I picked her up."

"Good on ya Mate!" Mike stated. "Babe, I'm gonna run out for some smokes, I'll be right back." He walks out of the restaurant and heads for the gate.

Edward sits quietly in search of an excuse to depart without insult but cannot contrive anything credible.

"If you need a girlfriend, I can arrange it," Aisha offered with a wink.

Edward changes the uncomfortable topic.

"Why are you with Mike? You realize when this contract is over he will leave."

Aisha takes a long look at Edward as sadness washes over her. He has insulted her but she understands that it was unintended. He is just stupid. She takes pity on his lack of compassion and smiles benignly.

"I know how these things work Edward."

"And you are okay with it?" Edward asked stupidly and Aisha tries to look past his ignorance. She realizes that Edward is not worldly.

"Mike has always been honest with me."

"But why you are with him? Is it because he has money? Because he is a white guy?"

Aisha contemplates slapping Edward for this impudence, but thinks better of it, and answers honestly.

"Mike is a sexy guy, good looking and a lot of fun, and he's good to me. It's that simple."

"But money is important to you, it's not really love is it?"

Once again Aisha considers a firm slap. She regards him for a long while before she responds.

"I will admit to you that it is easier to love a man with money, but not because of the money. It is the confidence. Maybe because of the money he is more confident, he is more sure of himself, and that is attractive in a man. I know I would love Mike if he did not have money, but perhaps having money is why he is as he is."

"So it is the money?" gloated Edward, pushing the contentious issue.

Aisha sighs, and wishes Mike would return. "Not the money per se, but the success maybe. He has a job, a career, a path he is following. He is sure of himself and his path. He is secure. I feel safe with him, as if the future is already written. We women are not so shallow as to be only interested in money, despite what you think of us." The tone in her voice warns Edward to leave it alone.

Mike reappears suddenly, "And what are we talking about?" He sits heavily and wraps a muscular arm around Aisha's slim shoulders. She appears smaller when he envelops her with his mass, and she nestles happily into his warmth.

"Love, Baby," she purred.

"Oh, good topic!" Mike laughed. "Tell me what I missed."

"Edward was saying that you will only love me and leave me."

"I see," Mike replied, and he looks at Edward with suspicion. "But I already told you that, didn't I Baby?"

"You did," she confirmed.

"You told her that you would leave her?" asked Edward.

Mike leans forward. "I did tell her my situation when we first met, that I travel a lot for work, and that I was looking for a girlfriend while I was here, but when I leave, that would be the end of it. I don't lie to girls, I prefer being straight up from the start."

Edward raises his eyebrows in surprise. Edward looks to Aisha, "You agreed to this?"

Aisha reflects before she eventually responds, "He's cute, and he looked like fun. We can have fun too you know. I appreciated his honesty. Most guys lie. They tell you anything to get you in bed. Still, this truth does not excuse his roughish behaviour."

Edward just shakes his head in disbelief. "So there's no love at all, you guys are just having fun?" He makes a face to flaunt his disapproval, but Aisha and Mike now converse to each other as if Edward is not even there.

"Yes, we say we agree with this truth he tells to us, we say we understand, and we smile and he takes us home, but we fall in love. How can one control the heart?" Aisha questioned as she stares into Mike's eyes. "We always hope you will find something in us to that you cannot do without. I know I am a stupid girl, that you told me true from the start, but you spread much pain Mike," she said, not angrily. "All women want a future. When we are young and beautiful you want us. And when we are old and not so beautiful, who will care for us?"

Mike looks at her sadly. "I have always tried to give more than I take, but you always want more, more than I have to offer. I have always told you the truth. I never wanted to hurt anybody."

"They never do," lamented Aisha.

"I'm sorry Aisha."

"I know you are Baby, it's all right."

Chapter 9

"I'm a helicopter pilot," Edward boasts to the security guard standing outside the terminal. The guard rolls his eyes. Edward believes his pilot's uniform affords him familiarity with airport security. The man is less impressed. Edward was sent to collect a new arrival, as everyone else had been busy, and base practice is for new arrivals to be met by someone in company uniform.

The guard tires and turns away. Edward hears the whine of the inbound Beechcraft. As it nears, the buzz of the turboprops swells then swells yet again as it turns onto final, followed by the roar of reverse thrust after touching down, then he listens to the long taxi in. He hears the engines shut down and raised voices and an aircraft door opening, his view blocked by the small rural terminal. A short while later passengers begin to spill from the terminal, mostly oil workers, many of them Filipino, that Edward might fly offshore to the rigs tomorrow. There are also African businessmen and a few affluent families, but no one approaches Edward. He stands there expectantly surveying every possible candidate, the embroidered company logo displayed loudly above his left shirt pocket. The passengers exit in clusters big and small then dwindle to the odd sluggish leftovers. There is still no pilot. Edward calls the manager on his cellular.

"Yeah, he texted me a while ago, he's stuck in security. Shouldn't be much longer," stated the manager.

Edward walks back to the terminal and pushes his face against the glass.

"Don't do that," advised the security guard.

"Is there anybody left?"

"One white guy."

Eventually a short, muscled and disgruntled man in a tight fitting t-shirt stumbles from the terminal. He drags his luggage haphazardly behind him and marches straight up to Edward. "Let's go."

Their vehicle sits alone in the now empty sandlot and Edward flags the driver. No one speaks as the vehicle arrives, nor while the driver loads the luggage into the boot. They get in the back seat and soon the driver is behind the wheel and they head off towards the hangar at the other end of the airport.

"Fucking monkeys, that was a pain in the ass," said the new guy.

"Monkeys?" asked Edward as he looks at the rear view mirror and notes the driver watching the new guy with a raised eyebrow.

"God damned security. Give them a uniform and they think they're better than us."

"What happened?"

"One of them asked what I had in my backpack and I told him to sod off, and that was it, next thing they've got me in an interrogation room and are going through my luggage. I told those fuckers I'd have their jobs if anything went missing. You got to let them know who's boss. Man, they dumped out all my luggage, opened everything, clothes all over the place, give those apes a uniform and…"

"I'm Edward by the way," Edward interrupted.

"Donald. What the hell is that stench?" Donald asked, his nose scrunched up as they pull into the hangar parking lot.

"Septic tank is overflowing. Apparently there's only one guy in town with a vacuum lorry, and it's broke down. He's trying to get us to buy the part he needs so he can come and drain our tank. Bit of a stalemate I'm afraid."

"Fucking unbelievable! They're really not too bright, are they?" Donald said as they exit the SUV. Edward casts an apologetic shrug at the driver. They leave the luggage and Edward takes Donald through hangar security and towards the manager's cabin.

"Christ this place reeks! What's with all the rat traps?" Donald asked as he motions to the metal contraptions every few feet along the hangar wall.

"We have a problem with rats."

"Don't they eat the snakes? Or is it vice-versa?"

"I really don't know."

"This place is a shit hole."

Edward knocks on the manager's door, then opens it for Donald.

"Wait till you see the hotel."

A hot and muggy East African evening welcomes the weekend and there are no scheduled flights on the roster until Monday. There are crews on standby but most look forward to a few days off. There are those who do not partake in frivolity, and would have spent the weekend in their rooms at the hotel regardless, so they volunteer to cover weekend shifts while the rest cut loose. As everyone gathers in the courtyard and restaurant, the mood is relaxed and festive with the television off and alternative music from the nineties blasts from a portable Bluetooth speaker paired to someone's tablet. A smattering of local NGOs had been invited, mostly German but Dutch and Americans as well. They often frequent the same local restaurants and bars. The faces are familiar. Moses the Chef has brought in fine cuts of beef, as well as chickens and large prawns and octopi . As per the custom most anywhere in the world, one of the South Africans has taken the helm of a BBQ, a large homemade contrivance that began life as a forty-five gallon drum. The bamboo screens that granted the restaurant a semblance of privacy had been rolled up and all is open. People converse in groups around the courtyard, for the vehicles have found other parking for the night, and folk mill about the restaurant and stand near the BBQ, conversing with the chef. They talk and laugh and smoke and drink beer.

Edward takes a seat by himself at the only uninhabited table, but Donald arrives and joins him. Once again he sports a t-shirt two sizes too small, flexing his muscles as he walks.

"White chicks!" Donald announced as he sits across from Edward. "I didn't realize that there'd be white chicks here."

"NGOs, the Peace Corps, a few involved in various projects in the area. We see them around town from time to time."

Donald stares at the girls in the group.

"Anybody tagging any of them?"

"I wouldn't know."

"What are they like?"

"Nice enough folk, helping the local community and all that."

"Missionaries? Religious types?" Donald asked with a disdainful look on his face.

"No, I don't think so. You can tell the missionaries from a mile away, they look overly wholesome and dress conservatively, and they stick together as a family. You see lots of them in town, but those NGOs like to party, or so I'm told."

"Interesting. Still, not much in common with us oil sluts I suppose."

"I guess not, but they seem friendly enough."

Donald nods as he continues his lecherous gaze.

An engineer walks into the restaurant with a local girl. Donald turns and watches them.

"That ain't right," he said.

"What isn't?"

"That lad there going native. Nasty."

"Oh no, that's the girl that runs the front desk of the hotel. I think she's the owner's niece. I believe they are just friends."

"I don't know about that, they look overly friendly. Lots of night fighters in here tonight," he said, surveying the crowd.

"Night fighters?"

"Whores. Prostitutes."

Edward looks around and frowns. "I don't think so, I'm quite sure they are all just local girls."

"Don't be naïve. They'd all shag you for a few bucks."

Edward looks around dubiously.

"I'm surprised you guys let them in here," continued Donald.

"I don't think they're prostitutes."

"Still, they don't belong."

"Local girls? We are in Africa, aren't we?"

Mike walks in with Aisha at his side. He carries two plates of food.

107

"Hey Guys, food's ready," he yelled for everyone to hear. The various groups saunter towards the line forming at the BBQ. Mike sets his plates on the table beside Edward and Donald and holds a chair out for Aisha.

"Beer Babe?"

She nods and Mike heads for the fridge.

"Hello Edward, how are you?" she asked with a smile.

"Fine Aisha, thank you," responded Edward. He nods a greeting from across the table.

She turns to Donald, "I'm Aisha." She offers her hand.

"Hello. Donald," he responds cooly. He takes her hand and shakes it languidly.

Mike eventually returns with five cold and sweaty beer bottles. He pops off the tops and hands one to Donald, then one to Edward and one to Aisha, and while standing he opens and downs a beer in one continuous gulp. He opens the fifth and places it before him as he sits.

"Thank you," said Edward. Donald raises his bottle to Mike and nods.

"Do you work out?" Mike teased as he takes a sip of his second beer.

"Yes, I do," said Donald proudly, flexing his muscles, oblivious to the taunt.

"So did laundry screw up or does that t-shirt only come in kid's sizes?"

Aisha and Edward laugh. Donald does not.

When everyone is fed, and many teeter on the edge of drunkenness, the music's volume inconspicuously climbs, and voices raise to carry the conversations. The volume is cranked again to be heard above the din of voices, which raise in kind.

Tongues untethered and thick with alcohol spout boastful tales and stretched truths, but no one balks. It's a game they can all play. The waitresses have cleaned the great mess of dishes and remove their aprons to join the party, and various pilots and engineers cover the cost of their drinks. Moses closes the kitchen and joins Mike at his table, from which no one has moved since dining. Mike tells a story.

"I knew a guy in a bush camp once, pretty far up in Northern Quebec. These poor sods were stuck in these damn canvas tents all summer long, up on these mountain tops without any trees higher than your waist. Of course I was flying back into town every night and sleeping in a hotel, but these guys stayed right there on the mountain, putting up communication towers through this remote region. Everything had to be slung up to them from the rail line running up the valley. It was a blast. The boss decided to give them all a little break about three months in, so I flew them all into town for a weekend. When we landed the boss headed straight to the bank and made sure everyone had their paycheques in hand. Big mistake! One guy we didn't see again for two weeks. And this guy I'm talking about went and bought himself five leather jackets! No shit! I flew him back without a cent to his name but he had these five leather jackets, every possible style you could imagine. Poor bugger, up on that mountain top with five leather jackets," Mike laughed. "The boss even offered to hold his paycheque for him until the end of the contract so he wouldn't do anything else so stupid next time they went to town, but he wouldn't hear of it. Crazy bugger, I don't think he took a cent home, but damn if he didn't have some leather."

"What would you do if you had more money in your hand than you ever had before?" asked Donald.

"Well, if I were you, I'd buy some larger t-shirts."

"Fuck you."

Mike smiles. "And maybe hire some people shorter than you to hang out with, so you wouldn't look like such a runt."

"What are you guys talking about?" interrupted the American, joining the group.

"What we would buy if we had money," answered Donald, scowling at Mike.

"I know if I had money I'd spend all my time hunting the Serengeti," said Mike.

"If I were rich, I'd buy me some Gucci underpants!" said one of the other pilots who had joined the conversation. Everyone laughs.

"I'd buy a dinosaur," said the American in his slow southern drawl.

"A dinosaur?" someone asked laughing.

"Well, just how rich are we talking here? I got myself a nephew, and he loves dinosaurs. I'd be his favourite Uncle if I had my own dinosaur." Everyone laughs.

"And what about you Moses? What would you do if you were rich?" asked Mike.

"There isn't any sense in wishing for what will never be," responded Moses. The group goes quiet for a spell.

"But if it were to happen, I certainly wouldn't be buying a dinosaur or Gucci underpants."

The lights dim as imperceptibly as the volume of the music swells until it is as dark and loud as any jungle bar. The people sway with the rhythm and someone vomits in the corner. The dancers' self-conscious restraint dwindles and they dance more freely, though still embarrassed. They shuffle their feet and wave their arms, yearning to unleash.

The new guys on base loiter around Donald to bear witness while he complains about Africans with a sharp tongue and puffed out chest.

One of the NGO girls approaches the table where Mike, Edward and a few of the senior base guys sit and asked, "A bunch of us are heading over to the new disco, anyone want to join us?"

"Damn straight!" exclaimed Mike. He and Aisha stand. "Come on Eddie."

Edward rarely drinks and his tolerance is low. He drinks his fourth beer.

"Sure," he answered in a slurred voice.

At first Mike is surprised, then a huge smile creeps across his face.

"Right on Buddy!"

Those seated begin to stand and Edward follows Mike and Aisha out into the courtyard and through the gates towards the vehicles parked along the dirt lane. One of the older NGO guys owns a beat up old Nissan pickup truck, and people pile into the open cargo bed.

Edward is anxious, but Mike and Aisha, a few of the other NGOs, plus the hotel waitresses, are already on board beckoning. He steps warily onto the tailgate and throws a leg over the dented and rusted rear gate, all the while apprehensive. His body moves forward in spite of himself. He squeezes into a small space that appears as others shuffle to make room. He sits on someone's feet. They lurch as the old NGO drops the clutch and stalls the truck. Others walk or attempt to hail *Tuk Tuks* or motorcycles from the nearby street. After a few false

111

starts, the old NGO, drunk and slurred speech, manages to get his overloaded truck rolling over the heavily undulating dirt lane. The suspension bottoms heavily and launches everyone into the air. Everyone laughs. Edward is scared. It is rough and uncomfortable. After one brutal jounce, they make the road proper and head to the disco. The old NGO floors the old truck and each shift of the gears causes everyone to sway fore and aft in rhythm with their momentum. With increased gait a refreshing breeze washes away the evening's swelter, tinged with recirculated exhaust fumes. Edward feels ill. The old NGO forgets the massive speed bumps along the route for they smack the first at great speed and with a loud metal clang everyone is launched high above the truck bed then roughly slammed back against the floor rearranged and discombobulated and no one laughs now. Someone has the presence of mind to bang hard on the back of the cab and yell for the old fool to slow down. Edward fears he will vomit.

The ride continues as everyone cringes in anticipation of the next jar, but lesson learned, the old NGO now slams on the brakes at each speed bump and they roll easily over the bumps. He then accelerates with the pedal to the floor and the engine strains against the load and pumps out great clouds of blue fumes, only to break hard for the next one. This uncomfortable procedure is repeated again and again. Eventually there is a violent swerve and the mass of bodies slide as one to the side of the cargo bed. The mass then slams forward against the cab as the old NGO skids to a stop. After a few moments to settle themselves and untangle, people crawl from the cargo bed as if escaping the grasp of a nightmare creature from another reality.

They stand about stunned and shake their heads and check their limbs and contents of their pockets. They have arrived.

From the crowded parking lot, Edward's nauseous eye is drawn to the flashing lights and laser show escaping the thatch-roofed and open-air disco, and even here, the heavy bass thumps through his very soul. Organizing themselves, others arrive via other modes of transport. Edward looks for Donald or Chet but they are not amongst the arrivals. Still their group is large and most of the faces are familiar, and en masse they head towards the entrance gate.

Edward finds comfort immersed within the group, yet approaches the bar uneasily. Local lads surround the gate, obviously the venue bouncers; large heavy set men with hard stares for those fearful souls who seek reassurance in a friendly smile. They scare Edward. Mike appears to have no such circumscription.

"What the fuck are you scowling at, you miserable cur?" Mike asked the largest of the bouncers. The large man responds with a weary smile.

"Hey Mike, keep out of trouble tonight, will ya?"

"Do my damnedest Kev."

They slap hands in some ritual handshake.

Like a sparrow in a large flock, diving for the middle of the mass, Edward tucks in to encapsulate himself within his adopted group.

Mike calls out the entry fee and everyone digs through pockets and purses and multiple hands pass forward torn and grubby local currency to satisfy the fare, then they migrate as a single entity into the crowded bar. Edward stops to catch his breath as he confronts the dancing sea of glistening black skin as bizarre colours reflect off the sheen amid pinks of open mouths and fluorescent eyes. The jumbled kaleidoscopic mass throbs as one to the heavy bass, which booms and courses through all and everyone and everything and the beat takes Edward's heart and controls it as its own. Edward shivers with trepidation. As his senses acclimatize to the onslaught, he notes that most males are shirtless, their lean muscular masses mix with the beautiful women in tank tops and bared shoulders. They sway with the rhythm and mindless, arms clawing for the heavens, lost in the here and now and the permeating African tempos. People bounce with the beat and in unison to impossible heights as heads roll wildly on their lithe necks, with no inhibition or restraint. To Edward, the scene exhilarates as much as taunts for his lack of life. The others in his group abandon him and absorb into the throng, and he finds he stands alone to witness the spectacle of debauchery, crawling from the bowels of Dante's maelstrom. The NGOs dance and find joy but with nowhere near the inhibition of the locals. Only Mike sacrifices his body to the demons coursing from the speakers.

They enter and seize him, and he meets their intensity and passion and carries it higher, higher than the Africans themselves dare tread, and Aisha is there with him. The others give berth to their dance with the devils, their bodies gyrating wildly to the African rhythm. A couple of NGOs with names he cannot recollect take Edward by the hand and drag him onto the floor, for he is desirous but lacks courage, and encouragement found, he resists only slightly. Embarrassed and certain all eyes are on him and him alone, he dances, tentative and awkward, striving to release the tension binding him to reality, and however ill at ease, he forgets and strives to match the exuberance of the others. Mike and Aisha drift into his field of vision lost to some ethereal dimension and are one and not apart from the music nor the crowd nor the essence of life itself. He envies them. Yet Edward is pleased to give witness to something intangible, at the edge of this life and teasing the next, and he wishes dearly to join but knows it is far beyond his capability. Teetering on the edge of what he is and overcome with the stench of body odour and an assault unlike his senses have ever known, the strobe lights now freeze the images before him in halting relief and together with the incessant hammer of the drums and deep bass resonating through the earth and all that is and Edward whirls and is lost.

When Edward awakes, he is in the parking lot, propped against a tree. Mike, Aisha and one of the waitresses hover over him.

"There he is! Passed out in the middle of an African pub from an evening of hard drinking, what a wild man!" Mike shakes his head and laughs. "I'll see if I can get a ride back to the hotel."

After a few minutes, Mike, Aisha and Edward jam into the back of a dilapidated old *Tuk Tuk* and head for the hotel. The humid night air is heavy in their lungs, tainted with fumes, and heavy rain drops tap heavily on the thin metal roof. Soon the sporadic becomes torrential and water finds its kin laid out across the landscape, unable to escape itself, and visibility wanes, affecting even this slow moving and rusted contraption. The driver finds every pothole, hidden beneath a uniform plane of rain splattered tarmac, as they drift through sheets of water riven from the heavens. Edward is soaked despite the scant coverage of the *bajaj* enclosure. The driver finds their hotel from directions shouted over the deluge, and Mike pays once again. They stand at the gate in the rain thoroughly waterlogged. Mike hammers on the metal gate to wake the sleeping security, and eventually the door opens, and they trod in sodden shoes across the courtyard and into the hotel. They climb the stairs dejected and forlorn, and *goodnights* are uttered as they disappear down their respective hallways.

Once in his room, reeling in that low feeling when alcohol's bliss departs, Edward stands, still drunk and unsteady, and disrobes. He hears a wail that carries above the noise of the heavy rain, hammering the tin roof relentlessly and echoing loudly throughout, and he approaches his window and peers outside. There is a young woman on the lane that runs beside the hotel, and she is on her knees in the mud. Her sodden clothes cling tightly to her small frame, and she pulls at her wet and matted hair and wails and throws herself facedown into the mud. Edward watches, and she appears to address one of the upper windows along his side of the hotel. She cries and beats her chest and throws herself into the mud again in a fit of despair, and Edward knows a heart has been broken by someone here. He knows not who. He is sad for the woman but too drunk to care, and he climbs into his bed and falls asleep.

Chapter 10

The sun sits high in the azure blue before crows skid down the hotel's tin roof and drag Edward from his slumber. Groggy and incoherent, he grasps for thoughts as they slip tween his fingers. His head throbs. He finds aspirin and places two at the back of his throat and washes them down with a litre of warm bottled water that tastes of plastic. He remembers the girl in the mud of the lane and moves towards the window. The brightness pains his eyes. He squints and searches but the rains had annihilated all trace of her. There are only the scrawny goats that nibble the brown grass and bay remorseful.

He takes a long shower then brushes his teeth. A clean and minty taste replaces the foul film he scraped off with vigour. He runs his tongue over his smooth teeth and satisfied and refreshed, he dresses and heads downstairs. The glare halts him as he steps into the courtyard, and the sun burns his scalp through his thinning hair so he hurries into the shade of the restaurant.

One waitress watches her Nigerian soaps on the television, and Moses sits by himself and smokes. Edward walks over and sits at the table, the plastic cover spotted with cigarette burns and sticky against his bare legs. A gecko runs across the ceiling.

"Hello Chef."

"Hello Edward, would you like me to cook something for you?"

"No, thank-you. I don't feel for eating, just for sitting. Have you seen any of the others?"

"I saw a few head out. I think maybe they went to the market, but it has been very quiet. I think most are still sleeping. Did you have fun last night?"

"Yes, I think I did," answered Edward uncertain, and he ponders the question and considers that yes, in fact, it had been fun. He smiles as the evening's events play out in his mind. He thinks of the girl in the mud.

"Do a lot of the guys here have local girlfriends?" Edward asked.

"A few do, but they are more discreet than Mike. Mike doesn't care what anyone thinks," he laughed. "The others, they do care."

"So who has a local girlfriend here?" Edward asked conspiringly.

"Ah my friend, that I cannot say. You would be surprised, that I can tell you."

Edward lets his thoughts drift amongst the faces of the crews, and Moses watches and knows he has given Edward something to speculate, a gift for his mind.

Cigarette finished, Moses stands and heads for the kitchen. Edward continues to sit, unsure of what to do with his time. After remaining stagnant for an age, adrift in mindlessness, the hysterics of the Nigerian soap begin to annoy him. He saunters back into the hotel, back to his room, and there he spends the rest of his day.

The crews lounge over the late Sunday morning breakfast, a far more casual event than their typical weekday feed. Shorts, flip flops and unshaven faces replace the uniforms of pressed black and crisp white.

"Anyone headed to the old fort today?" Dave asked.

"Yeah, we're going. I need a show of hands to figure out how many vehicles we'll need," said Mike.

A few hands reach for the sky.

"What's the old fort?" asked Edward.

"It's an old fort in the next village, about a twenty minute drive," answered Mike. "It used to be a fort and slave market, built by the Germans in the late 19th century. Some Norwegian bought the property and fixed it up into a hotel. There's a nice pool, and the food is great. Livingstone's last house, before he launched his final expedition, is right next door. There's a church down the hill too, sometimes you can hear them singing. It's a pleasant afternoon out."

"Okay, sure, I'm in," said Edward.

"We'll be heading out in an hour," said Mike to everyone. "Bring your swim suits, there should be no jelly fish in that pool." He winks at Edward.

They cram themselves into the SUVs then mince about to avoid skin to skin contact as they head out of town. Edward detests the pressure of Chet's damp warmth but there is no recourse so he concentrates on the African countryside. They pass motorcycles, slow overladen vehicles, and a large lorry toppled in the ditch, as men recover her cargo and load it aboard another. They cross barren salt flats and dusty gravel stretches of construction, and from time to time they catch glimpses of coast off to their right. Eventually they enter a small village, smaller than whence they came, and the SUVs toil in the deep sand of the narrow lanes, threaded between hovels from another era.

Edward spots a Swastika on one of the few cement structures. The driver notices Edward's gaze. "That's an old East-Indian building, the Hindi used that symbol long before the Nazis claimed it as their own. It's a sacred symbol that denotes prosperity, from long before Christ walked the earth."

The forest thickens as they climb into the hills, steeper and steeper amongst scattering children, until they encounter a gate tended by a uniformed guard. Credentials assured, they park in the lavish lot as butterflies dance on the breeze and stingless bees sample their sweat. With backpacks laden with swim gear, suntan lotion and novels for poolside they trek through Eden. Edward is enchanted by the beauty, surrounded by a lush and colourful garden of exotic plants, and cicadas chime amidst the whoop of monkeys that clamour in the high canopy. The old fort itself is grand and bright in fresh whitewash with dark contrasting doors and shutters of local ebony, and it is the Africa of Edward's imaginings. They stroll through the gardens hushed and reverent, along a stone pathway with more colourful butterflies and clucking chickens that strut arrogant and endemic. As they round the fort they meet the large modern pool of pristine water in azure blue. Amongst the hardwood tables scattered about in the shade are some NGOs from Friday's BBQ, and there are Indian families with children that scamper about and leap into the pool. There are a few local African families and it appears as if everyone knows Mike and

Aisha, for greetings call out from every table and Mike and Aisha respond in kind.

They locate a large enough table to accommodate them all, though some head straight for the poolside loungers. Shirts removed, suntan lotion applied and headphones adorned, they lay back and bake under the African sun.

Eventually a smartly dressed waiter makes his way to their table and records their orders. Despite a poor grasp of English, the waiter is patient and gracious amid the confused stream of words pouring forth from everyone simultaneously. It takes time and repeated clarifications before everyone is satisfied that their orders have been placed correctly, and he walks away content.

"Geez, that was painful," said Donald.

"He did all right, he's probably one of the trainees," said Mike.

"I'd fire his ass, I had to repeat my order four times. *Prawns and chips*, fuck sakes."

Mike ignores him.

"The food is quite good here, but have to wait an hour or more to get it," said Chet.

"Are you fucking kidding me?" asked Donald. "An hour?"

"What's your rush?" asked Mike, annoyed.

"An hour to cook some prawns and chips, it's bloody ridiculous!"

Mike stands up and peels off his t-shirt and dives into the pool. Aisha heads for the change rooms and soon wades in via the steps in a small white bikini. Most of the lads stop whatever they are doing and watch, their gaze veiled under dark sunglasses. Eventually Edward elects to change as well and afterwards, he takes the steps into the shallows, threading a course between the many Indian kids sprinting about. He tentatively steps in and finds the water pleasant, neither too warm nor too cool, and he slips below the surface and pushes off to glide along towards the deeper end, as the cool refreshing water draws away the heat of his body.

Movement catches Edward's eye, and he looks up into the canopy and sees a troop of small monkeys bouncing through the branches. They settle above the tables and watch the guests.
Donald swears and jumps up.

"One of those little fuckers is peeing on me!" Donald yells and he grabs a stone and hurls it into the trees and the monkeys screech and jump. They move a little further along before settling again. Edward watches as he treads the clear blue water. Small young monkeys cuddle with their mothers or suckle, and older siblings chase each other with great leaps between the sashaying branches high overhead. One monkey drops from the trees right on top of a chicken and there is a great tumult of screeching and clucking and feathers fly, then just as suddenly, the monkey vacates the battle and hops up into the nearest tree and scampers high into the canopy, leaving a pissed off chicken clucking about.

"Was he trying to eat it, fuck it or ride it?" asked Mike to those still at the table. They laugh.

"Probably a dare," said Chet laughing. "His brother probably told him *I bet you ain't got the balls to jump on that chicken*".

"I wouldn't recommend daring a monkey to do anything, they're crazy fuckers." laughed Mike.

After everyone had eaten and the dishes cleared, Mike leans towards Edward.

"Hey Ed, Aisha has to go into the village to see her Grandma, why don't you come join us for a walk?"

Edward looks about the pool as the guys soak up sun and snooze or read. He considers his anxiety over something precarious, possibly dangerous, but once again, he pushes aside the misgivings that obscure most of his decisions, and feeling proud, he nods and fishes his baseball cap from the recesses of his backpack. He sets it on his head to thwart the sun's searing heat then stands and follows them back through the garden.

They turn off on a different path, narrow and neglected, and Mike opens a small wooden gate and they head down the uneven rocks and into the village.

Threading through the brush under heavy foliage, they arrive at a dirt lane and turn left. They meet three young boys pulling homemade toys and Mike drops to a knee to inspect their wares. The youngest two pull empty water bottles with discarded caps acting as wheels mounted on wires passed through the body, with old dirty string as their teether. The oldest has a more elaborate affair which resembles a small wire cage, with metal caps off glass jars as wheels, and various paraphernalia stuck here and there that raise its status far above the basic vehicles of his younger friends. Deference is obvious. They all appear proud of their home made toys, and gloat that a big *mzungu* makes such a fuss. The boys brim with happiness and Mike gives them enough money to buy themselves ice cream.

They continue into the busier sections of the village, walking the narrow dirt lanes. The market stalls are tin roofed and misshapen, thrown together haphazardly with tied Acacia stocks, and hand dug ditches of refuse course here and there, and scraggy dogs sniff and lounge in the shade. People are preoccupied with activity and pay them little notice, though some show surprise at the white faces, not a frequent sight in these parts. They smile and wave and welcome. Swahili pop music plays from several small radios cranked far beyond their capability, and the speakers fart and crackle but the beat is decipherable, and kids dance beside their mothers as they peel corn or potatoes over plastic wash basins. When some children catch sight of the foreigners, they feign shock and run into the shacks, while the mothers laugh and smile and wave. It is a warm, friendly atmosphere and Edward feels relaxed and welcome. He is amazed at the happiness so prevalent amidst overt poverty. He considers that perhaps it is not squalor, depending on your frame of reference. Aisha stops at one stall offering a strange fruit and purchases a few and hands one to Edward. He tentatively tastes the pale flesh and swoons, ignoring his fears of exotic infection.

Edward warms to the place, for despite the dirt and garbage and rough living conditions, so far removed from his accustomed standard, the people seem content. In fact, the people appear to be happier than any place he has been. There is brightness and joy and a consuming happiness that permeates all despite the lack of material wealth, and Edward reconsiders his view of the world. The music distorts and crackles but there is indomitable African spirit, the traditional undertones tinged with modern flavour, underscoring the divine and the human condition. The timeworn harmony and melody of the music, rich in texture, blend and weave with powerful voices singing as if ordained by angels. The percussive beat and joy permeates the warm African afternoon. The call and response composition frolic as if taunting the gods, and the kids, mothers and shop keepers sing along and Edward wants to partake in whatever magic they have found. No one bothers them, no one is aggressive or withdrawn, they are only neighbourly and Edward is glad he came.

They continue through the market and garner a ragtag group of children that call out repeatedly in broken English *"How are you?"* over and over and the foreigners respond each time and laugh. Skinny and timid dogs accompany the children and Edward is unsure if they are pets but no one minds their presence, nor acknowledges them in any way. They follow and tails wag as the sun warms their hides, yet Edward refrains from petting the scraggy beasts. The foreigners leave the market area and head through the village and Edward notes that none give notice to the *mzungus* in their midst. He reflects on his preconceived notions and recalibrates his view. They eventually arrive at Aisha's grandmother's, and she has a small shop, though many streets away from the market proper. The elderly lady regards Mike with suspicion, raising an eyebrow at the tall *mzungu* on her Granddaughter's arm, followed by a subtle *'be careful of this one'* glance to Aisha. Then her hospitable leanings get the better of her and she invites them all inside for tea. They enter the poorly lit and threadbare domicile, not unlike those found in these parts over a hundred years ago or more, and it is dark and dank and ancient. She watches Mike with a wary eye as she prepares the hot water on a small burner set on a heavily leaning table. For Edward she takes a liking. He is perhaps unthreatening. She soon passes around tea for all and they sip while Aisha and her grandma converse in Swahili. Soon the sun lowers in the sky and with a nod and more false smiles they are led back into the street and make their way back to the old fort.

Others have packed their belongings and wait for them while one of the SUVs has already departed for town. Once seated in the rear seat, Edward reflects on his day, and on Africa, and realizes he needs to reconsider all.

Chapter 11

With a new outlook on life and Africa, Edward is renewed. The weekend had done him good. He reflects, what had an inebriated Mike told him the other night? *Challenge yourself, discover yourself.* Edward has faced challenges aplenty since his arrival, and surely he had grown, hadn't he? With new priorities, and wisdom gained from experience, he has seen the real Africa and is the better man for it. He shakes his head when he considers those who have not walked the markets of a remote African village nor visited aging grandmothers who served them tea. How could they possibly understand what he, Edward the explorer, had experienced? He is audacious, reckless and courageous, foolhardy and resolute, daring and valiant and heroic, and perhaps, a little dashing, and now, having tasted adventure, a step above those who have not, he brims with pride. He bathes in his exalted self-worth and decides to take more chances and live life fully, for therein lies wisdom.

On the ride into work Edward sits with Donald. Yesterday he discovered that Donald was already rated as a Captain in the company before his arrival, and only required a local line check to fly the line in a Command role. Edward is crestfallen.

"What a fucking shit hole," Donald comments as they pass through a slum on the edge of town, hidden behind tinted windows in air conditioned comfort, adorned in their pressed white uniform shirts and black trousers, with golden thread status bars proudly displayed on their epaulettes. "This lot will never change, best nuke the continent and start anew, eh what?"

Edward does not wish to offend so nods in reply.

There is excitement as they arrive at the airport, as a black mamba had been found under the portable fuel bowser. Edward and Donald head over for a look but there is little left of the snake.

"These lads go ape-shit over snakes, don't they?" laughed Donald. "What did I tell you? Get rid of the rats and you'll have problems with the snakes. Idiots."

They head for flight planning and prep for their first trip. Edward grows concerned about the weather as he reviews the government aviation websites. The satellite images portray thunder storms building in the area.

"Maybe we should carry some extra fuel for the weather, in case we get caught out?" Edward suggested.

"We'll be fine," said Donald.

They head out to their bird and fire it up as dark skies loom on the horizon. There are flashes of lightning and a few heavy drops of rain smack the windshield, but the mass of the storm cell passes them by.

They load their passengers and taxi out and soon depart towards the offshore platforms. Donald fires up their weather radar display and the sweeping arm paints the heavier of the storm cells ahead of them. The path to their rig is relatively clear but there is a great deal of activity and one of the heaviest weather days Edward had yet seen in this part of the world. The cruise checks are completed and they scrutinize the storms scattered here and there and some grow into solid reds and intense yellows and others decay and fade into nothing. Upon reaching thirty miles from their destination they contact the rig's radio operator and request current weather conditions and their return payload, and the radio operator happily complies.

Shortly afterwards Edward starts his descent, and more checks are completed and he maneuvers the bird until they are lined up into the prevailing wind and stabilized. As they slow and prepare to land, a rather large storm cell paints on their radar screen in yellow and red just beyond the rig. Donald forecasts they'll be on the deck before it's a real concern. Forked lightning framed in dark purple sky flashes on the horizon and static carries through their headsets.

"See that?" Edward asked nervously.

"Yeah, we're fine, continue with your approach."

Edward concentrates on the task at hand and bleeds off speed while he maintains his rate of descent, striving for a smooth steady profile to the platform. As they come over the deck itself, he flares off the remaining speed and pulls power as they settle, and Edward adjusts, and they are down. The wheels are chocked and passengers and cargo begin to unload. Edward watches the dark sky ahead of them, closing rapidly. It is a quick turnaround and the shore bound passengers load, the chocks are pulled and the take-off checks completed. Heavy drops of rain begin to smack the windshield and the wind sock off the bow flutters in conjunction with the renewed vigour of the winds. Edward looks to Donald for guidance but there is none so Edward pulls pitch and lifts into the hover. The aircraft twitches in the turbulence. He pushes the nose over and they accelerate into a hostile wall of rain. Forward visibility reduces to naught and heavy water from the skies slam into the aircraft and drowns out all and darkness envelopes them. Edward begins a left turn but his transition from flying visually to flying from sole reference to the instruments is not complete and he banks too hard and begins to descend.

"Watch your turn!" Donald called. "Check your altitude!"

Simultaneously with that frantic call Donald is on the controls and aggressively corrects. They are immediately wings level and climbing, with their radar altimeter warning light flashing at eighty feet about the sea.

"I have control!" Donald yelled. Edward releases his grip and his face grows hot and the stress almost overwhelms him. Donald glances at the radar and a second rig well outside their proposed track paints off to their left. Assured they are clear Donald relaxes somewhat, and with that risk negated he makes a small correction towards a brightness in the sky to their right, and they climb through five hundred feet.

"Gear?" Donald asked.

Edward shakes off his muddled thoughts and raises the gear and completes the rest of the after take-off checks. Donald watches him with concern.

"You almost flew us into the sea."

Edward does not reply.

"I'll fly back," said Donald. "Get on the radio calls and paperwork."

It takes a while before Edward finds sufficient trust in his voice before he responds. "Yes, I'll take care of it."

He now questions his own competence, a thought oft suppressed, yet now it confronts him in full relief. He deigned to ignore the many criticisms levelled towards him over these past weeks, but forced to reweigh his opinion of his own self, he considers; *perchance this life is not for him.* His heart quivers at this possibility but then some internal mechanism governing his self worth quells the thought. Like the passing storm, his insecurity displays its worth then dissolves into nothing.

"I think there was a down draft," Edward stated.

"Hmmm, or maybe you just fucked up." Donald looks over at Edward's morose face. "Listen mate, transitioning to the dials immediately like that? It's a bad scene that many would struggle with. I'll have to bring it up with Dave but don't sweat it. They can throw a few dozen inadvertent IMC scenarios at you in your next simulator session and you'll have it sorted."

That brightens Edward's mood somewhat, but he realizes he almost flew them into the sea. Another complaint about his flying on file won't do him any favours either. The adrenaline still courses through his body and his legs begin to quiver. Experienced pilots speak of the dreaded leg shake in hushed voices , the *tell* that they have danced with death, but for Edward, it is a common affliction. He is unable to admit to himself that he is prone to panic, that he does not handle stress well. Yet he knows, somewhere inside of himself, he knows. As in everything, momentum carries him forward, and he leaves his doubts behind.

"We didn't pull on anything too hard," continued Donald. "The Flight Data Monitor is certainly going to flag though. You can't hide anything anymore."

Eventually the thin line of the shore crests the horizon. Dark skies abound and another storm cell paints yellow and red on their weather radar screen. It appears to lumber towards the airport. Edward glances down at their fuel status and his chest tightens in panic yet again.

"I don't think we'll make the airport before that weather hits," said Edward.

"You may be right."

That is not the response Edward expected and fresh pangs of anxiety attack his bowels.

"I'll bring the power back to mins and slow down to conserve our fuel," said Donald. The aircraft raises its nose and the wind coursing over her smooth lines slacken as they settle into a more leisurely pace. Edward calculates their endurance at the reduced power and fuel burn. The results are dire in his mind and he runs through the numbers repeatedly. He can barely speak through his distress.

"We've only got thirty minutes fuel left," Edward manages to croak.

"Cool, that's plenty."

Edward's eyes open wide.

"But, but…we'll be into our reserve fuel any minute!"

"Yeah, that's what reserve fuel is for. That storm will be through in twenty minutes or so."

The storm cell is relentless, painting crimson and darker in their weather radar, and the sky itself is a deep, dark purple and forked lightning connects the heavens to earth in dazzling clarity.

"We'll land with barely ten minutes fuel left!"

"Uh-huh. Tell the passengers we have to delay for weather, revise the ETA."

"I'm really concerned about the fuel."

"Jesus man, we can always set her down on the beach somewhere if it gets too low. Relax. We may have the low fuel lights on and even more paperwork after we get down, but we'll be fine. Relax."

"I wish we had carried an alternate," cried Edward.

Donald rolls his eyes.

"Suck it up man. Grow a pair. You do realize nobody wants to fly with you, don't you?"

Edward's face grows dark. "Why?"

"You're a bundle of nerves Ed. You raise the stress levels in the cockpit though the roof. You've got to chill."

"Nobody wants to fly with me?" asked Edward, snivelling.

"It has been mentioned."

All of Edward's doubts tucked away so deeply rush to the forefront, and tears well up in this eyes. He repeats in his head; *'be a man, be a man, be a man,...'*. He recalls more of Mike's advice, *'Be who you want to be'* and he continues the mantra hoping it will take. Fear of running out of fuel cuts the mantra short and he almost vomits.

"I need you here with me Buddy," said Donald softly. "I need some help. Can you make sure we got all the checks done, and I'll circle out here and wait for the storm to clear out of the airport. Don't sweat it, we'll be fine. We are only a few minutes out and there are plenty of places to land if it comes to it."

Edward shakes off the crippling doubt and runs through the checks despite his quivering.

The low fuel lights come on, one followed shortly afterwards by the other. Edward's bowels clench. After they complete another orbit, they watch the edge of the airport materialize from the plum hue of the storm, as the tail end of the heaviest

133

rain continues its journey along its route, chasing the massive purple and flashing behemoth across the jungle.

"We're good," said Donald, and he turns into the airport to land. "It'll be clear by the time we get there."

They touch down on the tarmac with ten minutes left in the tanks.

Edward is the last to arrive at supper that evening. He collects his meal from the waitresses at the food table with nary a nod. With his head down and remorseful he shuffles over to a quiet corner and sits alone. Donald watches and collects his plate and utensils and sits with Edward.

"How are you doing Edward?"

"I've been better."

"Yeah, rough day for you, I know. What did Dave and the manager say?"

"Well, they said that there'll be a note on my file, and probably some more training, but I'll be keeping my job, for now at least. There's a meeting with the customer tomorrow morning."

"That's good news, the customer shouldn't be a problem. Just keep your head down and get on with it. We aren't expected to be supermen you know. As long as you learn from your mistakes."

Edward considers this, and it comforts him somewhat.

Donald continued; "What's that they say? *'What doesn't kill you, makes you stronger?'* We nearly bought the farm today, didn't we?" He laughed. "I wonder if the closer you get to getting killed, the stronger you get?"

Edward isn't quite as jovial but returns a smile. Mike finishes eating and joins them.

"I hear you faced certain death again today Eddie," Mike said. "How are you doing?"

"I'm all right." He had to admit that he did feel passably adequate. It was a lesson learned, a chance to grow. Edward starts to feel proud again, having stared into death's eyes and conquered yet again. In a fleeting moment he realizes that Mike has a calming effect, but the thought passes before he fully captures it.

"Where is Aisha tonight?" Edward asked.

"Dinner with her sister, but I might see that little jungle bunny later."

"Jungle Bunny? You can't say that man!" said Donald.

"And why not you little runt? It's one of our pet names for each other, she likes to call me *Twinkletoes*. Honestly, she doesn't mind."

"You could call her anything and she wouldn't mind Mate, you're her ticket out of this hole."

"What?"

"It's racist. *Jungle bunny*. Geez."

"You're calling me racist?" Mike laughs. Donald's verbal diarrhea slandering the locals at every opportunity had not gone unnoticed. Mike did not care about Donald in the least. He was concerned about the disciples he'd been collecting. It did not bode well for the base.

"Listen Mate, I don't mind you tapping a local *darky*, but calling her your '*jungle bunny*' is a tad much."

Mike raises an eyebrow. "*Darky?*"

"A *non-reflective*. Dark skinned. Negroid. An African," continued Donald.

"Well, Donald, your approval means a lot to me," said Mike sarcastically.

135

"Thinking with the little head, I understand," continued Donald. "An easier catch than one of those white NGO girls no doubt."

Mike stares at Donald and considers punching him in the face. Edward eats his meal.

"Just be careful, you don't know what those local girls carry," advised Donald. He finishes eating then stands and leaves. It is then that Mike notices Moses had been sitting right behind Donald's seat at the next table.

"Hello Moses."

"Hello my good friend."

"Sorry about the racist comments."

"Do not bother with that my friend, you said nothing wrong. I know your heart. People are so obsessed with the notion of race, but it does not matter." Moses waves his hand as if warding off a bad scent.

"Africans don't care about race?" asked Edward.

"I do not speak for Africa, only for myself, but I care not for differentiating over race, or over anything that separates mankind from one another. *Us and them*, it is a distasteful sentiment." He leans towards Edward and speaks in a low voice. "Even amongst us Africans, your shade of skin is seen as a sign of status, but for me, race is not an issue."

"Status? Because lighter skin is closer to white?" asked Edward.

"Perhaps, but I believe it is more complicated than this. It is true that most white people have good jobs here and more money than mosts Africans, and you are generally considered affluent, and that is a desired trait, do not get me wrong, but it goes deeper than this. We have women that bleach their skin to be lighter toned. The bleaching creams are very popular, but I am not so sure that it is race related. You see, if you are very dark, you probably spend a great deal of time in the sun, like a farmer or a manual labourer, and this is a low status to possess, but if you are lighter skinned, perhaps you do not get so much sun, perhaps you work in an office out of the sun and you are someone of importance, or at least, someone educated. Of course this is only a broad generalization, as you can be born with any shade, depending on your parents' lineage, but many women bleach their skin, and I think it is for this reason. Who understands women? Maybe in their minds the lighter skin is more desirable, but I do not believe this to be true."

"Aisha is very dark, and she carries herself with such confidence," said Edward, and he looks over to Mike to assure he hasn't offended.

"Yes," continued Moses. "Aisha is very beautiful, one of the most beautiful girls I have ever seen, but you see, the shades are not so important to us men. Beauty is beauty despite the darkness of one's skin. It does not matter about these things, but women can be vain."

"Skin colour doesn't matter to me," said Mike. "I grew up in a multicultural environment. I was completely immersed since birth. Race holds no sway with me."

"Oh, but it does my friend, but not in a bad way. I see how you look at the white girls from the Peace Corp, and they hold no attraction for you, but I see when you look at an African woman, and there is lust in your eyes."

Mike smiles. "I do find the African ladies incredibly sexy."

"Yes, I know this. I don't think this is racist. You have a preference, that is all. You treat everyone with respect, as equals, this I know."

"I try."

"I know you do. Even through you guys fly those crazy contraptions high in the sky, still you treat everyone well and with respect. This is why you are my friend. It is why you are everyone's friend. But the others, even though they may be polite, I can see, they carry false thoughts in their heads, and for this, I pity them. Like your friend Donald, he carries much arrogance." Moses fans his hand as if swishing away something unpleasant. "Don't worry my friend, I know racism, even if it lingers below the surface, but I do not see this in you. Racism is not an unnatural thing I'm afraid, I am old and have seen much, and I think about these things. Man has tribal tendencies, for this I am sure. We seek to belong to something that separates us from others. In our time, the idea of racial difference has been proven false, as we now know that it is simply a matter of skin pigmentation, and our differences are highlighted more by the differing environments in which we are raised, but this particular difference is clear in the colour of my skin. I am African, and I am proud, as I should be, but we are poor compared to the West, and I can see how the racist sentiments are generated. This attitude of superiority, of arrogance, is distasteful when the differences are racial, as we can accept that one has little choice of one's parents, but it is acceptable when applied to one's circumstances, or even choices. Let me explain." Moses takes a long draw on his cigarette. "People seek a kinship with those of similar economic standing, or with those professing to have certain religious beliefs, or political views, or even with those that prefer a certain sport, or a particular sport team, or even with those who prefer country music to rap or rock, or any other inane reason to feel superior to a fellow man, to feel part of some community with similar values, to validate the choices one has made, or perhaps, have been made for us. Tribalism runs deep I am afraid. I am saddened to say that I understand, even though I do not like it. It is a nice thing to be proud of your country, or beliefs, or tastes, but this separates from those who do not share the thing that makes you proud. This attitude seems to prevail in uneducated and untravelled people, as if education and travel has a power to wash this tribalism away, or perhaps it is strength of character from being exposed to more of the world." Once again, Moses takes a long draw on his short cigarette, and blows the inhaled smoke into the warm African evening.

"Do you think I would choose to be born a poor black man in Africa? Or would I rather have been born a rich white child in America? That is a question I am glad I did not have to ask of myself, *even though I just have*," he said softly with a wink. "Life has set its path before me and that is the life I have lived, and how could it be any different?"

Bewildered, Edward scrunches up his face. Mike smiles.

"I prefer to not think about these difference," continued Moses. "Whether those difference be skin colour or as inconsequential as where one happened to be born. I prefer to think of us as a people that share this space in time." Moses opens his arms in an all encompassing flourish. "We all share *now,* and what could be more than this? Why can we not come together as a people facing the challenges of today and not seek out differences that separate us?"

Moses flicks his exhausted cigarette butt into the void and sips his beer. "I believe the challenges to be met today are the inequalities that cause a man to consider himself better than his fellow man. Instead of gloating in one's good fortune, one should lift up his neighbour. We should not be considered separate for the colour of our skin anymore than for our social status or economic standing, or anything that separates us as human beings, causing us not to act together towards a common goal. When we act in our own interest, or in the interest of the group that we feel we belong to, we cause ourselves harm. I believe when that challenge can be answered, the world will be a better place."

Mike claps.

"The beer, it loosens my tongue. Too much I am afraid," said Moses.

"Well," said Mike, "I'll be honest, I grew up in a home where everyone was equal and that was the end of it. I've never seen racism like I've seen since I've been touring overseas. Racism is far more prevalent than I had ever imagined."

"Then you are a lucky man to have been raised this way. I can see this acceptance in you my friend."

"Yeah, racism is evil," said Edward, throwing his hat into the conversation.

"I forgive as is my place for evil is not absolute, and it has its time. What is evil now may not have been evil in the past, and what is good now may be evil in days to come. But some refuse to accept what is now accepted." Moses said, and he shakes his head. "How could we know something before it has been learnt? Tribalism played a large role in our development, for who could stand alone in the days before history? I believe tribalism had its place, it had its time, but that time is now past. Slavery for example, it was a dark time indeed, but it was the moral standard in its time, and many nations prospered because of it. Who else could have built the pyramids? They did not know then that what they did was evil. At the time it is what was done. How could it have been wrong? To look upon it with today's eyes is a false condemnation, for those of that age were only living the moral standard of the day. There were the weak and there were the strong and that is how it was done. Now we know better of course. Now slavery is known to be detrimental to our common good, and we have stamped it out, because we have learnt how to prosper without the use of slaves. Now the practice of slavery is evil, but I don't believe you can judge the past with today's eyes. Today, those who refuse to learn, who cling to their sense of superiority because of race, these I do not forgive so easily. Now it is a different time. It is our time, all of us sharing this planet here and now, and I have no patience for those who refuse to accept this truth."

"Yeah, it'd be nice if we were all a little more on the same page, but the world is not always good, " said Mike.

"This is true, people will be people, and people act in their own self interest, and this is to be expected, but I would like to see more equality," said Moses.

"You think that's possible?" asked Mike.

"I do not know. Greed is at the root of man, and proves a difficult foe." Moses finishes his beer and Mike hands him another. Moses nods in thanks. "You can legislate against greed, to thwart the very desire of man. We write laws to curb those fierce appetites. What do you think birthed religion? The great mind control of the masses, designed to mankinds very nature, be it intentional or simply a byproduct of baser desires, this I do not know. I do not wish to give those who have gone before us too much credit. Many things happen for reasons that are not known at the offset." He takes another long pull and lets the cool liquid sooth his throat. "Do you think man would not follow his true nature if there were not repercussions? That is what law is. That is what civilization is. There must be consequences for actions that are deemed detrimental for society, so men, they write laws."

"So laws will help Africa?" asked Edward.

"Perhaps. Foreigners come and take our resources and they get rich and we, for the most part, remain poor, and so it is. Our laws are not fully developed yet to stop this sort of behaviour. There is corruption, there is lack of education, lack of good healthcare, there are many problems. Ours is not a developed nation. But we are getting there Edward. We are moving towards this. Maybe someday we will have a modern society free of poverty. But I do not grieve for man being what he is. No, it is a process, and it is not yet complete. But it is moving in the proper direction I believe. Maybe it will not be perfect in our time, or the next, but that is the struggle, isn't it? Moving forward towards something better."

Chapter 12

The flying continues day in and day out. Pilots ferry changeover crews from shore to rigs and back again. At times they fly engineering specialists or geologists, or some critical mechanical part. Sometimes meritorious senior management teams travel offshore to unveil enhanced safety programs, or to annoy the oil workers with renewed deadlines and realigned cost cutting measures. The offshore exploration world's myriad of moving parts; contractors, cooks, service personnel, engineers, roughnecks, drillers, *toolpushers*, *derrickmen*, *floorhands*, *motormen*, *worms*, medics, radio operators, and sundry all work on scheduled rotations though some are beckoned for specific tasks. Oil exploration is a dynamic and fluid endeavour. The sea floor holds mystery and peril, with hydrocarbons concealed deep in the substrate under extreme pressure that is difficult, and often dangerous, to control. The helicopters play a roll, however subsidiary. Theoretically the men could be transported by boats, an option oft employed when fog or poor weather makes flying impractical. Supply vessels move back and forth from shore to rig, hauling pipe and bunkering fuel, and if the need be, they can move people, but it is impractical and time consuming. With profits paramount amongst all things, it is cheaper overall to move people quickly and on time. Overtime is expensive. The pilots and engineers play out their roles and collect their paycheques. The helicopters cross the coast line often enough that the townsfolk rarely lift their heads to watch them.

Edward's tour meanders along with early mornings and flight after flight after flight. The initial shock of all that is Africa fades for Edward because Africa and his imagination have found common ground. The variances to everything he knows have become the familiar. He calls his wife whenever the internet permits. The calls are never warm, nor reassuring, but they are Edward's lifeline to home and his life before any of this place.

Late in the week Tor catches Mike walking across the hangar floor.

"Are you guys finished for the day?"

"Yeah, I guess, just the two flights on the schedule."

"Damn pilots, must be nice to be finished work before lunch."

Mike ignores the derision, for it is too common a complaint between pilots and engineers to acknowledge.

"Do you need something?" Mike asked.

"Yeah actually, I wanted to let you know your bird is grounded."

Mike looks across the hangar at the helicopter they had flown earlier. All the cowlings are open and an engineer lies askew with legs hanging from the front door, his head up under the dash.

"Did you guys find something?"

"No, your co-pilot wrote up that auto-pilot snag we've been troubleshooting. It's in the logbook now, so she's grounded."

"Understood," said Mike angrily. He turns and walks away.

Mike stomps into the pilot's cabin. The other pilots sense the foul mood and stand and leave.

"Did you write up the auto-pilot snag?" Mike said to the remaining pilot after the others had left and closed the door.

Edward looks up from his paperwork, oblivious to Mike's mood. "Yes, I did. It went offline twice today. It needed to be written up."

"First of all," Mike replied angrily, "I'm the Captain and if something goes in the logbook, it'll be me putting it there. That's my signature going in there, it is my responsibility. I won't tolerate you going behind my back and adding things afterwards. Understood?"

Edward has a worried look on his face. He nods nervously.

"Second, we have been trying to track down and troubleshoot the cause of the auto-pilot issue by swapping out various components to see how they fare, to help identify just what causes the auto-pilot to drop offline. Once you've entered the snag in the logbook, the aircraft is officially grounded."

"I was taught to always put every snag directly into the logbook immediately after the flight regardless of the consequence. My job is to enter the snag. It then becomes someone else's problem."

Mike's face turns red. Edward continued nervously. "It is the safest method, I don't care if the aircraft is grounded. If it's broke, it's broke."

Mike chews on his bottom lip as he turns that over in his mind.

"Broke may be broke on a huge base in the North Sea, where you have a ton of aircraft and a warehouse full of parts, but this is Africa. It can take weeks to get a part through customs, and we have people to move. The customer is working on a tight schedule and if we can't get the job done due to an unserviceable aircraft, there are companies that can and will replace us in a heartbeat."

"That isn't our concern. It says in the operations manual that snags are to be entered immediately."

"Listen, if it affected the safe operation of the aircraft, I'd agree with you. We have two redundant systems, and one of those systems kicking offline twice in a two hour flight hardly constitutes a safety hazard. You push a button and it reengages.

And, you should have talked to me first."

"That's the rules," protested Edward defiantly.

Mike rubs his hand over his face and grimaces.

"Okay, you are an idiot, that has already been established. For the most part, I can put up with that. When you start making me look bad, or even worse, make the company look bad and negatively affect our performance, and possibly have the customer start looking elsewhere for their needs, that pisses me off. I understand that you come from a very controlled environment where you blindly follow the rules as if they were handed down from on high, and that you are a slavish adherent to anything written down…"

"Rules are the cornerstone of society. Rules took us from the dark ages to the modern age. Rules are the fabric of modern life! Without rules we are nothing!" sputtered Edward.

"The fabric of life?" scoffs Mike. "I think I'd prefer the dark ages Eddie. You can't blindly follow the rules, you have to know the reason for the rule in the first place, what that rule is trying to circumvent. Seems nowadays every time someone screws up they try writing a new rule to prevent some other idiot from making the same mistake, then you get a bunch of these newer guys thinking these rules are handed down from on high and I swear they'd shoot themselves in the foot if they could find a rule telling them to do it."

Edward looks bewildered. Mike sighs and turns and leaves the office, leaving Edward wondering what he had done wrong.

Mike heads into the engineer's office and sits down. Tor glances up from his desk as another engineer inputs data into a computer program that tracks aircraft hours. The engineer looks over his shoulder at the pilot.

"Hey Mike."

"Hey Danny, how ya doing?"

"All right."

"I apologize for my co-pilot guys, I know this complicates things for you."

Tor responded, "Yeah, I already spoke with the manager. We've got parts inbound already. Hopefully we get them through customs in short order and one of them fixes the issue."

Danny swings his chair around. "You fucking pilots, such prima donnas. Nothing but fucking trouble, you lot." He smiles warmly and winks. "Can I tell you a story?" Danny doesn't wait for a reply. "When I was a young lad working on the farm, working on my Dad's old tractors and decrepit trucks, every now and then a helicopter would fly by and I'd look up at it and think; *how cool would it be to work on one of those things?* You know? That was my dream. So I worked hard at school and saved my money and got myself into a technical college to be a helicopter engineer, and I was so damn happy. It was perfection, here I am going to school to work on the coolest contraptions ever to grace this earth, and I'm learning about turbines and fluid dynamics and all these systems and how to fix them. There were all these cool tools and I could travel the world, and I was in seventh heaven, I tell you. But you know what none of the instructors ever told me?"

"No, what?" asked Mike with a smile.

"That I'd have to work with you fucking pilots. If I knew then what I know now, I would have stayed on the fucking farm."

Edward takes another sick day for a bad stomach. He sleeps in, despite the early call to prayer and the crows sliding down the tin roof of the hotel. He lays in bed, half asleep, and listens to heavy wood doors open and close, followed by the screech of the downstairs door and raised voices. The diesel engines of the SUVs roar to life and their doors slam shut, and the gate opens and closes as the rest of the crews head off for another day's work.

It's a lazy drawn out shower, with plenty of hot water, and dressed casually in shorts and a short sleeved shirt, plaid and buttoned to the neck, Edward heads downstairs to procure an omelette from the kitchen. He sits and Donald stumbles in and joins him.

"Why in hell do I need a day off in this shit-hole?" asked Donald as he sits across from Edward in the empty restaurant.

"I think it's a customer requirement. Pilots are required to take one day off every five or seven days. I forget."

"Fucking stupid. Have you read the news about the processing facility?"

"No."

"Well, it seems the locals are in an uproar as the government wants to pipe all the gas they found here to the city to be processed there. Of course, the locals want the processing facility built here, for local jobs and whatnot. They figure the gas is here and they should reap the rewards."

"I hadn't heard."

"Yeah, nasty bit of business. If they decide to process in the city, I think the shit will hit the fan."

"Really?" asked Edward with concern.

"And you know what? They'll be coming straight here."

"Who will?"

"The locals. They know where we are. They'll fucking attack us and we'll be machete fodder, mark my words."

Edward's eyes widen. It's the first he heard of this.

"Those fucking security guards we have are useless, I doubt *Aids* even has bullets for that ancient rifle of his. We should ramp up security and right quick. They should issue each of us a gun."

"*Aids*?"

"The old fucker at the gate."

Edward glances over at the skinny old man.

The waitress brings Edward's his omelette. Donald looks up. "Where's mine Sweetie?"

"It's coming." She hurries away.

"Fuck sakes, how long does it take to make a fucking omelette?"

149

Edward struggles to make a face of agreement with a hint of disapproval.

"This place is a walking time bomb, let me tell you Edward. The security risk with local girls prancing around here all hours of the night is stupid. I swear, those gals are telling all the local guys about what we have and where our stuff is, about our lack of security, about how unprepared we are."

"We have security."

Donald laughs. "That old fuck with the rifle? I asked him what he had for bullets and he shrugged his shoulders. I doubt a full on riot would even wake him up, and if it did, he'd go hide behind the trash bin. We got nothing here Ed, no razor wire over that wall, nothing. Man, they could be up and over that thing quicker than a blink of an eye, and the hotel doors are just glass. That won't even slow them down."

"Our room doors are wood and lock," argued Edward.

"I could bust your door down in a second. Mark my words, they are going to get in here and murder us all in our sleep and it's all because of these local whores running around willy nilly and the complete lack of security, and I tell you what, the company will be liable for all of it."

Edward frowns. He hadn't thought about that.

"We have a safety reporting system, and I'm going to damn well use it, and I think you should too. The more of us the better. State the risks and they'll have to do something."

"Yeah, I guess."

"And that idiot Mike, who knows what diseases that local whore of his is carrying? I know she's got this place scoped out for the local lads. I saw her in town talking with some of them."

"Some of who?"

"Some hoodlums. Looked to me like they were hatching up something."

Edward is nervous now. Why would management even let local girls into the hotel? They turn a blind eye. They don't care for my safety. There are rules and they break them and no one says a thing. He gets angry.

"I'll put in a report too," said Edward.

"Good idea, Edward. They have to get this place under control."

Edward gives Donald his sternest face, to confirm his solidarity. Donald gives a slight nod in reply. A long awkward moment passes before Edward breaks the silence. "I was thinking of heading into the grocery to get some toothpaste and a few things, if you want to go for a walk?"

"I'd be keeping a low profile if I were you, maybe wait till the guys get back and take a driver and a vehicle. Even then, I don't think we should be seen around town."

Just then, Aisha walks by the dining area towards the gate.

"Hello Edward," she said and waves. "Hello Donald."

Edward waves and Donald nods. She passes through the gate after a brief word with the old security guard.

"Do you believe that shit? She was up in the hotel alone and Mike is flying! She could have been going through all our rooms!"

"My door is locked."

"Oh, she could get in when the cleaning ladies are up there. They've got all the keys. It wouldn't be difficult for her to get in."

"Couldn't the cleaning ladies steal just as easily?"

"No, they'd get caught, though I don't trust them either. I'm going up to my room and check through my shit. I recommend

151

you do the same. Those whores shouldn't be allowed here at all. It's jeopardizing all of us."

"I agree," said Edward. Donald stands, flexes his pectorals, then strides into the hotel. After the door closes, Edward gets to his feet and ambles into the courtyard then stands in the shade wondering what to do. He had planned on a trip to the grocery store, which was just around the block, but there was no way he'd brave that gauntlet now. The gate opens again and Tor walks in with a shopping. bag

"Aren't you working today?" asked Edward as Tor passes.

"Should I be? Are you lazy pilots the only ones who get a day off?"

"I'm sorry," Edward apologized.

"I'm joking Ed. Of course I'm working today, we engineers **always** work. I'm going in after lunch. We have a late night tonight. I can't get started on some heavy maintenance until the birds are finished flying."

"Okay," said Edward, unsure of himself. "You know, I don't think we should be out walking around."

Tor scowls. "Why the fuck not?"

"Well, the riots they've been talking about. It's dangerous for us to be seen."

"Who the hell told you that? Nobody gives a fuck about us."

"Well," Edward stammered. "If there's a riot, what are our options? What if they come for us?"

"You can hide under your bed."

"Really? You think that's a good idea?"

Tor looks at Edward with sympathy and humour. "Probably for you that is a good idea." Tor turns and walks into the hotel with his groceries, shaking his head.

Edward languishes in his hotel room as crows claw at the tin roof, drowning out the mournful cries of the goats, another beautiful East African day wasted. Frequent trips to the toilet are interspersed with lengthy chugs of lukewarm spring water, tainted with plastic from too long in the sun. Later the gates open and the Toyotas return from the airport with the crews. Edward heads downstairs for a soda. Moses leans against the wall of the kitchen chatting to a waitress. They both wave at Edward. Edward returns the greeting and stands in the shade and watches the activity and sips his soda. After a short time, an engineer and pilot walk out of the hotel and exit via the gate carrying beach gear. Edward frowns.

Completely bored, his stomach much improved, Edward heads downstairs while the sun settles towards the horizon, having bore its mass high in the African sky for yet another long day. Despite the late hour, the heat and humidity punches Edward as he steps from the hotel . Surprised to find Mike and a few others standing around the Toyotas, he saunters over.

"We're headed over to that restaurant by the beach for some *sun downers*, then we'll stay for the BBQ tonight. Why don't you join us?" asked Mike.

"I don't think we should be going out. They are expecting riots."

"Bullshit. Who the fuck told you that? Come on Eddie, we're ready to go." He holds a door open and Edward reluctantly gets in. Mike hops into the driver's seat.

"You can drive?" asked Edward.

"I can fly a helicopter, I think I can drive."

"No, I mean...I thought we weren't supposed to drive here? We have drivers."

"I gave them the night off."

More arrive as they pile into the SUV, so they end up taking two of the Toyotas. With everyone jovial and in good spirits it's a fun and relaxing drive, with crass jokes and pilot versus engineer taunts. They arrive at the restaurant and Mike backs into a tree causing fits of laughter. They spill from the Toyotas and are swarmed by tail-wagging mongrels. Few brave petting their mangy hides. The crews strut through the foyer with smiles and waves then head out to the open-air dining area that overlooks the sea. It is busy tonight. The group follows Mike out to a long group of tables that run along the beach-side rail. Aisha and some of her friends sit and chat, awaiting the new arrivals. Mike sits with Aisha, and while casual, it appears preordained when a few of the guys greet the ladies already seated at the table. They nod at a few oil workers and ex-pats at nearby tables. Edward sits with Mike and Aisha.

"It seems like most of these guys have local girlfriends," said Edward.

"No, not at all, but a couple do," said Mike. "The others are just friends. Quite a few of the guys don't go in for the local ladies, but they don't mind the company either. And don't forget half the guys stay at the hotel and never go out. They're just here to work, collect a paycheque and head home. Shame really. This place has got a lot to offer."

"You seem to enjoy the place."

"Yeah, I really do. I could settle down here. Life is more immediate here compared to back home, with all its superficial bullshit. I feel more alive here. The place gets under your skin."

The waiter comes to the table and the majority of the crew order gin and tonics though a couple order the local beer. Edward orders the beer.

"The local beer here is kind of nasty, gives me a headache," warned Mike. "There's rumours they use formaldehyde as a preservative due to the lack of refrigeration, but I doubt that'd wash, even here. There's deaths every year from home brewed beer but the stuff sold in bottles has to have some standards. One would think anyway. Still, I stick with the old tried and true gin and tonic, an East Africa tradition. The venerable *sundowner*. I believe the British East India Company's Army came up with it, as the quinine in the tonic was believed to suppress malaria. I think *James Bond* had one in *Dr. No*, and that's good enough for me. Hemingway wrote about them too. Regardless, and maybe I'm just a hopeless romantic at heart, but I enjoy a gin and tonic while watching the sun set."

Edward wishes he had ordered one.

The drinks arrive and everyone cheers another evening in Africa. Mike turns to Edward.

"So why did you think it was a bad idea to go out?"

"The riots."

"Riots? Trust me Eddie, if they riot, they won't be after us, they'll go for the government offices. Don't worry about it."

"Well, the security is atrocious at the hotel, and everyone knows where we are."

"Have you been listening to that idiot Donald?"

That idiot Donald? Edward reconsiders the report he put in that afternoon with Donald's coaxing. His face flushes bright red when he realizes it could directly affect Mike and Aisha.

"You're turning fifty shades of red Eddie, what's up?"

155

"Well," stammered Edward, "Donald should know about security, he's ex-military. I think he was security in the military. He's been to war you know."

"Oh, for fucks sakes, yeah, that's what he's been telling anyone who'll listen. Those security guys are obsessed with that shit. It's their job, but this isn't a war zone. There's tourists walking all over this place. He's being an ass. And having been to war doesn't carry any weight with me, either you have a pair or you don't."

"A *pair*?"

"Nads. Balls. You either have them or you don't, and Donald don't. Having been in the military doesn't count for anything in my book. Seriously, I think Donald's too short to have been in combat. There has to be a minimum height requirement," Mike laughed.

"What are you guys talking about?" asked the American.

"What a bunch of fucking losers you ex-military wankers are," laughed Mike.

The American looks at Mike with a raised eyebrow and doesn't smile. It's not often that anyone raises any sort of reaction from the American as he doesn't care much about anything, other than the local girls. He has a different one under his arm every other night.

"We're you in the military?" asked Edward.

"Over twenty years in the U.S. Army."

"Are you concerned about security at the hotel?"

"Fuck no. Have you been talking with that idiot Donald? Don't compare him to me. I don't think that little asshole could stop talking long enough to secure anything."

"He was in combat," argued Edward.

"Doesn't mean a thing. Either you're a dickhead or you aren't. Combat won't change that one way or the other," said the American in his southern drawl.

"It seems our buddy Donald has been spouting off about hotel security to everyone. We heard his spiel all the way to the airport the other day. We just ignore him," said Mike. "Be careful with that one Eddie, he's got some ideas that could get you in trouble over here."

Edward considers this and remembers the reports he had sent in earlier that day. He feels low. One of the oil industry guys from the shore base approaches to talk with Mike and Aisha. He crouches between them and speaks in a hushed tone.

"Hey guys. Aisha, remember that girl that was with you the other day? Would you mind giving her a call? I'd like to see her again."

"Sure, I'll give her a call," said Aisha sweetly.

"Thanks. Enjoy your drinks guys."

As the horizon devours the African sun, the sky blooms into warmer hues of pink amongst massive thunderheads far, far away. Conversations suspend and heads from every table turn to witness the fleeting spectacle, for some sunsets will tug at your very soul. The pinks deepen into strong reds with yellow bands artfully brushed across the sky as the fiery brim of the sun wavers. Then the clouds and all the sky churn into a maelstrom of crimson and nary an eye dare blink. Edward is awestruck, for his imaginings are not capable of such things. His heart quivers as all face their own reckoning, mesmerized by the beauty. The intensity quickly fades and darkness seizes the night, and the conversations renew with vigour. Either from alcohol or from the equally liberating absence of light, the night swallows reservation and allows for villainous sentiments to flow freely from unrestrained mouths, an intoxicated atmosphere where thoughts flow unhindered. Edward switches to gin and tonics.

Then she arrives. Aisha's friend, the girl the ex-pat had requested, struts into the restaurant and none can deny her bearing, for every soul at that place turn to watch. Tall and thin and beautiful, she has accented her powerful aura with absurdly high-heels and she towers, her long legs strong and confident despite her dubious footwear. Ones eyes are lead up those long smooth legs to gold shimmering *short-shorts* tight as if spray painted on her lithe little body. This low waisted garment does little to hide what nature has bequeathed beneath, and as the eyes continue their journey upwards, for surely those legs beg precedence, there is a glittering jewel in her navel, framed with her taut skin over a trim belly, and continuing upwards there is a blue sequine halter top that sparkles in the restaurant lights. The smooth dark skin of her chest, nestled between narrow shoulders, draw the eye to the wild and teased hair, three times as wide as the rest of her and dyed a glowing unnatural baby blue. Her calculating and provocative eyes seduce behind fluttering false lashes that extend far beyond her petite nose, and her lipstick is blue and garish on her full and voluptuous lips. A pink tongue emerges and languidly caresses her upper lip, moistening it further, before slipping back whence it came. The first viewing complete, one cannot turn away, and further scrutiny reveals a face and upper chest sprinkled with glitter. Her nails are painted bright metallic blue, obscenely long and curled, and between those long fingers rest a cigarillo which she draws upon with flourish and poise. She struts and swishes her cigarillo with overblown confidence that carries her extravagance, justifies it, and is unapologetic. She looks about and spots Aisha.

"Jesus, its *Super-Whore*," said the American.

She saunters over and greets Aisha, then Mike and Edward. She daintily takes a seat with them.

The ex-pat that requested her presence sneaks over and goes directly to Mike, intentionally avoiding the girl. He leans in to speak privately.

"What the hell man? I can't be seen with her looking like that! My boss is at our table."

"I'll take care of it," answered Mike discretely, and he laughs, shaking his head. He leans over to whisper something to Aisha and she nods then speaks with her friend. The friend stands up in a huff and struts back towards the door and disappears.

Donald arrives later with another pilot and sits with Edward. Aisha's eyes darken and she stands, as do all the girls as if by an unspoken command. They head off towards the washrooms.

"Got yourself a live one there mate," said Donald. "You do know she's just after your money, right?"

"It's not my good looks then?" Mike scoffed.

"Don't fool yourself. She is taking advantage of you mate, she likes the prestige it gives her to be seen with a white man."

Mike smirks. "Well, I guess being taken advantage of by a beautiful African gal isn't the worst thing that can happen to me. Why do you care? You should concentrate on your own problems."

"What problems?"

"Like getting yourself a woman, so the rest of us don't have to listen to you jerking off all hours of the day and night. The walls are pretty thin at the hotel. We can hear you spanking and grunting in there."

Donald's face grows dark. "You are brave, I'll give you that. Tagging African gals. You must have a death wish."

"What are you guys on about?" asked Chet, arriving with a wobble, beer in hand.

"Bravery," said Mike.

"There's a fine line between stupidity and bravery," slurred the American, joining the conversation. "Depends on your point of view."

"And the results of the endeavour," said Chet.

"Bravery is farting in Africa!" added the American. They all laugh.

"Depends on the results of *that* endeavour," added Mike and Chet chokes on his beer.

As the tide recovers from the moon's pull, the surf pounds against the rough coral shelf that runs alongside their table, occasionally sending a spray of saltwater skyward. A light refreshing breeze courses through the rustling palms and cools the sweat on their skin. They dine on BBQ prawns and octopi and jovial chatter. Shore based oil workers and some NGOs have joined their table, and it becomes another party, not unlike the weekend prior, yet more restrained for all work the morrow.

Donald attempts to chat with a couple of the white NGO girls but they quickly find reasons to move on. The hours pass and the crowd dwindles until excuses are made and friends depart. Despite a yearning to maintain the perfection of the evening, better judgement prevails and the crews pay their dues and head home, leaving the restaurant empty. Rain splatters the windows of the Toyotas as they near the hotel followed by a deluge of water that reduces visibility to zero as they park in the courtyard. All run for the hotel and soak their feet in the standing water. The rain relents slightly when Edward reaches his room and sheds his wet attire. The soft tap of heavy drops of water on the hotel's tin roof echoes thoughout as he prepares for sleep. He attempts to call home, and the phone rings and rings and rings and Edward does not understand why his wife would not be home at that hour. He tries twice more then gives up. Then the intensity of the rain builds and builds, and the power goes out. Water cascades from the heavens and soon becomes a roar that drowns out any capacity for thought. The sky flashes brightly and KABOOM! Lightning and thunder assault with an intensity Edward can hardly fathom, and if one were to let imagination run free, one could easily envision the end of days. The room is awash with repeated flashes of bright purple light and the air seems to collapse as yet another crack challenges the roar of water beating the tin roof, and the air rushes to refill the gap from the thunderbolt with a hardy snap.

The storm does not wane. The intensity surges as time creeps forward despite the attack from the heavens, for hour after hour the storm does not slacken. After a time Edward is carried to the underworld, and he sleeps the sleep of the dead, the demons thrashing beyond his conscious. The tumultuous assault does not relent and one is vexed concerning its provocation. It carries on with its quarrel with all and sundry well into the morning, well after the sun has risen to face its adversary. Eventually, the sun wins.

Chapter 13

All of the morning's flights are cancelled. Remnants of the cyclone pester the village until the bulk of its energy drifts Northward and finally it is done. Steam wafts from every water logged thing as the storm relinquishes its captives to the sun. The humidity intensifies and scalds as the temperature climbs. Moisture permeates all. Edward slept late as the rain hammered the hotel. Now in his sun brightened room, he stands at his window and regards the devastation. The village's drainage is overwhelmed. The yard and lane are submerged and the goats are gone. Flotsam flushed from every nook and cranny drift among wading locals and cattle, and cars push waves of brown water as they search for shallow passage. Edward ambles downstairs for breakfast and wades through knee deep water across the courtyard to the restaurant. A few other hardy souls had braved the water and the waitresses manage a serving of local fruit and cereals. The manager arrives.

"They may have cancelled the morning's flights but we still have plenty of people to move. It's looking to be a busy afternoon. Everyone scheduled to fly today be ready to head into the airport in thirty minutes."

They grumble and finish their food and disappear into the hotel.

Thirty minutes later the drivers park as close as possible to the hotel door and the crews navigate the high spots of the courtyard to avoid soaking their shoes. The water levels subside a little. Once loaded, they head out the gates. All gaze aghast at the sea of brown muddy water as they exit the lane, yet the activity of the village continues unabated. Each small cellular hut is half-submerged and water is still well above the floors of the shops they pass. Yet people waddle along, often to their waists in the brownish-red murk, their wares above their heads, and *Tuk Tuks* persevere with wet footed passengers while SUVs plow through, their wake scorned by the pedestrians. Water seeps into the passenger compartment as they cross through deep water and circumnavigate washed out roads. Jammed against the door of the crowded SUV, Edward captures a glimpse of what has always been, his short life span bearing witness to a perpetual event. He imagines floods are common in these parts and have been for eons. His mind grasps at something greater. *The seasons and the rains are timeless, and man is the guest* thinks Edward.

As the crews unload the manager asks everyone to meet in the passenger lounge for a quick meeting prior to prepping for flights. The pilots drop their bags in flight planning and grab a quick coffee. After a few minutes they sit in the lounge, well before the passengers arrive. A few engineers skip to inspect the aircraft.

"Okay Gents," said the manager, "we've received complaints about the girls overnighting at the hotel, and unfortunately they've gone straight to head office. As you can imagine, the complaints have not been well received. The folks across the pond don't have an inkling of life abroad, they just worry about corporate responsibility and how we are perceived locally, and they've taken a hard line. Basically, and this is from on high as of this morning," he looks down at the paperwork in front of him and reads, "*there will be no females allowed on the hotel premises, and breaking this rule will result in immediate termination.*" He looks up with a grimace and gauges reactions. "Sorry guys, but it's been pushed to the top and I have to deal with it."

"Surely they mean *local* girls aren't allowed? No problem with white girls, right?" asked Donald.

The room goes silent. Some would later swear that they could hear crickets chirping.

"I don't think we can differentiate between local girls or otherwise Donald," said the manager after an uncomfortable silence.

"Well, thats bullshit," said Donald.

"Yeah, as if any of the NGO girls would have anything to do with you, you short little racist fuck," said Tor.

Edward's stomach churns and he can feel the heat in his face as he blushes profusely. He hopes no one notices.

"Did you get one complaint or a few?" asked Mike.

"Sorry bud, I can't say, but I can't ignore it."

"Understood," said Mike.

Activity at the airport is hectic as the electricity throughout the area remains out, making operations and communications troublesome, and there is damage from the storm to contend with. Melancholy prevails despite the suns warmth and the deep blue of the sky. The mood is somber and subdued, and animosity builds between the old guard and the new.

Flights depart and the helos vanish into the scattered white clouds, remnants of the massive influx of moisture forsaken by the passing cyclone, driven up into the atmosphere as the sun's rays cook the mud and foliage. Later those helos return at odd intervals. They flare and land and dislodge their cargo and passengers in a hive of activity and noise. The weary pilots grab a quick visit to the toilet and replenish their water bottles while the engineers inspect and refuel the aircraft. They launch again and the day is long, with everyone finishing in ebbing light, as the sun kisses the horizon.

That evening while the others are downstairs at dinner, Edward attempts to call home again. This time his wife picks up but she is distant and preoccupied. Edward senses something is off but is afraid to ask. He tells her he tried to call the evening prior but lies and claims the call did not go through. She offers no explanation to satisfy his curiosity and he does not inquire further. This night he does not sleep well.

Edward's mind is elsewhere the next morning. He is tired and worrisome. He sits beside Donald in the crowded Toyota for the drive into the airport. Donald spouts his incessant diatribe over the shortcomings of the locals. The weaker minded chuckle at his antics. Some strive to avoid Donald, while others wear earphones and lose themselves in portable music for the drive to work. There are those taken in with his sharp wit and derogatory tirade. He speaks what others dare to think. He has become popular on base, his non-stop rant a welcome and humorous distraction. The derision between the old African hands and the new additions grows, and Mike senses the shifting tide. The base has lost its charm.

Edward flies with Chet again today, unaware the frequent pairing chafes at Chet's patience. Chet notes Edward's lack of focus, and tires of constantly prompting the pedantic fool for radio calls and checklists. Chet considers commenting then decides against it and accepts the task at hand, albeit with a wary eye on his copilot. It is another long day.

That evening Edward tries to call home again. He mock dials a few times before he builds up the nerve to let the call ring through. He wants to discuss the distraction in her voice during the previous call, and to question why she wasn't home the evening prior. He also fears upsetting her. She can be so unpredictable and moody. He has learnt that a conversation will never go as he imagines it will. Somehow everything ends up being his fault. This time he lets the line ring and ring and he is about to hang up when there is satisfying click. There is no voice at the other end.

"Hello?" said Edward.

"Yeah?" his wife asked breathlessly.

"It's Edward," he said, sounding uncertain. His heart pounds in his chest.

"I know who it is," she said in a condescending tone. "You don't have to call so often, I'm busy. My life doesn't revolve around you."

"But I like to hear your voice."

He hears her snort and then he hears something else.

"Who is there with you?"
"There's nobody else here."
"I heard a male voice."
"It was probably the TV. You're breaking up, I can barely hear you."

And the line goes dead.

Edward wakes with another bad stomach and takes the day off. Uncertain if his ailment's cause is something he had eaten or his nerves, meagre sleep was the result either way. Not wanting to face his unsympathetic coworkers, he waits for the noisy diesel engines of the Toyotas to fire up and for everyone to leave. He ambles downstairs with a sore backside. The American is the only one in the restaurant. Shirtless and tanned, he leans back on a plastic chair with his feet raised and reads. He doesn't look up so Edward sits by himself. Shortly afterwards, Edward's standard cheese omelette is served and he eats, but there is no flavour. He wonders if his omelette lacks flavour or if distraction thwarts his palate. While he eats, a large and angry black man stomps into the restaurant and stares hard at Edward. Edward stares back, frozen. The African snorts and looks over at the American, obviously a better candidate for his fury. His nostrils flare.

"You!" he yelled in a heavy voice congruent with his bulk. The American looks up slowly, annoyed at being distracted from his novel.

"You leave my wife alone!" yelled the large African. The American regards the man with boredom. Edward watches with mouth agape.

"Who's your wife?" asked the American after a long pause, in his slow Southern drawl.

167

"Jasmine!" yelled the African. His eyes bulge from their sockets and his temples visibly throb. There is another long pause.

"Jasmine the waitress?" asked the American after an age.

The African's eyes swell and tension courses through his body and evolves into a perceptive force.

"Yes, Jasmine the waitress!" screamed the African, spittle flying from his mouth.

The American watches the guy for a moment, standing there quivering in anger, damp with sweat, chest heaving. The American's eyes drop back to his novel. Almost as an afterthought to dismiss his guest, he said, "Yeah, no problem."

The African stares for the longest time, unsure of himself. Eventually he snorts and stomps from the restaurant. Edward feels for the man as he watches his angry march across the courtyard and his own heart races. He thinks of his wife and the possibility she is cheating and his stomach churns. He turns and notes the chef behind him. He had come to watch the confrontation. They both watch the angry man leave through the gate.

"Hello Moses."

"Good morning Edward, how was your omelette?" He sits at the table.

"Fine, thank you."

"You know, I heard this man on the local radio station this morning."

"Really?"

"Yes, he called in and was complaining about the white men coming here and taking their African women. He was very upset. I did not know it was our own Jasmine's husband. I will have a talk with her."

"Jasmine is nice, my favourite waitress," offered Edward.

"Yes, yes, she is nice. Do not worry Edward, she will not lose her job, but she was stupid to go with this man," motioning with a thrust of his chin towards the American. "He has different girls back all the time. I think maybe he is a little crazy."

"Mike brings back a local girl," said Edward. "At least he used to." He feels guilty about his report once again.

"Yes, he does, but Mike is different. It is not different girls all the time. It's as if this crazy guy is trying to quell some fire within himself, sleeping with all the girls of the town. But perhaps it is better to be like this. Poor Mike, he falls in love too easily. He loses his heart."

"Isn't it better to love just one woman?" Edward asks, thinking of his wife and his heart breaks anew. He conceals his sadness.

"Yes, I am sure it is. Love is a sacred thing, this is sure. Mike and I talk often of these things. He wishes he could be more like this naughty fellow. He wishes he was colder and could take his pleasure and walk away without remorse, without conscience. But it is not his nature. He gets attached and gives his heart, which is a splendid thing, but I fear that he breaks more hearts this way."

"How so?"

"Well, he is a scoundrel, and he tells the girls this truth from the start, but then he gives them his heart and the girls think maybe this scoundrel is not who he claims to be, and they allow themselves to love him as he loves them. Of course, in the end, he leaves. Mike gives hope then takes it away. This man before us gives very little hope. The girls know what they are getting with him. Perhaps it is the better way."

Edward's mind is restless. He heard a male voice in the background while talking with his wife…certainly, probably, maybe, or perhaps not? Sufficient to sow seeds of doubt in his addled brain, the more he dwells on it, the more excuses he finds to explain both sides, settling nothing. Stress upon doubt begets more stress. It was just the television. Could be. Had he been negligent? Was he not the ideal husband? Was he not devoted and dutiful, or perhaps he was overly docile and submissive? Perhaps she needed more than he could offer? Perhaps he was a weak man after all? Perhaps he deserved to be cheated? Did he have a right to be angry? Was there anything to be angry about? His heart pounds as these thoughts race unfettered through his mind. He can only quell them with activity. He needs to go for a walk. Another day spent idle in the hotel will drive him mad. His stomach somewhat stolid, he elects to walk to the beach. He even decides to walk there alone.

That conclusion alone does wonders for Edward's mood. He had found bravery and recklessness again, and do not forget, here he was in Africa, goddamnit. Only the bravest of souls dare tackle Africa, This was the trial of manhood he had sought. Even his wife's supposed indiscretions laid weight to the trials before him. It was all good. He would endure and be stronger.

Edward elects to take the bare minimum for the outing, just in case he is robbed. He dons his swimsuit and feels wicked for walking to the beach in them, though they are baggy trunks and none would be the wiser. He buttons up one of his plaid short sleeve shirts and dons his sandals, purchased in the market the week before. He then stuffs one of the rough and stained hotel towels into his backpack, plus a novel he had found in the lobby. With just enough local currency for a tea at the restaurant and a return fare for a *bajaj*, just in case, he is ready to depart. He feels brave. As he crosses the courtyard with a confident step he proclaims to one waitress peeling potatoes that he is going to the beach. At least someone will know where to look for him should he go missing, and he wished to brag. He steps through the gate, and the old man closes the heavy metal lock behind him and fear takes Edward again. *This is stupid* thinks Edward. He considers returning to the hotel to spend a quiet day in his room. He pushes down the fear and puts one foot in front of the other and his momentum carries him away from the hotel and out into the world. Edward walks down the dirt lane and out towards the street and marches with feigned purpose, as if he belongs, or at least, how he imagines one would look if they belonged. He turns and walks South along a dirt path under the shade of large mango trees, and ignores the prolonged stares at the *mzungu* out on his own. Despite himself, he quickens his pace. He passes all the young lads at the car wash, an area of dirt and mud and piles of rags and multiple plastic buckets and forty-five gallon drums of water. The washers sit idle on a low cement wall and watch him pass and he unconsciously increases his pace further. Then he reconsiders, for to show fear invites folly so he slows and falls into a confident pace much like he would imagine Mike would strut, were it him out here so exposed. *Pretend to be the person you want to be and it will become so.* His swagger is overblown and laughable but gives him confidence. Under the shade of another tree a group of Maasai sit together and sell crafts. Edward recognizes one Maasai from the beach restaurant and waves, feeling embolden. The Maasai takes this as an invitation and jumps up and is soon at Edward's side, begging for money. Edward shakes his head and makes a motion of having empty pockets.

"I'm going to the beach for a swim, I have no cash," said Edward. The Maasai smiles but is disappointed. He falls back and takes his place in the shade of the tree. Edward bursts with pride and swings his arms and puffs out his chest. He handled that well! Awhile later along the footpath, Edward comes across a beggar with his deformed legs on display before him, with his hand out and flashing an imploring smile. Edward fishes coins from his pockets and drops them into the dry withered hand. The beggar clasps his hands together in mock prayer and he bows to Edward repeatedly in thanks. Edward feels even larger now. What a great guy he is! He is out on his own and warding off aggressive Maasai warriors all the while helping those in need. There is a bounce in his step now as he proceeds on his journey to the beach.

As Edward walks he spots Tor exiting a small shop with a plastic shopping bag. Edward frowns, reconsidering his bravery.

Leaving the shade behind, Edward steps into the morning sun's fury and strolls along the side of a busy road. *Tuk Tuks* and motorcycles honk and their drivers wave in hopes of a fare. He fends them off with aplomb. He passes a school and teenagers watch his passing and make him nervous but he realizes they are only curious. This realization helps him calm his frayed nerves and his feet continue to pull him forward along the path. The sun is hot on the top of his head and sweat trickles down his sides under his shirt. He passes giggling women from the fish market with colourful plastic bins balanced on their heads overflowing with foul smelling seafood.

He continues past the fish market and into a more affluent neighbourhood, with security fences and security guards who watch him pass, suspicious and wary. As he turns on the last dirt lane leading to the beach restaurant he encounters two rough and large caucasians. They look lost.

"I say, you fellows lost your way?" asked Edward, brimming with confidence for finding himself among white men.

"Where can we get a beer?" one of them asked.

Edward smiles. He knows this place. "Come with me!"

They follow him down the dirt lane.

"I'm Edward, by the way."

"I'm Big John," said the smaller of the two large men.

"And I'm Bigger John. My Mom calls me Johnathon."

"Big John and Bigger John?"

"That's what everybody calls us," said Big John.

"What are you guys doing here?"

"We provide anti-piracy security for that vessel there," said Big John, pointing towards a large container ship anchored in the harbour, just coming into view through the trees. "We run cargo from Mumbai to Durban. We had some mechanical issue so we tucked into the port until they can sort it out. We're just on walkabout."

"Pirates? In this day and age?"

"Oh yeah man, they are notorious all along this coast. One of the guys in the port said they were attacked last year."

"Pirates attacked the port here?"

"That's what the man said."

"That's the first I've heard of it. Are you guys military?"

"Ex-South African Special Forces man. Our buddy runs this security company, we contract out to the ships running this coast. It's a pretty lucrative gig."

"Ever have to shoot anyone?"

"Can't say man."

Edward is happy to take on the role of tour guide, and relishes the opportunity to portray himself as a brave and adventurous soul roaming this remote corner of Africa. He describes his job as a helicopter pilot and the unfathomable risks he faces daily, and he praises the local disco and its decadence and the relaxing pool at the old fort. As they walk he warns his audience about the risk of riots and chronicles the obvious lack of security at their hotel. The anti-piracy security team listen politely and eventually they arrive at the beach restaurant. They pass timid curs that scurry ahead with tucked tails and Edward waves to the colourfully robed Maasai security lounging in the shade.

Edward had his mind set on a swim but this chance encounter provides an excuse he desired. He did not relish braving jellyfish today. He realizes that he had not worried about his wife in a good while.

They walk through the dark foyer into the open air restaurant with the thatched roof and head for a seaside table in the shade.

The place is empty.

"Goddamn I need a beer," said Big John.

When nary a soul arrives after a prolonged wait, the security team whistle and clap loudly. After a few minutes a uniformed lad emerges from the dark kitchen and before he reaches the table Bigger John stops him with a raised hand.

"Three beers my good friend," he said in a booming voice.

The lad turns and retreats into the kitchen.

When the sweating bottles of beer arrive the waiter sets them on the table and digs in his pockets for an opener but the security team grab one each and pop the tops off on the edge of the table and inhale the contents before Edward can blink.

Edward waits for the waiter to find his opener and his beer is handed to him, while Big John orders a second round. The waiter scurries away.

"How's the pizza here?" Big John asked Edward.

"I don't know, I've never had it."

"Three pizzas!" yelled Bigger John towards the kitchen. The waiter's smiling face pops out and he nods.

"I'm sure they have more than one type of pizza," said Edward.

"Don't matter."

The second round of beer arrives and goes a little slower than the first, but they are soon empty and Big John yells at the kitchen for another round. Edward still sips his first.

As the waiter walks towards them with three more cold beers, Big John said, "If you're going to keep sneaking off we might as well order another round right now."

"Better yet, bring six next time," said Bigger John. "Then we won't have to bother you so often." The waiter smiles, sets the beers around the table, clears a few of the empties and disappears again.

The waiter soon returns with a full tray of beer and Big John helps him set them about the table. "These aren't cold."

"Sorry sir, but we have small fridge. You drink all the cold beer."

"No worries mate," said Bigger John, laughing. "This *is* Africa."

The pizzas arrive as Edward starts into his second beer. The waiter clears the empties and Bigger John orders another double round for all of them, and orders another pizza. The waiter walks away and Edward looks over at Bigger John's empty plate.

"Where's your pizza?"

"I ate it."

"But it just arrived."

Bigger John shrugs his shoulders. Edward digs into his pizza, and nurses his beer and soon another pizza arrives for Bigger John. Watching closely this time, Edward discretely observes as Bigger John rolls the pizza up into a scroll and stuffs the end into his mouth. He chews while forcing more in with each impossible bite. The entire pizza disappears in seconds. Bigger John then grabs another full beer and downs that as quickly as the pizza.

Still wearing sandals and swim trunks and quite drunk, Edward realizes that the day has passed and the sun has set and the restaurant is setting up for its BBQ. They order the BBQ over more beer, their table overflowing with empties. Edward worries about his exposed skin and lack of bug spray, but a light breeze off the sea carries away the thought as another round is placed before them. Dining on poor fatty cuts of steak and prawns and dry chicken that sucks the moisture from their mouths, they drink and talk loudly and make little sense but no one cares. There are NGOs and oil workers around but they give the newcomers wide berth. The evening of merriment passes and the restaurant shuts down and the cook goes home and Edward glances at his watch and realizes he isn't wearing it.

"Do you guys know what time it is?"

"Almost midnight."

"Damn."

"Hey, lets go hit up that disco you keep talking about!" suggested Big John.

The happiness courses through Edward's body, fueled by alcohol and new friends and a perfect evening seaside in Africa, and he can think of nothing more desirable than hitting the disco. Somebody grabs the waiter and requests the bill.

The bill arrives after an age, and the restaurant is quiet and lights turn off. A large rat runs along the rock wall enclosing the dining area then scampers up into the thatch roof. Edward digs into his pocket and remembers that he only brought enough cash for a tea and perhaps a ride home. His heart jumps and his bowels tighten. Panic simmers but doesn't boil over. He tries to find some method of escape but seeing none, he jumps in with both feet.

"Uh guys, I don't have any money."

The anti-piracy security teams' faces cloud over and they stare hard at Edward. Edward shrinks in his chair and fears he may wet himself. He imagines what they may do to him, and his imaginings are anything but pleasant.

"I'm good for it!" he reassured them. "I can get to the bank in the morning and meet you anywhere," he pleaded.

They both stare at him a while longer, then look to each other and shrug. "Yeah, okay. You told us where you live so we know where to find you," said Big John ominously.

Big John settles the bill and they walk out into the parking lot. There appears to be no *Tuk Tuks* in attendance. They look up into the sky and spot the disco's spotlight dancing in the sky, and even from the hotel they hear the rumble of Swahili rap. Nothing is said as they head down the lane on unsteady legs.

They arrive after a pleasant walk under the East African skies, awash with stars creating a vista unlike anything Edward had ever witnessed. His head spins. The disco looks busy for a week night and they locate the entrance. A drunken man stands ahead of them with a live chicken under his arm, and he argues with the bouncers. Apparently he didn't have time to cook supper and hoped that someone in the bar could fry up his chicken. The bouncers take the chicken and push the man away. Angry and unsteady, he berates the larceny of his dinner and the heavens and the disco and his lazy wife and stumbles and falls into the bushes. Chickenless, the South Africans and Edward approach and pay the requisite fee but Edward is stopped when the bouncers notice his inappropriate attire. Big John slips the large man some additional currency and they soon find themselves inside as multicoloured lasers flash in the dry ice fog and heavy base thumps through their very core.

They find a table to lean against and watch the pretty girls writhe to the beat. Dark skin and sweat glisten in the blue lights and lean men shirtless with arms raised above their heads sway lost in the rhythms and people stare at the *mzungus*, as if spectacles on display. Body odour and cigarette smoke permeates the thick air. The chicken the bouncers confiscated runs past. They didn't notice Bigger John disappear, until he returns with a tray of shots and sets it before them.

"*Konyagi,*" he said. "Some local drink. It isn't vodka, it isn't gin. The girl said they make it from sugar cane, and its cheap!"

Each takes a shot glass and downs it, then the second. Tor makes an appearance at their table as if an everyday occurrence and Edward offers to buy him a round with the South African's money. There are girls at the table and they order more shots and beer. They dance and they laugh and Edward is happy.

Chapter 14

Edward is unsure which malefaction awakes him the next morning, either the scrape of crows on the tin roof or the brilliant sunlight beating on his face, or perhaps the foul dryness in his mouth. He is hot and damp with sweat and notes the air conditioner is off. His head hurts. He groans and sits up slowly in his bed, easing his feet to the floor. With his head in his hands to stabilize himself he realizes he is still very drunk. Edward craves copious amounts of water, yet despondently realizes there are no bottles of drinking water in his room. He aches at the roots of his eyeballs up into his temples and he rubs them in an attempt to ease his discomfort. He raises a butt cheek to let a fart seep out but realizes too late that he got more than he bargained for. He puts a hand tightly over his bare bottom as he stands with clenched cheeks and he does not wish to turn to witness the damage done. It is then it catches his eye. There's red fabric on the floor. It appears to be a skimpy dress, and he scrunches up his face in confusion, struggling to understand why a red dress would be on his floor. Still clutching his bare bottom he turns slowly towards the bed.

There is an African woman asleep in his bed, on her stomach with her face turned away. His bowels lurch again and he shuffles to the toilet.

His bowels addressed for the time being, Edward wraps a towel around his waist. He dampens a smaller towel as quietly as possible in the sink and sneaks back to the side of the bed and cleans most of the mess where he had been sitting, and he heads back into the washroom and rinses the towel and throws it into the dirty clothes bin. He looks back to the woman in his bed and is overwrought. With a deep breath he approaches the bed and peaks under the cover. As he feared, she is completely naked, and his eyes drift over her bare body under the raised cover. She is overweight with dark stains like bruises all across her skin and scabs from recent open sores scattered across her backside and down her thighs. Edward suppresses the urge to vomit. He lowers the cover and looks around the room and takes stock. Her dress is on the floor and her black panties are on his laptop. His swim trunks are on the floor to the side of the room and his shirt drapes over the desk chair. Edward knows he didn't have condoms but maybe she did. He searches but can't find any wrapper or indication of what transpired. Fear grips his heart again, and he turns away from her and opens his towel and bends his head over as far as possible and tries to smell his own genitals. There is a musty scent but he can't be sure, as he stinks of body odour and shit.

His bowels surge again and he hurries back to the toilet. After flushing he runs the tap and waits an age for the water to warm and wets another towel's corner and scrubs his privates as well as he can, lathering on soap furiously and rinsing and scrubbing some more. He pours far more mouthwash into his mouth than he can handle and it dribbles from the corners of his mouth and he swishes it about vigorously for a full two minutes before he spits. He hears a groan and dares a glance and the girl rolls onto her back and snores. He sneaks over again and takes a long hard look, and try as he might to convince himself otherwise, he has to admit that she is not an attractive woman.

Edward cringes and shudders and his heart races and he wants her gone, and he wants a hot shower, and he desperately wants to go back in time.

First things first; Edward needs water. He doesn't want to leave the woman alone in his room but all of his valuables are locked into his small safe since before the beach outing yesterday. Leaving her here is not ideal but Edward needs to replenish some liquids sooner than later. His head swirls and throbs. He appreciates that he stinks, but he hopes a dash downstairs will go unnoticed, and a shower may wake her up.

Edward isn't ready to face her yet. He pulls on his swim trunks and throws on yesterday's shirt and sneaks out of the room. Stepping into the hallway away from the unassailable situation in his room is a relief, and he heads down the hall in better spirits. Halfway down the stairs he meets Chet.

"Behave yourself today Edward, there are bigwigs here from head office, surprise base inspection."

"What?" Edward exclaimed. "Today?"

"They're here now. I guess those reports someone sent in about base security and women in the rooms has gotten someone's attention. You don't have a girl in your room, do you?" Chet laughed with a wink.

Edward's legs nearly collapse, and he grabs the rail for support. Chet eases past and continues up the stairs. After passing he stops and turns back. "Jesus man, you stink."

Edward frowns and continues down the stairs in a dejected forlorn state. He peaks through the glass door before opening it and sees no one, so he eases it open yet it squawks loudly and grates his nerves. He heads into the unattended office and finds the stash of one litre water bottles, thankful they have recently resupplied. He immediately drains one down his parched throat. It is warm with an unpleasant plastic taste but he is past caring. He grabs two more bottles and sneaks back across the courtyard and up the stairs.

Edward enters his room, and the girl is awake. She sits up and rubs a hand roughly over her head. Her small empty breasts sag.

"Good morning lover," purred the girl, awash with happiness. Her smile is so bright and warm Edward's heart sinks. He vaguely remembers her from the disco.

"Good morning," croaks Edward. He clears his throat and struggles to create the gentleman he aspires to be. He doesn't know what to say. Edward stands there and stares with a lost expression, and she regards her befuddled lover with raised eyebrow and a naughty smirk. One of the water bottles in his hand slips and he catches it.

"Would you like some water?" He holds the bottle out to her, inching towards the bed. She reaches for it and takes a long swig.

"I'd like more of that lovin'," she said, with her head tilted downward, striving to be seductive. Edward scratches his head.

"Listen, I was really drunk last night."

He witnesses the moment her heart breaks, but she conceals her disappointment with practiced indifference. In a last ditch effort she throws the covers off and lays nude before him. Edward turns his head and looks towards the window.

"Silly boy," she said, feigning confidence. "You weren't so shy last night."

"I have to get ready for work," he lied.

Sadness washes over her and it's horrible to behold. Edward's heart aches when she sheds a tear. She pulls the covers up and hides her body. Edward stands stupidly. She sighs and drops her feet over the other side of the bed and stands, taking the cover with her. She wraps it around herself then thinks better of it and lets it fall to the floor. She struts past him naked and unashamed, straight into the washroom, and she closes the door. After a few moments her head pops out.

"There's no water."

Edward frowns. "We had some earlier." He pushes past her into the washroom and tries the taps and arrives at the same conclusion. She struts back into the bedroom, finds her panties and pulls them on, then dons her dress. She gets on her knees to find her shoes under the bed. Edward looks out the window and sees a Caucasian man and woman talking with Moses in front of the kitchen. His heart races.

"You have money?" asked the girl. She stands now fully dressed. Her purse hangs in the crook of her arm and she taps a foot.

A grimace grows across Edward's face betraying his disgust. "You're a prostitute?"

The girl sighs and takes a deep breath before she replies.

"No, I need cab fare home."

"Um, yes of course," said Edward embarrassed. "But you can't leave just yet."

She raises an eyebrow. "Why not?"

"We aren't supposed to have girls here, and there are people from head office looking around, and they're downstairs right now. I have to sneak you out of here."

She looks at him unimpressed, but she sits on the bed and digs her phone out of her purse. She starts texting.

Edward's head throbs.

"I got it!" he said. "I'll go find one of the cleaning ladies and you can leave with her, pretend you are one of the cleaning girls!"

"I'm wearing a red dress and high heels honey."

"I can ask Moses to ask the cleaners if any of them have spare outfits you could wear, just wait here!" Edward whisks out the door. The girl frowns.

Edward flies down the stairs two at a time. He stops at the glass door and peaks. He notes the two Caucasians have finished their chat with Moses and they walk towards the hotel. Edward braces himself and opens the door. It squeals.

He meets the Caucasians halfway. They stop to greet him but he dashes past with a quick *hello* and hurries into the kitchen. The Caucasians turn to watch.

"Moses, I have a problem."

Moses looks up from the table where he prepares a meal. "I'd say most definitely you have a problem. Amina is still in your room."

"Amina?"

Moses regards Edward for a moment. "You don't know her name?"

"I never thought to ask," replied Edward. The hotel door screeches and Edward and Moses watch Amina strut out of the hotel in her red dress. The two Caucasians stand shocked, then one of them addresses the girl.

Edward frowns and they watch.

"Amina is a nice girl," said Moses.

Amina waves her hand to dismiss the inquisitive Caucasians, then she struts across the courtyard and out the gate. The newcomers watch her depart then turn towards the kitchen. They aren't happy.

"Shit," said Edward.

"Yes, that is probably the proper sentiment."

Edward sighs and walks out to meet the angry folk from head office.

"Hello, I'm Edward."

The man checks the clipboard he has nestled under his arm. He pushes out his bottom lip when his finger finds Edward's name.

"Are you the Edward that put in the complaint about girls on the base?"

"Surely I was not the only one."

"Well, yes, you were the only one to send in a report, but we take these things seriously. Did you see the girl that just left the hotel?"

Edward considers that for a moment. "No."

The man consults his clipboard again and flips through some pages and reads some more. The woman looks serious and unsure whether to scowl at Edward or befriend him. They decide to believe him, for he filed the complaint.

"Do you know Mike?" said the man, reading from his clipboard.

"Yes, of course."

"I think he's the one I need to talk with, seems he is rather public about bringing ladies back here. I gather that he regularly disregards the rules?"

Edward tries to think about the report he wrote and doesn't recall specifically mentioning Mike, but he appears to be off the hook if he plays along. He decides that valour is the most appropriate action, for while he has no intention of taking the blame unless forced, he isn't about to nail his friend to the wall either. That is valour enough for Edward.

"I don't know," Edward shrugged.

There is a knock on Edward's door as he attempts to snooze after lunch. He stumbles out of bed and opens the door. It is one of the waitresses.

"There are men here to see you."

Edward shakes his head to wake himself but it causes pain. He groans. He ambles down the stairs and meets the two South Africans from the evening before.

"You look like shite mate," said Big John. "You owe us some money."

Edward wants to sleep, but he decides he best settle this debt first.

"I'll get my bank card, just a second."

He runs back up to his room and quickly returns and they walk together to the nearest ATM. The sun is relentless and Edward's head throbs. There is a huge line and they queue up and wait. Nobody talks. After an age Edward steps into the small glass booth and gags on the stench of body odour. The heat is twice as intense as outside and he breaks out in a profuse sweat. The old faded black-and-white screen reads "OUT OF ORDER". He steps back out into the fresh air.

Mike looks thoughtfully at Edward, lost in despair. He puts a hand on his shoulder.

"You'll be fine mate. You aren't going to catch anything after one drunken shag."

"Are you sure?"

"Nothing is sure in this life Eddie. My guess is you're fine."

"I am such an idiot."

"Hey Eddie, don't sweat it. You're a guy. You can't apologize for being a guy, can you?"

Laden with guilt and worry Edward recalls the bruises and scabs and his stomach churns. He desperately wants it to have never happened, but knows that sort of wish is effort wasted. Mike smiles with compassion. They continue to eat their meals in silence. Edward's phone beeps with another text.

The roosters beckon the sun and she answers the call. Another day begins anew despite Edward's distress. He listens as others below his window talk and laugh as if his world had not come crashing down. For the failings of man, for his weakness, for his drunkenness, oh how he suffers. Edward imagines he can feel the disease spread through this body, elated with fresh and innocent blood to assail. He feels the hideous demon ride his own lifeblood to his core and multiply and negate his existence. These notions plagued him all the night and when he finally drifted off, those same notions birthed nightmares he dare not voice. He awoke in sweat and heavy of breath with his heart racing and he swore not to sleep again, yet sleep dragged him back into the depths of his despair again and again. Thank goodness for the sunlight to drive the demons back to the underworld. Thank goodness for the dawn of another day. Edward drags himself out of bed and into the shower and this morning there is water, although tepid at best. He washes and scrubs and the water carries the sweat and filth and evil thoughts that had dried to his skin down to mix with the suds collecting at his feet. Together they swirl down the drain and away from his tattered soul. Edward dries and dons his uniform and departs his stank and condemned room, out into the hall and he ambles dejected and forlorn down the hall and down the stairs and the door screeches in mockery of his self-pity.

No one notices Edward enter the dining area for breakfast and if they do, they do not acknowledge him. He orders his omelette from a waitress and pours some hot water from the electric kettle into a cup with a tea bag. He sits by himself. His phone beeps but he doesn't look at it.

Chet and Donald walk in a few moments later and sit with Edward, continuing a conversation they had engaged before entering.

"I hear the riots are imminent," Donald said, with no greeting.

"Yeah, I've been hearing that too," agreed Chet.

"Mark my words, we are sitting ducks here. I told my wife that if anything happens to me, to sue the living shit out of these assholes," said Donald.

"At least head office sent out someone to have a look at the place," said Chet.

"Lots of good that'll do. This place is a security nightmare," said Donald.

"I hear they had a sit down with Mike yesterday. I think they are sending him home," said Chet.

That perks up Edward. He almost spits out his tea.

"What?"

"Yeah, apparently they asked him about bringing local girls back to the hotel and whatever he said they didn't like. He's done, poor bugger. They are sending him home. Honestly, I don't think he cares much, he's got jobs lined up everywhere," said Chet.

"Who is headed home?" asked Dave as he sits.

"Mike," said Chet.

"Serves him right, tapping that bush meat, stupid fuck," said Donald.

Chet stands and shakes his head in disgust. Donald takes that as an endorsement for his statement rather than a criticism of his opinion. Dave follows suit. They load into various SUVs and head to the airport.

The day is busy yet everyone realizes something is amiss. Edward moves through the day in a daze. His heart pounds every time he thinks about Amina and the risk that disease courses through his body. It sickens him to consider it yet it clouds every waking moment. News of Mike's fate does not warrant space in his addled mind, for Edward worries only of himself. The strong scent of turbine fumes and the loud roar of whirling mechanical mayhem and his dominion over the elements offers no comfort on this day, nor does the escape of gravity's purchase by his own hand, nor the languid blue East African skies, nor passing over the lush landscape of the wet season, nor the lines of red dirt connecting grass roofed domiciles as children run in the clearings, nor the azure blue waters of the Indian Ocean hinting at life laden reefs, nor over the deep grey of the sea beyond the shallows, concealing secrets untold, nor even when those massive marvels of engineering and man's offering to the unrelenting quest for resources and riches loom on the horizon, nor as those abominations grow larger and larger and threatening, nor the command of his craft that passes above it all. He thinks only of the girl in his bed.

After the day's flying is complete, Edward enters the pilot's cabin following post-flight maintenance with the engineers. He walks in as others sit and discuss the day. He files his paperwork in its allotted folder and listens to the conversation.

"Mike is a damn good pilot, a natural, and the hardest working guy I've ever met. It's a goddamned shame," said the American in his drawl.

"I'd agree with that," said Dave. "He doesn't have to think about it, he doesn't give a shit for any of the stuff the rest of us worry about, he gets on with it and gets it done. You know, I have to work at it. I study all the time. That's why I got into training, for more exposure to the procedures and emergencies. I figure I need that extra exposure to improve, but Mike just seems to have it."

In their own minds, each considers himself to be the best, sovereign of others' comprehension, for they deem the skills they possess most vital to mastery of the craft. Even Edward considers himself superior to the others, for his strict adherence to the rules and regulations that govern their trade. But those rules and regulations are written by others for his adherence, and he pays no heed to the whys and wherefores, he follows them blindly as if decreed from the gods. They are all pilots, proud and confident, arrogant and self-reliant, and to be amongst so many like-minded souls is a joy and an abomination. But here they are, biting their tongues and co-existing in harmony, for they have little choice. In a feeble attempt at humility, they sometimes praise their co-workers.

"You sound like the fucker is dead," said Chet. "He's already got a job lined up on the other side of Africa; the Congo I think. You can't imagine all the connections that guy has. He can get another job anywhere in a heartbeat. I think he told me once he had flown in over forty different countries."

"He talks about West Africa fondly, probably not breaking his heart to go back. Don't think he liked the Middle East much, and I know he has no use for Europe," said Dave.

"Or most Europeans," laughed the American.

Chapter 15

The pilots load up in the Toyotas, day bags stuffed in the back or underfoot, and they begin the trip back to the hotel. They pass shoeless riders aboard old bicycles from the fifties, standing on the bare pedal shafts and shifting their weight to propel their steel steeds forward, their home-made panniers loaded with large bags of coal. Most carry three bags, while the younger lads manage only two. The odd load of four bags will generate praise from the apathetic crews. Five bags is rare indeed. Today they pass a skinny old man hauling a load of six bags and the guys hoot and holler. Dave has their driver pull over at the bottom of the next hill where the rider has to disembark to push his huge load to the top of the next. The rider eventually approaches then slips off his bike. He approaches the Toyota warily and is uneasy when the uniformed *mzungu* steps from the SUV. Dave approaches with a smile and places a wad of cash into the old man's hand. Dave then opens the rear hatch of the SUV while the bewildered old man counts the cash. The old man questioningly raises one finger, then two, then three. Dave motions for the entire lot. As the old man unties the load Dave piles the bags of coal into the back of the truck. The old man counts the cash again and then hands most of it back. Dave shakes his head and closes the man's hand over the entire wad. Dave points to the top of the last big hill before the long descent into town, and motions for the man to meet him there. The man appears confused but nods. Dave hops back into the SUV and they haul everything up the steep hill and pull over again. Eventually the old man meets them with his unladen bicycle and Dave begins to unload the bags of coal. The old man laughs and shakes his head, then loads it all onto his bicycle again.

"I hope that made his day. He has no pedals on that thing, bare feet on those thin metal spindles, jeez," said Dave laughing. "I said if I ever saw someone with six bags I'd give him everything I had in my pocket. That's hard work, that is."

"I think you confused him boss, but he looked happy," said the driver.

They drove the downhill section of the route and watched the speeding coal bearers in awe, the cautious applying one bare foot on the front tire to slow their steads, while others clung to the shimmying bars with dread. They wonder if it's as scary as it appears, and often they spot bikes and loads in the ditch, and road rash aplenty. These riders make the trip a couple of times a day for mere cents. They'd ride about the village and ring their bell and the womenfolk would buy their wares, and once their bags were gone, they'd turn back onto the road and out past the airport and up into the hills and forests for more.

They eventually arrive at the hotel and the pilots spill from the Toyotas and make their way inside. Edward notices someone in the dining area as he passes, so he steps inside. It's

Mike and Moses and they look up as he walks in. His phone beeps but he ignores it.

"You're still here?" asked Edward.

"You guys haven't gotten rid of me yet. They wanted to fly me out today, but I had promised Moses that I'd help with his school this weekend."

"His school?"

"Yeah, he saved up some money and is building a school for his old village up in the hills. We poured foundations last week. I'm going to help with the framing this weekend."

"I had no idea!"

"Mike has helped a great deal," said Moses. "He financed many of our supplies, and has helped me secure donations from some of the local ex-pat businesses."

"Wow!" said Edward. He was legitimately impressed. He sat with them at the table. "Is this something I should get in on? Is it a good investment? Do you stand to make some money?"

Both Mike and Moses laugh.

"There will be no money I am afraid, it is a bad investment for one to make money, for there is none. I invest in the future, to help the children of my community." Moses stands. "I must go and prepare dinner."

"Okay Brother, see you later," said Mike. He stands to shake Moses's hand. Edward smiles awkwardly. When Moses is out of earshot, Edward leans across the table towards Mike.

"I'm sorry to hear about the trouble you had."

"Don't worry my friend, onto bigger and better things. I don't get my nose out of joint over such nonsense. The time has come to move on."

"I heard you already found another job."

"Yeah, in the Congo. I know it well. The pay isn't as good but honestly, as long as I'm flying I'm happy. And flying in Africa? This place stirs my soul like nowhere I've been, and buzzing around in a helicopter, low and close amongst the tree tops, like the birds themselves." He shakes his head and smiles and stares off into the blue skies above the breeze block wall.

"I'm sure you know. The novelty of it never grows old. I love this life. It is what I am, and I have based my short stint on this planet around this romantic ideal, set in my head as a farm kid on the prairies. Maybe I've been duped by my own imagination but hell, what a ride! My actions have satisfied my imaginings, and what is a greater accomplishment than that?"

"It's just a job for me. Pays the bills."

"You live a passionless life my friend."

"Maybe, maybe. Are you upset the company let you go like this?"

"I'm just an asset like an aircraft or a fuel bowser, a part to be used to generate revenue, and for me, they are simply a source of a paycheque, a means to ply my trade. There is no loyalty either way as long as we satisfy our agreed commitments to each other. I guess they feel I haven't lived up to my end of it, and that's fine by me. I know I broke the rules, but I'd do it again."

"Well, I'm sorry it turned out this way."

"Me too, I was having a blast here, but I could see the writing on the wall when Donald showed up. When I first started touring overseas, I was surprised at the racism amongst the Europeans. Not all of them mind you, but it was far more prevalent than I ever imagined. Growing up was extremely multicultural for me. I never saw skin colour as an issue, but there is a ton of hate and fear out there. I know it's just

ignorance and lack of exposure, but those racist fucks have always pissed me off. It took some getting used to when I started working overseas, as I had no idea it was so rife, and I certainly don't like it, but fighting it is wasted breath. And Donald, well, people are susceptible to strong personalities and opinions. It's like they want to be told what to think. Like water off a ducks back to me but some folk soak that shit up. I just let them get on with it and live my life the best I know how.
 Small minds. Anyway, he got a few susceptible souls on his side of the table and that's all she wrote. Some people complained and here I am, moving on. *C'est la vie.*"

Edward blushes and hopes Mike doesn't notice. He changes the subject. "What about Aisha? She'll be upset."

"Yeah, but once I get settled, I might send for her."

"Really? I figured you'd just find another one when you got there."

"Well, it's not that difficult to be honest, lots of ladies out there to love. My Dad always told me, *Be the flame, not the moth*, and that's worked for me since high school, but being white and having money? It's like shooting fish in a barrel in Africa. I'm not stupid, I know how it works. I do my best not to abuse the situation. I try to give more than I take. But you know, you find someone like Aisha; she's a pretty switched on chick. I really do like her. She's got nothing holding her here." He looks back to the sky and considers it for a moment. "I'd fly her to The Congo in a heartbeat."

"You like the African girls, don't you?"

"In my learned opinion, white girls tend to think that what they have between their legs is some great gift to the male species, but the African gals love sex without all that bullshit. It's pretty simple for them; they like you, you like them, you knock boots. There's none of that complicated bullshit. No games. It's such a natural and easy thing for them. I guess it's the fault of the guys back home that worship women like they do, putting the girls up on pedestals. The African guys don't bother with any of that shit. Go in on equal footing and you'll do okay. The African guys generally don't treat the women all that well, and there's tons of screwing around, and the girls know this. You treat these fine ladies with some respect and they fall all over you. You know, I was raised to treat a woman well, and that attitude gets a ton of mileage over here. And to be completely honest, the dark skin drives me wild. I have never seen a sexier woman than an African woman in all my days, and I have loved a lot of women. I love Africa Edward!"

"I know Mike, I know," said Edward laughing. "They are pretty, but it's not my thing." He blushes. "Do you think you'll marry her?"

Mike laughed. "I hadn't given that much thought to be honest. I'm not much of thinker, more of a doer." He rubs his chin thinking. "Maybe I'll make an honest woman out of her, who knows? She's a good egg."

"Maybe she's the one?"

"I don't believe there is some perfect match out there for anyone, but she does tick all the boxes." He smiles as he considers Aisha. "Honestly though, it's all chance and compromise who you end up with. There is no ideal person out there, it's who you meet in your travels and what you can put up with. What if I never came here, and we never met? What if I hooked up and fell for some girl in North Africa, or somewhere in South America, or the Middle East, or even back home? I was here, she was here, we met, we liked each other, I took her home, we make it work, so far anyway. No, we are very adaptable my friend, more so than most appreciate, *love* for all the love songs is merely deciding what's practical."

"So you're a romantic when it comes to flying but completely practical when it comes to love?"

Mike smiles and considers that for a moment. "Maybe because I don't idolize women. I've always found that if I wanted one, I could find one, and I don't consider them some great prize to be held onto whatever the cost. I just be me. If they want some of me, so be it. I don't get too out of sorts one way or the other. Plenty of fish in the sea Edward. What about your wife? Have you made her indispensable?"

Edward's face flushes again. He thinks of the male voice he heard in the background the last he spoke with her. He thinks of the girl in his bed. He considers his risk of exposure to disease. He considers how his heart aches for all of it.

"I guess I have."

"Well, I'm no expert but I think that's a mistake. You have to be your own person. Rely on no one. If someone wants to share the adventure with you, so be it, but don't count on anyone beside yourself to make you happy."

"You're a loner Mike."

"I don't think so, I hate being alone. I enjoy having a lady friend around, and not just to keep my bed warm. They add some excitement to the mix, some drama. But yeah, I know I'm brutally practical. Drives Aisha crazy how practical I am. Like death for instance. Aisha gets all upset at how I view death. My sweet Jesus, I can't believe how out of sorts folk get over dying. Like you know it's coming, don't you? Everyone that has ever graced this planet has died or is going to, but we can't seem to get used to the idea. It blows my mind." Mike shakes his head. "But I'm changing the subject. Yeah, maybe I'm cold, but I can love too. I know I have a strong personality and I'm sure of myself, and some people aren't so much. So I always strive to give more of myself than I take. Maybe it's right, maybe its wrong, but I sleep well at night."

"I'm glad to hear you are considering taking Aisha with you, she is really sweet. Does she know about the other women?"

"She is well aware that I'm Satan incarnate, and she is no innocent herself either. I'm not a fool but neither is she, and maybe we can find a life together. If it goes sour, well, I regret nothing and never will. I'm not really one for regret. I like moving forward." He rubs the back of his neck and twists his head around. "So tell me about you Eddie, how are you adapting to life in Africa?"

Edward blushes again and looks at the floor. "I'm kind of worried to be honest."

"About what Bud?"

"Amina. I wonder if I caught anything. You know I don't want to take anything home to my wife."

"Well, go get checked out then. There are a few Doctors in town. Dip it in enough ladies, you'll get something eventually, but I imagine you're okay." Mike notes Edward's downtrodden expression. "Honestly, I wouldn't be too worried about catching anything from Amina, I'd be more worried about her brother."

"What about her brother?" As if on cue his phone rings. He doesn't answer it.

"Well, I hear he gets pretty upset about guys messing with his sister, especially white guys. He beat the crap out of one of the ex-pat oil workers here who took her home from the bar one night. He's connected too, got off scot-free. Actually, I don't want to scare you, but Aisha said something about Amina's brother last night. Sorry, I wasn't paying attention."

Edward groans. "Really? What have I done? I really wish I could just go back in time and undo everything."

"Don't worry Eddie, I make bad decisions all the time. You know sometimes, I know a decision is a bad one, that there'll be trouble on the other end of it, but I go for it, regardless. Sometimes you want to challenge yourself, see what you're made of. Bad decisions make good stories."

"I wasn't trying to challenge myself, I was just drunk."

"Well, that happens too. You're a guy mate, shit happens. Suck it up. Keep moving forward."

Edward drops his head and holds it between his hands. He groans again. The stress is too much for him.

"Grab the bull by the horns buddy," continued Mike. "What's a life worth that hasn't faced challenges, and if you ain't got enough challenges, go and create some. Poke that bear. It's the best way to grow, to see what you're made of. I don't give that bear any rest." He laughed.

"I like things simple and uncomplicated. I was happy with my life," sputtered Edward. "I don't want to grow or be challenged, I want to go home."

"Yeah, maybe you aren't the type to go around poking bears for amusement," Mike shrugged. "But Amina's brother? You have poked one mean bear my friend."

That evening at dinner while everyone is busy eating and watching rugby, Mike saunters in.

"Woah," said the American. "Are you still here?"

"I am, clearing out later tonight."

"There's a flight out tonight?"

"No, I'll be in country for another week or so, heading up into the hills with Moses this weekend."

"Up into the hills? Are you fucking mad?" asked Donald.

Mike ignores him and heads over to sit with Dave and Chet.

"Are you seriously considering helping that little shit with his school? You can't help this lot," continued Donald. "It's wasted effort, this place is going to hell."

No one takes any notice but he continues.

"Why help these losers? You know, they really are a different species, it's a fact. They're fucking monkeys mate."

A few watch now, then look to Mike for his reaction. Donald flashes his self-satisfied smirk and takes another bite of his dinner. Mike has had enough. He stands up.

"You racist little fuck. Why the hell are you in Africa anyway? Why would someone who is so goddamned racist even consider coming to Africa?"

"It's a job, isn't it? Not like these sorry fucks could do it on their own."

"If these people had the same prospects we did, the same upbringing and opportunities, I'm sure they'd kick our asses at all of it."

"Yeah, you keep telling yourself that mate." He stands to meet Mike as he rounds the table. "You are a fucking idiot mate" continued Donald, wiping his mouth with the back of his hand. "If you had kept your head down and hadn't paraded around your, your , your *proclivities* , you might not have lost your job. You lost your job for a fucking piece of bush meat."

Mike punches Donald in the head and Donald goes down. Everyone watches in silence. Mike stands over an unconscious Donald.

"Fuck."

The next morning Edward steps into the courtyard enroute to the dining area and notices Moses in the kitchen. He walks over and steps inside as a waitress passes with breakfast omelettes.

"Good morning Moses. I thought you were headed up to your village last night?"

"Yes, I was," said Moses, scrambling eggs. "Unfortunately the other chef was not available this morning. He called last evening about a death in his family. I swear his Grandmother has died a dozen times this year alone," he laughed, shaking his head.

"What about Mike?"

Moses regards Edward with suspicion then his face softens. "He is staying in my village. He is quite capable of getting things done at the school without me, and I think it is best he keep away for a while."

"The police were here last night, I believe they are looking for him."

"They are not looking too hard I think. The police know Mike, and they know Donald. This is a very small town and the staff talk a great deal. The police will not bother Mike. Now if Donald were to create some trouble, let me tell you!" He whistled.

"May I ask you something?"

"Of course Edward."

"Do you know Amina's brother?"

Moses regards Edward for a moment before responding.

"Amina's brother is trouble. I think he may even be with the secret police. I would not recommend crossing him."

Edward's stomach leaps and his face flushes. His phone beeps.

"I think maybe he might be angry about the other night. Mike said something, but he wasn't sure."

"Oh well, then you may be in for some trouble. He is not one to have against you."

A horn honks. The guys are ready to head to the airport.

"I can make some discreet inquiries for you if you would like?" offered Moses.

"Yes, please." Edward hurries out the door and hops into one of the Toyotas.

As they drive Edward finds it difficult to focus on any one thought as so many conflicting concerns race through his mind. He does notice that they take a left turn that he did not expect.

"Where are we going?" he asked.

"We are going to be taking a different route every time we go to or from the airport, in case anyone is watching our routine. One of Donald's security measures," said one of the other pilots.

"That guy is a fucking ass," said the American.

Edward watches out the window as they pass through different neighbourhoods he's unaccustomed to. They appear rougher than the main route, and he grows nervous. As they pass through an area of shops he is surprised to see a Caucasian, and even more surprised when he realizes that it is Tor, talking and laughing with some locals.

"There's Tor!" Edward said. No one pays him any mind.

"Where's your *bug-out* bag?" asked Chet as they passed out of the unfamiliar neighbourhood and onto the main highway leading to the airport.

"*Bug-out* bag?" asked Edward while deleting texts and missed calls from his phone.

"If the riots actually break out, we may have to bug out to the capital. Didn't you read the memo?"

"I've been distracted."

"For a guy who loves rules, you should pay more attention. Basically the memo said we should keep a bag with us in case we have to leave in a hurry, you know; a change of clothes or two, toothbrush, any valuables you don't want to leave behind."

"I missed it. What's going on with the riots? I haven't been paying attention." Edward finally puts his phone back in his pocket.

Chet gives Edward a disapproving glare. "Riots in this neck of the woods should not be taken lightly. They can turn ugly in a heartbeat."

Edward looks concerned. He feels that familiar panic build once again but manages to control it.

"Maybe we should leave now?"

Chet huffs. "I doubt the company would go for that. We still have a job to do."

"I didn't sign up for this. If it's not safe, I want to head home."

Chet shakes his head. "You agreed to come to Africa, you know this place is unpredictable. Suck it up buttercup."

"Aren't you worried?"

"Not really. I've been working in African for years, it goes with the territory. You take a job like this, you throw the dice, you get what you get."

They pass a few cyclists heading back up into the hills to collect more coal.

"Hey, I heard that the brother of that girl you brought back to the hotel the other night is after you."

Edward's face turns ashen. "I didn't bring a girl back." He feigns an indignant face while struggling to figure out how anybody besides Mike knows about her.

"Yes, you did, and you blamed it on Mike and he got kicked off the base because of it. You're an evil little bastard."

Edward drops his head and holds it his hands and groans.

"I hope her brother seriously fucks you over. That shit is not cool."

Edward contemplates opening the Toyota door and rolling out, as they cruise at high speed over the rough coral gravel road; take all the road rash and bruises and just run off into the jungle and disappear.

Hyperventilating and still holding his head, struggling to control his racing heart, Edward asked, "What did you hear about the brother?"

"Just that he was looking for you, and that he is a serious dude. Serves you right."

Chapter 16

Edward strives to shake the demons that plague him, sandwiched between two pilots on the rear bench of the Toyota, enroute to the airport firmly embedded in the morning traffic. Their shoulders touch in that confined space and despite the air-conditioned coolness none like to feel another's heat. They pass excited uniformed school children with packs containing notebooks, pencils, crayons and lunches lovingly packed by caring mothers, then slung over slender shoulders for the walk to school. The driver watches carefully, and stops to allow the smallest of them to safely cross. They pass brickworks of shirtless men, their sweat glistened bodies caked in white powder, resembling some primal tribe. They pass the furniture shops as hard men with hand tools hew heavy local timber into workable planks and beds and tables and desks and chairs. The daily life of the locals exists beyond Edward's scrutiny, for Edward considers his dilemmas and nothing else. He worries about the disease that could now, this very moment, be coursing through his body, and he dwells on his guilt for having cheated his wife, and this weighs heavily on his conscience. He dwells on his jealousy for his wife and the possibility of her unknown guest, and it pangs his heart. He considers his fear of the ominous riots looming just beyond the morrow, as well as his fear of being hunted by Amina's connected and fearful brother. He even considers his guilt over what troubles he has created for his friend Mike. Edward struggles to grasp it all, to contain it and harness it and to put it all neatly away for another day.

He remembers reading a trick, and it served him well when he faced the fear of coming to Africa, and perhaps he even used it subconsciously dealing with his hateful peers back home, who ridiculed his concerns and his mannerisms and all that he is. Break it down Edward. Break it down into something you can handle. Analyze and consider each concern separately. He ponders and reflects and they pass through the East African village and he is not a part of it. He struggles to compartmentalize his fears as thoughts race through his addled mind as wild horses he cannot tame. Focus Edward. Focus. The disease. He admits that he doesn't know if he has a disease and has entertained the thought in spite of himself. Knowledge is the key. He admits he knows little about the subject, as he is not one to brave indiscretions, not so much for lack of desire, but for fear of exactly what he now faces. He decides to research just what the various risks could be and to get checked by a Doctor as soon as possible. He accepts his ignorance in the matter and having decided on a course of action and a realization that whatever damage there could be has already been done; he places the concern aside for the time being. *Man up* Edward. He tells himself these things and believes them and feels stronger. Next in his long list of demons is the fact that he has cheated on his wife, and the guilt of this act, even if he cannot remember any of it. The act weighs heavy. His heart leaps at the thought of the grave error, and his bowels tighten. As Mike had said, he is but a man and it's a common enough folly, especially as alcohol was most certainly involved. Men have dealt with this weakness for ages so it cannot be insurmountable. This thought gives him further confidence, but it still causes consternation. Now the jealousy. How does one deal with that devil? He has doubts, and the emotion is real enough, almost as if it were more than merely a thought, as if jealousy was a physical ailment. Tears well up at the consideration, at the image of his wife intimate with another, but then again, can he be so hypocritical? Had he not known the flesh of another, even if he had not intended upon it, or could even recall the act? Perhaps Edward could brush aside her indiscretion along with his own? Perhaps this is a common thing? Perhaps this is how long married couples survive? Surely he is not the first, nor the last, to face such questions, and this realization comforts Edward somewhat. The riots. The riots. Having never been exposed to something so primitive and wild, how can he know how to react to its threat? How will he deal with it when faced? How bad will it be? Perhaps it is only the uncertainty that concerns him, the fear of the unknown? Perhaps it is no big deal. Surely they will not hack him to pieces with machetes. Surely there will be civility. Then he remembers that he is in Africa and that thought causes his heart to race again. Fear grasps for him but he tells himself that he is a logical man and he will face this challenge like any other, for he is a man who had challenged Africa when all his compatriots had not. He was a brave man. The Toyota lurches to a stop in the sandpit beside their hangar and it's time for work. Edward feels unease for not having solidified his thoughts, for not being able to continue with his breakdown and resolution of his distractions, nor being allowed to apply his logic to quell the many fires that burn within. Chet impatiently pushes him towards the door so he can exit the vehicle. Edward struggles to retain the progress his thoughts have attained but as he is pushed out of the vehicle, the progress all but disappears as if embers rising from a fire.

Flight planned and prepped and all the pre-flight tasks in hand, the crew sit in the muggy cockpit and checklists complete, run up the helicopter. A warning flashes on the caution panel so they call the engineer. It's suggested that they shut down and reboot the entire system.

Edward wants the aircraft to be broken, to require serious maintenance, to release him from his duty on this fine East African morning. He desires a quiet place to sit to resolve his issues but he goes through the motions as requested. Unfortunately for Edward the reboot works and the spurious warning disappears and with a clean panel they load the passengers and are soon airborne and flying out over the Indian Ocean.

After the day's flying is complete, Edward walks into Dave's cabin, feeling brave and renewed and aggressive, as any African helicopter pilot should. Contemplating his troubles while flying through the African sky had done wonders for his confidence. For in his mind, Edward had tackled challenges far beyond the comprehension of his colleagues, unappreciative that all men face adversity. Edward does not consider the challenges of his colleagues, nor of the daily challenges of the locals, nor of anyone beyond his worried self.

"Dave," he said, addressing the training pilot with bravado and confidence, thinking that makes all the difference. "I'm ready for that upgrade to Captaincy."

Dave doesn't look up from his laptop as Edward has requested the upgrade to Captaincy almost daily since arriving.

"The flight went off perfectly, you can ask Chet. I was told by head office that I was hired as a Captain, and I demand to be designated as such," Edward said with finality.

Dave sighs. He appreciates his position demands patience, and he reminds himself that he has patience in surplus. He forgets sometimes. "Yes Edward, when everything goes well you do a fine job, but when things go awry, you consistently fall apart. To be honest, and I think your daily visits here have only helped me to make up my mind, you are *un-upgradeable*." Dave cringes as he is not certain whether he has just made up a word or not.

"*Un-upgradeable?*" asked Edward angrily, trying it on in a mocking tone, but his confidence is shaken.

Dave smiles when he hears the word repeated, giving it credence.

"As a matter of fact, yes, and I'll be drafting a letter to head office stating as much." He decides there and then on the matter.

Edward scowls and his face turns red. Dave idly returns to whatever he had been doing before Edward had stormed in, dismissing Edward by ignoring him. Edward wishes to argue the point but is unsure of which tact would swerve the decision. He looks at the floor. Edward's phone buzzes in his pocket. He ignores it. After a long moment he looks back at Dave who appears to be completely absorbed with his laptop. Edward turns and stomps out in a huff.

They arrive back at the hotel and spill from Toyotas. Moses steps out of the kitchen and summons Edward.

"Hello Moses."

"Hello Edward. Amina's brother was here looking for you today."

Edward's face turns red. A panic attack builds.

"I told him that you were working but surely he will return."

"When? Tonight?" asked Edward with a fearful grimace.

"I do not think tonight, maybe tomorrow or the next night."

Edward's phone beeps in his pocket. He ignores it. His shoulders drop and he hangs his head. He shuffles morosely into the hotel.

Later that evening, while the others are downstairs eating, Edward tries to call home. He wears the heavy cotton shorts he bought with his wife that never dry around the waist band in this hot muggy climate. They remind him of shopping with his wife and he feels even more guilty. His heart races and he fears his wife might suspect, or even know, that he has cheated, for Edward suspects all women of possessing some strange female perception beyond logic. Surely she can tell. His palms sweat and his heart beats wildly in his chest. The phone rings and rings and there is no answer. Edward is relieved. He fears her knowledge of his indiscretion more than the threat of her own wanton behaviour. Everything is shit. He shakes his head at his own weakness and decides to be a man. Move forward. Get on with the task at hand. He sprays on his bug dope and heads out his door and downstairs for dinner. As he steps outside his phone rings. He doesn't answer it.

The next morning Edward is off the schedule again. He's called in sick with a bad stomach so frequently he's exhilarated to have a day off bereft of guilt. After Edward's late breakfast Moses pokes his head into the dining area.

"Good morning Edward."

"Good morning Moses."

"I am heading up to my village for the day to work on the school, and to give Mike a little help," he laughed. "I have to be back before supper as the other cook is still unavailable. Would you care to join me for the day?"

Edward ponders the offer. It might be better to get away from the hotel with Amina's brother looking for him, but he has other concerns. His face twists in indecision.

Moses notices. "There is a problem?"

"The riots? I thought we aren't supposed to be out."

"There will be no riots today."

"Well, I did want to visit a doctor today to be honest."

"It is on the way, I can take you and wait. We can go from there to the village."

"You know what, I'm in. I'll go upstairs and change, I'll be back in a few minutes."

"I won't leave without you Edward."

Moses sits and waits outside the doctor's office in his beat up Daihatsu. Edward had first frowned at the neighbourhood, then at the old ramshackle building with bizarre signs spouting all sorts of quackery, and the rusted metal bars on the broken windows. Risk of rumours of his possible affliction had he attended the medical station that served the ex-pat community held greater fear. They might even fire him if they found out. He bravely walks down the dirt path through the cement gate and into the open door. The receptionist looks slightly distraught to see a *mzungu* but he is seated and not long thereafter whisked in to see the Doctor.

A small local Doctor of advanced years shines a small light into his eyes and asked; "Did you shiver? Do you use air conditioning? How do you feel about the Queen?"

Edward comes out after a half hour and does not look happy. He slips into Moses's Daihatsu and slams the door. Moses starts the car after a few attempts and drives off through town towards the hills.

"Bad news?"

Edward frowns. "No, not really. He can't tell me anything."

"What is the problem, if I may ask?"

Edward ponders this for a moment before responding.

"Well, I was a little concerned that perhaps I picked up *something* from my evening with Amina."

"Ah."

"Yes, well, the doctor told me that it takes time before anything will show up in any tests. He said to come back in two or three weeks to get checked, but I'll be back home by then. I was hoping to know now."

"I see Edward. Would it not be better to take Amina and get her checked, then you will know? You will not have to wait two or three weeks."

"I haven't talked with her. I don't want to talk with her."

"I see." Moses frowns. "I really think you should talk to her. It's very true to be a little concerned, but you really should talk with her. It is not something to be feared. You made love with this woman, you should not be fearful of talking with her."

"I'd be quite fine if I never saw her or spoke with her again."

Moses shakes his head in bewilderment. Sometimes he just doesn't understand *mzungus*.

"Why do you fear that Amina gave you some disease? Do you have some symptom? From what I know, she is a good girl."

Edward huffs. "No symptoms. Not yet, anyway. If she was a good girl, would she have gone home with me from a bar? A guy she just met?"

Moses thinks for a moment. "Did you not take a girl home from the bar that you did not know?"

Edward frowns at that. "I was drunk."

"Ah, a convenient excuse."

"I'm sure I'm not the first to use it."

"Nor the last!" They both laugh, but Edward takes the point.

As they drive out of the town and into the countryside, Edward picks up a local newspaper from the floor of the car and peruses through the pages. He reads chatter concerning the riots and about the Chinese hoarding all the labour and about corruption and about men giving themselves sexually to their male superiors to advance their careers.

"Is this for real?" Edward asked Moses, showing him the article.

"Unfortunately it is, letting a superior sodomize you for career advancement is more common than many think. It is a problem."

"I've never heard of anything so barbaric!"

Edward continues to read through the paper and finds another article about rural witch-doctors and bizarre rituals involving albinos. The dark trade on body parts is rampant. He is shocked to learn that parts are considered more magical if harvested while the albino is still alive. There are brutal photos that shock Edward.

"The news is horrible," Edward said in disgust. He throws the paper back on the floor. "I'm going to have nightmares after reading that."

"Of course the news is bad, who wants to read about good news?" Moses laughed. "Good news might make you happy but it will not sell newspapers. They want to sell newspapers."

"But this is horrific. I cannot believe people could be so cruel."

"Yes, it is true. People can be incredibly cruel. The government is fighting some of the more disturbing activities that take place. Do not be troubled Edward." He reaches over and pats Edward on the leg. "I will tell you a story; When I was a young boy, I had a school project that required that I follow a certain news story in the paper. Everyday I got the paper and read about this thing and wrote my report. I never missed a day. I became so stressed about the news, the things were all so terrible. How will we even survive the week? I was concerned that all would end. It bothered me greatly. Then I finished the project, and I did not read the news for many months and do you know what happened?"

"No."

"Nothing bad happened. Life went on. Then I started to read the papers again, I do not remember why, and once again it was all so horrible, and I feared for all our futures, but of course, nothing happened again. It took me a while before I figured it out. *Stop reading the news*! They sensationalize everything far beyond common sense. It is all about ratings and selling newspapers and getting advertisements to as many people as possible. Yes, bad things happen, that is certain, but do I need to know about it all? I do not think so. You can say of me, *there is a man with his head in the sand*, but I am a happy man. My concerns are my concerns. I do not want to worry about what they tell me to be worried about. The papers are too full of opinion anyway. I don't need to be told what to think. Some people, I think they like it. They like to be told what to think. I believe maybe they must enjoy the fear the bad news gives to them. It is good to be informed, but it can be too much. There is too much evil in this world for me to ponder."

"Yes," Edward agreed, still upset. "Africa is a pretty messed up place."

Moses regards Edward for a moment, then looks ahead and watches the road.

"It is worse in America I think."

"What?" laughed Edward. "What do you know about it?"

"I lived in America for twenty years Edward."

Edward stares at Moses. "Really? Where?"

"In Toledo, Ohio."

"Wow! I had no idea. Why did you leave?"

"I did not enjoy it there. Yes, it was cold, I do not like the cold. More important, it was not my home. I missed my people. I missed Africa. I had family here that needed my help, so I came back."

They hit a large pothole and the Daihatsu bounces.

"You chose to live in Africa over America?"

"Yes, Edward, I chose Africa."

"And you say it is worse than here?"

"Maybe not worse, I do not know, but they worry about silly things. They talk endlessly about things that do not matter. So many things were strange to me. They have so much yet they are always unhappy."

They pass a series of shops set back from the road and small children chase each other and laugh. Moses honks his horn and a man and woman wave back enthusiastically.

"You see how happy everyone is here?" said Moses laughing.

"Yes, I have noticed."

"And the news was just as bad there. Maybe they don't show the bad photos like we do, but they highlight the things that should not be highlighted; the racial tension, the fear of immigrants like myself, like we are some invaders coming to conquer their land, but we are only seeking a life for ourselves.

Anything that is even slightly different to their way of thinking, they highlight and ridicule it. It is as if no one is allowed to have a different opinion on anything. They want everyone to think the same. Instead of educating people about the things they do not understand, they highlight the differences and they highlight the problems." Moses shakes his head. "I never felt like it could be my home. I could not contribute. I did not understand how they think, so how could I help anybody?"

Edward scrunches up his face in confusion. "Why did you want to help?"

They round a corner and Moses slows and stops as shepherds in threadbare and colourful wraps herd their cattle across the road, making clicking noises with their mouths as they tap their staffs against the ground.

"I want to help. I want to contribute. I want to make a difference in this world. I have lived many years and I think I have something to give, but in America I was nothing. Here I am a man with experience, and people respect me for the things I have done. I know I am not the wisest of men. My education is sorely lacking, but I truly desire to be able to help people move forward. I desire to do good. To share the things I know."

"Is that your religion? You have to help people?"

Now Moses turns and regards Edward. The cattle have completed their crossing, and the way is clear, but Moses does not put his car in gear. After a moment's reflection, he pushes in the clutch and shifts the gears and they begin to move again.

"It is not religion Edward," he said, with a tinge of anger in his voice. "If it is in your ability to help, should you not do it? That is why I missed Africa. Here everything is about community and helping, not about doing better for yourself."

"Maybe because life is so rough here, you have to help each other to survive?" said Edward hopefully.

"Maybe Edward. Maybe the West do not need each other like we do. Everyone can take care of themselves easily enough so they can concentrate on advancing their own concerns. It is okay my friend. I understand differences. I have my path and you have yours and that fellow has his," he said, pointing at a man walking along the road as they drive past. "The pace was too hectic for me, everyone hurrying to get ahead of everyone else. I prefer the African way; the sense of community, of family. It has nothing to do with religion."

"I understand."

"I want for nothing here. My life is full, and my heart bursts with helping others. My life is very fine. And because my life is very fine, I can take some time and help my village. It is what makes me happiest."

They make a turn onto a small dirt road and continue to climb into the hills. The bush thickens into jungle.

"Now that I am talking so much Edward, can I tell you another thing?"

"Of course Moses."

"People are too concerned about skin colour and other things that separate us, but I believe that is fallacy. We have to concentrate on what we share, not on what sets us apart. The thing we share is right now, this period of time. If you must identify with differences, think about those that are alive now versus those that have gone before, or those that will follow. Everyone living now, we are sharing the most important thing we can share. What matters beyond now? Why should I care for a future that isn't mine? What should I feel for those who have passed? All we share is this place in time, and for that we should be striving for harmony. We should feel kinship with everyone we meet because we are all in this together. I think if people think this way, maybe it can be better."

"Life is short, its best to enjoy it, do what makes you happy."

"Yes, Edward, I know of this sentiment, but I do not totally agree with it. First, life is not so short I think. My time on this earth is all the time that I have. My life, from my point of view, is the longest period of time that I know. From my perspective, it is anything but short. It is all that I know. I do agree that we should try to be happy with that time, to do what we feel is right with the time that we have."

"Helping others?

Moses laughs. "For me, it makes me happy. Maybe for you happiness is bringing strange girls home from bars?"

Edward laughs and gives Moses a gentle push.

"Mike has it figured out," continued Moses. "You do not need to be so introspective, once you have it figured out, you can just get on with the living. Does understanding give peace? Does being introspective and cognizant of consequence yield some greatness, some progress, into the human condition? Am

I happier for questioning everything? I think not. What bothers Mike? He is always happy, is he not? He finds joy in everything, and what more can one demand of one's life? I think he is blessed in his vision of this world. You find a happy person, a solid person, a person sure of themselves and what they know, this is a person to emulate, not to envy. Jealousy is for the small minded. I see envy amongst your colleagues."

"Among other things."

"Yes, among other things. I understand the need to work to provide for your family, but I do not understand some of the people who come here and they do not like Africa, they do not like the place, nor the people. They do not even try to understand, they just do their work and stay in their room and hurry back home with their paycheque. How can that be a satisfying life? I do not understand."

"The pay is better if you come to Africa, much better in fact."

"And what is money if you cannot taste life? What do riches give to anybody? Riches are fallacy if you do not enjoy your life. And what use is a rich man? He wishes to relax and enjoy his wealth, and takes little chance, whereas a poor man, a hungry man, has no such compulsion. He has nothing to lose. There is a useful man. Give me a poor man any day."

"You know what Moses? I was afraid of coming to Africa."

Moses laughs. "And what about now Edward, the man who brings home strange girls from bars? How do you feel about Africa now?"

"I am beginning to enjoy it."

Moses laughs and pats Edward's leg again. He turns onto a smaller road that winds through the trees and the bush becomes thick. They come into an open area and construction and Moses turns into a busy sand lot and shuts off the car.

All heads turn when Moses and Edward pull into the lot, and the children stop their games and scamper towards them. As they step from the car everyone waves and Edward returns the greeting. He looks around at all the activity; the heavily laden wheel barrows pushed this way and that amidst piles of cement blocks and freshly cut lumber, women with all manner of load balanced atop their heads, their full bottoms swaying beneath colourful fabrics. Edward notes that the outer cement walls are up and men inside build walls for classrooms, and the framework of the rafters is well under way. He spots Mike balanced precariously up amongst the timbers and local men pass him plank after plank. Timid and unsure, Edward remains close to Moses. The children are not shy, and they pull at his hands and fish in his pockets and the only word he recognizes over and over again amongst the children's flurry of Swahili is '*mzungu*'. Everyone laughs, and the happiness is infectious and Edward laughs in spite of himself. Men approach Moses with serious faces and advise him of problems, and Moses listens closely, then makes some suggestions and the men move back to their work satisfied. One of the children offers Edward a soda, and he responds with *asante* and the children giggle.

Soon Mike is at his side.

"I'm surprised to see you here Edward. I am happy you came." He grabs Edward firmly on the shoulder. "Are you here to work?"

"I'll do what I can," said Edward.

They give Edward various tasks. He proves inept at most everything. No one seems to mind, and although he does more harm than good, everyone seems pleased to have him amongst the volunteers.

They take a break in the afternoon and Edward and Mike sit together in the shade of a large acacia. A smattering of children that had attached themselves to Edward sit and play amongst themselves.

"I am starting to understand why you like it here," said Edward.

"You get good postings and you get bad ones, depends on your outlook. You can find the good in any place, and you can find the bad just as easily. It's all on you. *Wherever you go, there you are*, sounds stupid, but there's truth in it. If you find you don't like a place, perhaps it's you and not the place? Think on that. Some people make the most of everything, the cup half full folk, and others? Well, I think you know. The trick is not to get too attached to any place because it never lasts." He looks up into the tree for a minute deep in thought. "And don't let yourself get spoiled neither, because I've stayed in some five-star beach resorts and hardly worked and sat all day by the pool, to tents in the desert where you flew your ass off and there was a wood plank with a hole in it to shit out behind a dune. You generally don't get to choose."

"You've done a lot of touring overseas?"

"Christ Edward, I've been everywhere, I've whored the back alleys of Mombasa, Dar and Istanbul, all across Eastern Europe and all along the Amazon, the Congo, the Ganges and the Seine too, from the high Northern reaches of Scandinavia to the Southern tip of South America, and all through the Far East, and you know what?"

"Tell me."

"Everywhere I went, there I was."

Edward laughs. The children join in, not understanding a word.

"One of things I've discovered about myself, living in all these third world countries, is that it doesn't really matter where I am. I've found that I can adapt to anything and anywhere. I can live anywhere. Seriously mate, it doesn't matter. To be honest, if I had the choice, I'd probably live somewhere in Africa." He gives Edward a wink. "It gives me confidence, knowing that I'm not beholden to my country of birth, that I am a man of the world." He throws his head back and laughs. "I can adapt to most anything. You may not realize what kind of confidence that can give a man. The entire world is mine. I can make my home in it anywhere. Yes, I have my preferences but I have been around enough to know that for me at least, it doesn't really matter. I will make the most of whatever life places in front of me. I've only got what? At most eighty or ninety years to account for, and I'm well over half way there. What do I have to worry about? Slap me down and there I am. Here is as good as anywhere."

"This is my first time away from home, so it's all quite intimidating."

"Well, you are doing all right then Edward. You take to Africa like a duck to water."

"I don't know about that. I feel pretty hopeless most of the time. I see how well suited you are to the place and I try my best to understand."

"Edward, the trick to understanding Africa is to search out the similarities with things you know rather than the differences. Try to identify with the people, see things from their perspective. The folks here are trying to get on with their lives, feed their kids, pay the bills, have a little fun. If you can place their hopes and desires into context, take your hopes and desires and imagine the same in Africans, you will have a better understanding. Not just here but anywhere you go, the same thing applies. People everywhere are just like us and until you grasp that we are all part and parcel of the same struggle, you will never fit in. Consider yourself lucky to have this experience. I think it was Mark Twain that said, *Travel is fatal to prejudice, bigotry, and narrow-mindedness.*"

Mike takes a sip of his soda and looks over at Edward. "For your first trip abroad, I'd say you are doing all right."

Chapter 17

Edward wakes the next morning in his own bed, having driven back to town with Moses the evening before. As Edward lies in bed, he listens to his stomach burble and senses a familiar twinge in his bowels. He clenches his butt and hurries to the toilet. Finished and sweating, he washes his hands and splashes cool water on his flushed face. He then calls the manager.

"I have a bad stomach this morning."

There is no response for a time, then Edward hears a sigh.

"I'll get Chet to cover your shift." The line goes dead.

Edward crawls back into his bed, not overly concerned about disappointing anyone. He pulls his sweat dampened sheets over his shivering body and listens to the morning activity as doors open and close amid undecipherable chatter. Boots stamp on the stairs and there's the squeak of the door, and finally the diesel-engined Toyotas fire up and the heavy metal gate opens, then closes again, and all is quiet. He tries to doze but the pangs in his stomach jolt him awake. After repeated frenzied dashes to the toilet, he gives up on sleep and takes a shower and dresses. There is another unpleasant voiding, but he feels better afterwards and considers heading downstairs for something to settle his stomach when he hears a loud boom off in the distance. The ill-fitting windows of his room rattle and a car alarm goes off nearby. The loud noise is accompanied by smaller more compressed blasts and he hears a sharper staccato pop that sounds like gunfire. It is nearby. Edward crouches and sneaks up to his window and peaks outside. He sees dark smoke billow above the palms a few streets over. Something akin to the air raid sirens from old *War War II* movies begins to wail and movement catches Edward's eye. He watches as a group of youths with bandanas over their faces scurry across the lane between two adjacent buildings.

"Shit."

Edward panics. A wave of dizziness passes through him and his knees weaken. His bowels clench. Fearing he may pass out Edward allows his body to settle to the floor of his room in a disheveled heap, and there he spots a hiding place. For lack of a better plan, he elects to stash himself under his bed.

Awkwardly he slides across the worn linoleum and grabs the heavy wood braces that suspend the mattress, then he pulls himself underneath. It's a tight fit, and he has to turn his head to one side, but with great difficulty, he manages to get himself well ensconced. Feeling somewhat calmer nestled in under his bed, his phone rings. It's in the pocket of his cargo shorts but it takes effort to work his arm around in that confined area. He eventually retrieves it, but then cannot get the phone to his ear. Swearing, he pulls himself out from under the bed. Before he can answer, it stops ringing.

He looks at the screen expecting it to have been Amina, but it's the manager. He redials.

"Edward, where are you?"

"Under my bed."

The line is quiet for a long moment. "Yeah, right. Well, you have probably figured out by now that the riots have kicked off. We passed them setting up road blocks on the way into the airport, and I've been told that all the roads are impassable now."

Edward gulps and another spell of dizziness passes over him.

"You're the only one back at the hotel, so just sit tight and keep your head down and we'll figure something out."

"I'm the only one here?" quivered Edward. Tears well up and he tries to push them back.

"I'm afraid so, not an ideal situation I admit. Just sit tight, we're working on it."

The phone line goes dead and Edward stares at it for a good while before he gets under his bed again. He listens to the sirens and the gunfire and listens for steps coming up the stairs, and he falls asleep.

When he awakes, it is not so bright in his room, and although the sirens still wail, he hears no gunfire. He looks at the door of his room, the little he can see of it from under the bed, and realizes that hiding under the bed is perhaps not the smartest place to be. If they came in, they would only have to bend over to see him. He has to pee anyway, so Edward struggles and pulls and manages to get out from under his bed, and checking his watch, he notes it is now late afternoon. He crawls across the floor to avoid broadcasting his presence to anyone who may be watching the windows and slips into the toilet. He chooses not to flush for the noise may alert someone lurking in the hotel, assuming such a possibility exists. Crawling on the floor again, he reaches up and brings his laptop from the desk to the floor and attempts to call home. For the moment his wife's imagined infidelity is forgotten, for he needs to hear a comforting voice, but there is no internet connection. He hears chatter and crawls over to the other window of his room and peaks over the sill. A fierce local man argues with a waitress in front of the kitchen. He is well dressed and angry. As Edward watches, the large man points an accusing finger at the waitress then stomps out the gate. Edward decides to brave the downstairs courtyard to find out what's going on.

He stalks down the stairs, peaking around every corner before committing. He watches through the glass door before gently opening it, doing his best as he pulls to avoid its loud squeal. Outside, the sound of the sirens and people yelling is much more immediate. He shivers in fear but braces himself and walks across the courtyard to the kitchen. He steps inside.

"Edward!" said the waitress. "You are still here?"

"Yes, I am the only one left."

"Ah, Tor was here most of the day then left a while ago."

"Tor was here?"

"Yes, he went to the beach for a few hours."

"The beach? They're rioting!"

"Yes, I think someone pointed that out to him. He said no one riots at the beach. I think he wanted to go for a swim."

Edward stares at her in disbelief. Gathering his senses, he asked, "Is he back now? I'm confused."

"He was back, then he left again. I think he went to the airport to join the others."

"How? I thought the road was closed, and why didn't he take me?"

"You know Tor likes to bike to the airport. I think he takes the trails and backstreets. I don't think he could take you on his bike. I don't think he knew you were here anyway. I did not know."

"I stayed back, I wasn't feeling well."

"Ah, that explains it. Tor must have thought you were on the schedule."

Edward looks at the ground between his feet and shakes his head. He hyperventilates.

"Amina's brother was here to see you, he is very upset."

"Amina's brother? That guy who was just here?"

"Yes."

"I thought he was Police? Isn't he busy with these riots?"

"I think he is secret police, and he has found time to look for you. I told him you were at the airport. I thought that is where you were."

There is another loud boom and a smattering of small arms fire. It is much closer than before. There is some hectic activity just outside the gate as another group of teens run by yelling. Edward's knees weaken again. He tries to call the manager. It takes quite a few tries before the call goes through.

"How are you doing Edward? Still under the bed?" joked the manager.

Edward considers swearing at him but thinks better of it. Before he can respond the manager continued, "I'm afraid I've got some bad news for you. The police claim all the roads are closed and there is no getting through. The company doesn't like having the birds sitting here exposed at the airport, you know how security is up here, so we are gearing up to fly them to the Capital for the night."

"What!" Edward screamed into the phone. "You guys are leaving me?"

"I'm afraid that we don't have much choice Edward. There is no way to get you, and even the police claim they can't get through. The company is quite worried about the aircraft, they want them out of here as soon as possible. Things are going for a shit rather quickly I'm afraid."

"You can't leave me here!" Edward cried. There is no attempt to conceal the panic in is voice.

"I've already spoken with head office and they aren't happy about it one bit, but we don't have a choice. We have been trying to get the police to come and get you, even if it was to take you back and keep you at the police station, but unfortunately they are quite busy at the moment. Not to mention, the police station is probably not the safest place anyway, I heard it is directly under attack."

Edward barely hears the words over the roar of blood gushing through his ears, muffling the noise. His heart pumps wildly in his chest. He forces himself to think.

"Is Tor there?"

"Yes, he arrived on his bike a while ago. We have talked about your situation at length and everyone figures your best bet is to keep your head down at the hotel. The military should be in here in a day or two and…"

The line goes dead. Edward looks at his phone in disbelief. He pounds it a few times and looks at the waitress.

"Is your phone working?"

She digs it out and checks, then shakes her head.

"Sometimes they turn off the cellular services when there are riots, so the instigators cannot communicate."

Edward stands there breathing heavily. More gunfire goes off just around the corner so he runs back into the hotel and bounds up the stairs and back into his room. He frantically pulls on his long trousers and a long sleeve shirt, and puts on socks and his running shoes, then grabs his small backpack and stuffs in a change of clothes, his bug dope, a hat, his passport and his money. Edward looks about his room one last time, backpack in hand, then stuffs in his small laptop, a phone charger and his *Leatherman*, a toothbrush and some toothpaste. He sits on his bed to take stock. There is a clunk as the hotel's electric relay snaps open. Edward notices it is darker and much later than he thought. He peaks outside and notes it is not just the hotel. The entire neighbourhood's power has gone out.

There's more activity outside and then a hotel window breaks. Edward looks at his bed and considers crawling under it again but he really does not want to be caught here alone. He considers trying to make his way across town to the customer's offices, or at the very least, downstairs with the hotel staff.

He opens his door slowly and steps into the hallway, his *bug out* bag over his shoulder. He creeps the length of the hall and peaks down the stairwell, wishing he had left before. Edward starts down the stairs then freezes as another window breaks. He stops and listens to the commotion of the large crowd outside the hotel. They aren't inside yet as far as he can tell. He continues down quickly as it seems penetration is imminent, hoping to escape via the courtyard out the back. Just as he gets to the ground floor the front door smashes open and people rush in. Edward shifts right out of their view and there is only a closet. He slips inside and shuts the door, hoping they didn't spot him. Trying not to make any noise, he hides behind numerous mop handles then crouches and pulls a spare blanket over his head just as the closet door opens and Edward freezes.

He holds his breath while listening to the pandemonium coursing through the lower floors of the hotel. There's a creak and someone looks into the closet, but with no electricity it's very dark. Edward shivers. The rabble heads up the stairs and footsteps pound above his head amidst laughter and kicked in doors. Edward wonders if he is alone again. He braves a peak from under the blanket, so scared that waves of nausea cause his stomach to heave. His eyes adjust and there's no one else in the closet. Scared yet knowing action is required, he stands and sneaks back to the hallway. Peaking around and seeing no one, he slips from the closet and sprints for the rear door. He peaks into the courtyard then someone yells behind him. He turns and sees the white eyes and black face of a youth, then another, and they come for him and he knows not why. He bursts through the door and bolts across the courtyard. The security guard stands when he sees Edward run towards him, seemingly unaware of the looting taking place inside the hotel. Despite his obvious confusion, he opens the gate as is his place, and Edward dashes through and heads up the lane. The old security guard now spots the youths as they spill from the hotel in pursuit and stands to block them out of professional duty, and unsure, they stop and frown. The security guard, emboldened with stopping the troublemakers, steps forward and the youths turn and run back into the hotel. Rather than follow, the security guard sits back in his chair.

Edward runs down the lane unsure of his next course of action. As he comes to the first bend, he dares glance rearward. With no one in pursuit his heart recovers somewhat, but still, he is a white man in Africa in the middle of a riot. His body quivers from the adrenaline. He is anything but secure. The sirens wail off towards the market area and there's sporadic gunfire and the booms of what? Percussion grenades perhaps?

Shotguns firing bean bags or rubber bullets or maybe even tear gas? He doesn't know nor does he want to. He moves off into the deeper shade of a large tree and takes stock. He checks his cellular phone and there is no signal. Just as the waitress told him. He thinks about the kitchen staff and perhaps they could help but he doesn't dare return to the hotel. He thinks about the restaurant on the beach which is in the opposite direction of most of the activity, as far as he can tell, but it's a long, exposed route. Rowdy people move up the lane. The boisterous crowd approaches and he considers hiding behind the tree, but he reconsiders and moves along, towards the beach.

Edward passes from the shade of one tree to the next, for it is almost fully dark, and the trees offer some concealment. As he nears the main road he is disappointed to discover a great deal of activity. There are police vehicles, fires and a large crowd pushing forward. He spots a quiet area behind all the frantic activity and at least it gets him away from the sound of gunfire, cracking sporadic in the distance, so he slips from tree to tree as innocuous as possible. He must cross the main road and expose himself, but the more he finds himself out amongst the rioters, the braver he becomes. Bracing himself, he pulls his baseball cap low over his head and struts out into the open with purpose and walks across the road and although a few heads turn no one bothers him, and Edward is soon back amongst the dark areas of a quiet lane. It is almost completely black now so Edward braves the side of the road and walks on, not sure where he is headed but in the general direction of the beach and away from the melee. He passes many excited people headed in the opposite direction and although some look, no one stops him.

He stumbles as the uneven dirt lane before him undulates but he soldiers on for no other purpose than to remain on the move.

Spotting a glow off in the distance, it catches his attention and in spite of himself, he gravitates towards it. There are lights and he is confused. Then the sound of a generator resolves the query. He approaches tentatively and as he comes around the corner he finds a jungle bar. There appears to be lit Christmas lights surrounding the perimeter, yielding a festive atmosphere, and one rotating disco ball flashes dots of dancing lights throughout the foliage. Swahili rap plays at the typical volume far exceeding the capability of the stereo's speakers. Despite the riots playing out all around, *Tuk Tuks* and motorcycle taxis come and go and discharge party goers in front of the bar, and there are a few SUVs parked in front. Edward watches a while from his cache in the trees along the lane, then asks himself; *what the hell? I need a beer.*

Edward smiles gleefully and proud as he struts into the rudimentary jungle bar nestled deep in the trees on this lonely lane, in the middle of a riot no less. His stress washes away as new found confidence takes hold. If people could take the time to have a relaxed beer in the middle of all this why can't he? A bravado previously unknown captures his psyche. Once again he sees himself conquering his fears. He is a man among men. He imagines the others in a hotel in the capital, fearful of the riots, discussing poor Edward stuck in the epicentre all by himself, and here he is, walking into a bar for a beer. None of the other patrons pay any notice and he seats himself at a table made of an inverted and hand-carved longboat. He slips his backpack off his shoulder and swings it between his feet. A young waitress soon arrives and takes his order. Edward looks about the open air bar nestled in the trees, still well within the confines of the town but wooded enough to offer seclusion. He sits amongst the other jovial souls seemingly far removed from the riots. As Edward waits, he checks his phone again and there is still no service. His beer arrives sweating and cold and he drains it blissfully. The cold liquid washes the dryness and heat from his throat and settles cooly into his belly. He orders another.

As Edward sips on his second beer, savouring it and his surroundings, he notes as two expensive and rugged SUVs arrive, and the local men who disembark are well dressed and serious. Just then a group of youths run past the bar with bandanas over their faces and a police truck passes afterwards in pursuit. The noise of the riots draws nearer as the minutes pass. Edward steals a glance at the new arrivals, now at the standing bar, and they are all turned and looking directly at him, drinking their beers. Edward quickly looks down. He risks another glance and one of them walks directly towards him.

His mannerism doesn't appear overly aggressive but there is determination that sets Edward ill at ease. Edward smiles nervously as the large man approaches. The man smiles back reassuringly. He sits down across the table from Edward.

"Good evening Sir," said the man, the deep timber of his voice resonates with confidence and some malevolence. The man portrays an aura of ease and unrestrained authority, and Edward perceives that he is *Police*.

"Good evening," Edward stammered.

"How are you on this fine evening?" the man said, clearly enunciating each vowel with strong emphasis.

"I am good."

"So I see this, out enjoying a beer. Should you not be home instead of out and about when people are acting mad in the streets?"

"My hotel was ransacked, I had to leave."

The man scratches his chin thoughtfully. "Where are the others from your hotel?"

"I am the only one, they all left this morning."

"I see," said the man nodding. "I think I know the hotel that you speak of. Does a Jasmine work there as a waitress?"

"Yes, that's it."

"Aha, and Moses the chef?"

Edward nods.

"The helicopter people?"

"Yes."

There's commotion as another large group of agitated people march past but the man does not turn his head. He does not appear to blink. He stares at Edward who quivers beneath his gaze.

"You know Jasmine is my cousin's wife. That is how I know this hotel."

Edward thinks back on the altercation between the American and Jasmine's husband.

"You are not American I think?"

"No."

The man looks at him and nods. He enjoys making people uncomfortable. He continues to stare at Edward and says nothing. It does not take long before the other is compelled to speak. It saves the policeman from asking numerous questions.

"I'm Edward." Edward sticks his hand out to offer a greeting, trying to lighten the mood. The man does not take it and his gaze hardens. There is anger in those eyes as he scrutinizes his quarry. The man's eyes grows small, and he involuntarily gives too much away, a mistake he doesn't often make. Edward sees it too. The man stands without saying another word and walks back to the standing bar with his comrades. Edward watches from the corner of his eye and one of the larger men appears to grow agitated as they talk. They all stare at Edward from across the bar.

 There are screams and Edward spots an orange glow through the foliage concealing the bar. There is a crackle and pop and embers fall onto the road. More and more people run along the lane that passes the bar and gun fire cracks through the music. There is a shift of wind and acrid smoke flows through the bar yet quickly fades. People start to leave in a panic. Edward tries to motion the waitress for his bill so he can leave, but can't catch her eye. He never considers simply leaving. As Edward waves his hand about at the scurrying waitress, he now sees another large black man headed towards him, the agitated fellow. Edward doesn't know if he should be scared or not. He decides that he should. The man sways menacingly as he rolls his hips, shifting his mass from one leg to the next, his long arms loping at his sides. His head is down so he stares up at Edward as he approaches, menacingly. People run now and flames have taken the building next door. There is more gunfire and screams. The man appears familiar but Edward can't place him. The man's aggressive demeanour fades as he sits in the same seat the other man had vacated. He smiles at Edward.

 "Hello Edward," he said in a low booming voice, thick and slurred from whiskey. Edward watches the man's friends depart the bar unhurried, despite the mayhem unfolding around them. He watches them discretely while focusing his attention on the man in front of him, for he does not wish to insult this large inebriated beast. They all step into one of the SUVS and depart, forging ahead with little concern for the pedestrians on the lane.

"Hello," replied Edward nervously. Embers land on the straw roof and he spots smoke whisking through the dried grass.

"I am very excited to meet you Edward," said the large man. Now Edward remembers. It is the large man who had been arguing with the waitress at the hotel. It is Amina's brother.

Chapter 18

Smoke from the fire consuming the building next door blows through the open air bar and stings Edward's eyes. He coughs but Amina's brother does not flinch. The grass roof smoulders above them. People run in the streets and there are shouts and commotion. The flashing lights of nearby police vehicles reveal the dark recesses and lay them bare in eerie blue, and the red glow of high flames paints everything else in a fiery hell. There is sporadic machine gun fire nearby and concussive booms of tear gas grenades.

"My dear sister was so excited about meeting you Edward," said the brother, now laying his hand over Edward's wrist firmly. Is it a term of endearment or is he binding him to his presence? "She told everyone in the family about the nice man she had met, the white man who would carry her away." He looked at Edward with a raised eyebrow. "I like to see my sister happy Edward. She is my kin. I love her dearly. Do you understand?"

Edward nods nervously, watching the flames now lick through the grass ceiling and they are engulfed in clouds of thick smoke as the light breeze shifts. The brother holds his wrist firmly.

"Then I can see that she is not so happy." He makes an overtly sad face. He burps loudly and continues. "After a couple of days my sister is not so happy any more, so I ask her *what is the problem?*" He shakes his great head slowly, sadly. "She says to me that the man does not return her calls, that he slept with her but now he ignores her." He looks up at the ceiling but the flames do not seem to register. He looks back at Edward, firmly griping his wrist. "She was ashamed of what she had done, taken a white man to bed and then to be dumped like some whore, cast aside like some worthless thing." He spits on the ground beside him. "Please tell me Edward, why do you treat my sister like a whore?" His grip on Edward's wrist tightens painfully. Edward watches his massive head sway and realizes the man is very drunk. His voice is heavy and slurred. Edward is unable to quell his trembling. The rioters have realized that the bar is abandoned and youths course in and smash the bar and stuff bottles under their arms and into their pockets and packs. They leave Edward and the man alone.

"I need the toilet," said Edward meekly.

The man raises his eyebrows in shock, then his severe gaze softens in understanding, for are they both not men with common enough needs? He releases his grip on Edward's wrist. He appears completely oblivious to the mayhem playing out all around them.

"Of course Edward, the toilet is inside," he stammered.

Edward stands up relieved. He considers taking his bug out bag but considers it too suspicious, so he saunters towards the inside of the bar as nonchalant as he can manage. There are looters inside breaking glass and tearing things from the wall. They ignore Edward. It is all dark now for the generators have died. Edward goes into the toilet and pees into the lone urinal.

There is more gunfire now and there are clangs of metal against metal all. Edward flinches as bullets hit the stove and fridge beside him. He steps out of the toilet and wanders back into the looters and it is all dark. A large firm hand clasps his throat and thrusts him forcefully against a wall. Against his will he is turned about and pushed back into the wall face first and a heavy body pushes into him and he fears his ribcage will crack. He gasps for a breath.

The heat of another man is hard against him, with rancid alcohol-tinged breath against his ear. "Edward," the voice whispers, heavy and drunken. It is Amina's brother. A large hand takes his head and pushes it firmly into the wall. Edward fears his skull may crack under the pressure but there's little he can do. Another hand fumbles with his belt, and he is confused.

Despite the pain in his head and the large sweaty body pushing him into the wall, he senses that his belt is now unbuckled and his pants are being opened. He pounds his pelvis into the wall to try to thwart the offending hand but the hand is rough and powerful and soon his pants are open and pulled down. The hot breath in his ear speaks again.

"You fucked my sister Edward, you left her like a whore, and now I am going to fuck you like a whore."

Edward is frozen, as if trapped in a nightmare where you want to move but cannot. If only he could move his feet, or move at all. Edward is uncertain if it is fear holding him in his place, or if this massive man is truly in control. The man laughs loudly.

"I thought you had just peed Edward? And now you pee again?"

The comment doesn't register immediately with Edward, then he realizes that he must have wet himself in his fear. He struggles but cannot move. He feels the movement behind him and he knows that Amina's brother is opens his own trousers. He shivers in fear. Edward hopes someone will help him, but the looters have left. There is only the red glow of the fire and the blue flashes from the police lights in the lane, the cackle of flame and the suffocating smoke. He hears the hubbub outside, the yelling and the gunfire and the hectic commotion, and he knows no one will hear. Edward begins to sob uncontrollably. It's painful as his lungs are compressed by the weight pushed against him and he cannot get enough air.

"You white men think you can do whatever you want. I will show you."

Amina's brother grabs Edward's hand and forces it against his groin and Edward cringes as his hand touches the rough pubic hair and swelling organ of another man.

"Come on Edward, help me, and it will all be over quickly, and I will leave you be like you left my sister," he whispers softly into Edward's ear, his breath hot and laboured, stinking of cheap whiskey.

Edward hears the man spit and then feels a rough finger on his anus, and quivers in fear. It enters him roughly and he gasps but it is soon removed. Edward is hyperventilating now and struggling to catch his breath. His world spins and he wavers on the verge of passing out.

Edward feels it now, the head of a swollen cock, pushed against him. His heart beats out of his chest. He clenches his buttocks tightly and whimpers, "Please no, don't do this."

The force of the body pushing him into the wall slackens and the hand pushing his head into the wall releases him. The brother's head then slams into the wall next to him. Edward shifts his head slightly to try to make sense of what he sees. The brother's head is pulled back and his eyes bulge. Edward moves farther away and now spots another man behind the brother, and the head is thrust forcefully into the wall again with a sickening crunch. The brother falls to the floor in a heap with his pants around his ankles. Edward shuffles further away and has the presence of mind to pull up his trousers. Edward fastens his pants before he turns and in the darkness realizes that Mike stands over the inert brother's body. Mike digs through the brother's pockets and finds some keys. He dangles them for Edward to see and smiles.

"Let's go Eddie."

Chapter 19

"Can we leave him here?" asked Edward.

Mike looks at the unconscious brother for a moment. The entire bar spouts flames.

"No, I guess we shouldn't." Mike reaches under the brother's arms and Edward takes his feet and together they muscle the heavy body across broken glass and out the door amidst crackles, heat and darting embers. Once out of the smoke-filled building, Edward lets the feet drop and braces himself against a wall, feeling light-headed.

As Edward is somewhat discombobulated, Mike continues to drag the brother's body through the open bar. Smoke laden air burns the eyes and fills the lungs. The straw roof covering the open bar is engulfed in flames and large chunks fall to the ground in explosions of embers. They cough but continue to move towards the exit. Tear laden eyes guide them towards the lane. Mike drops the brother for a moment and grabs Edward by the shoulder and yells in his ear, "Do you have anything else?"

Edward thinks for a moment and then remembers his bag. He heads back to his seat and thankfully his backpack is still there, so he throws it over his shoulder and together they grab the unconscious brother and continue to drag him out from under the burning roof. Removed from the thick smoke and risk of fiery death, things are less hectic now, but the flames have carried over the bar and to adjacent buildings. Everything in the vicinity is ablaze. People rush about with armloads of assorted things, either from looting or struggling to save their meagre possessions. Edward and Mike leave the brother in the sand far enough away from the building to not have to worry about him burning, and Mike leads them to the only SUV left and opens the door with the keys taken from the brother's pocket.

"He must be well known, nobody has touched it."

Edward gets in the passenger seat. There are two shotguns mounted between the front seats and a police light on the dash. Mike slaps the light onto the roof and it's held in place by its own magnet and he fires up the engine. The blue light flashes all around them.

"Too cool. And a full tank of gas! Lucky days!" he laughed.

Mike looks over at the body in a heap in front of the bar and stares at it for a long moment.

"I think we should take him with us."

"What? Why?"

"I'm not completely sure, but I'd feel better having him with us, more in control of the situation." He continues staring and thinking. He puts the SUV into gear and drives up alongside the body, blocking the view from those still walking on the lane, and hops out. Edward reluctantly joins him. Mike jumps in the back and rummages around and finds some tie wraps, then fastens the brother's legs and wrists together. They then manhandle the heavy body up into the rear seat. Sweating, they both get back into the truck's cabin.

"We are driving around in a stolen Police vehicle, you know? How cool is that?" asked Mike.

"Yeah, now with a cop tied up and unconscious in the back," said Edward sardonically. Mike smiles and gives him a wink. He reaches down and cranks up the stereo. Swahili rap booms through the vehicle.

"Gotta look the part!" Mike yells. He throws the vehicle in reverse and backs up enough to turn around, then heads down the lane in the direction that the crowd appears to be coming from. The flashing blue light seems to warrant some respect, for people get out of the way as Mike and Edward bounce down the lane between the burning buildings. They soon face teens with covered faces throwing rocks. Mike pays them no mind and continues. The rocks crack against the front window but it doesn't break. The rioters yell and pound on the hood and doors but Mike pushes through. They eventually come to their first road block, with all manner of debris pulled across the road and lit aflame. Mike eases over into the shallow ditch and scatters angry people everywhere. He lies on the horn and people climb all over the vehicle but he plows through. Edward is fearful of the angry faces and pounding fists but the windows hold up.

"I'm thinking this beast is made for this shit," exclaimed Mike happily.

"Bullet proof glass?"

"I think so, she's taking a beating," he yelled over the pounding on the exterior of the SUV.

"How did you know?"

"I didn't."

"Jesus! What if they get in?"

"We're fucked buddy."

The vehicle rambles along and Mike eases back up onto the lane after passing the roadblock and the crowds eventually thin. "Fuck, I love the wildness of this place." He watches a few in pursuit in the rear view mirror but they soon drop back.

He takes a few turns down smaller lanes and the crowds dwindle and they run one more roadblock but it is less violent than the first. He turns down what ever lane presents itself.

"Do you know where you are going?"

"Not really, there's a compass up here," he said, pointing to the display in the rear view mirror. "So I'm basically working our way North and East. If we hit the sea, we've gone too far East."

After an age of bouncing over rough undulating dirt lanes, they find themselves on pavement again and heading through the outskirts of town. Edward turns off the radio.

"How did you find me?"

"We ran out of beer at the school so I drove into town for a cold one, and there you were with your pants down."

"Really?"

Mike looks at Edward and raises an eyebrow. "No, I spoke with Chet earlier and he told me about your situation, so I figured that I best come into town and find you. I tried calling but the cellular service is down. I stopped by the hotel and saw it's been ransacked, so I asked around. Not a lot of *mzungus* running around in the middle of riots. Someone saw you having a drink at that bar, you sneaky bugger."

"Thank you."

"Don't mention it little buddy."

"Do you think he's dead?"

"Nah, he's still breathing."

"Did you have to smash his head that hard?"

"Probably not."

"Do you think they'll come for us?"

"Yeah, I figure, after the riots die down they'll be after us. I think we should get out of dodge as quickly as possible."

"What about him?"

"Well, to be honest, I'm hoping he's out cold until we figure something out. I was hoping to just cut him loose with his truck and when he wakes up, we're long gone. That way he can save face. He can tell his buddies anything he wants, or nothing at all."

They drive through the night and the sky dazzles with stars. There is no one on the road.

"We're explorers Edward, like Franklin looking for the Northwest Passage, Columbus seeking the New World, or even my favourite, Richard Burton searching for the source of the Nile."

"Stanley and Livingstone!" added Edward enthusiastically.

Mike pauses.

"Livingstone not so much. He was a missionary trying to change things, and Stanley was hired to find him. Trying to push that Anglo-Saxon Christianity bullshit on the heathens; I got no time for that crap. No, I mean explorers in the sense that we play our small part to find resources and riches far from our homes. How about *Tippu Tip*? The great ivory and slave trader out of Zanzibar?" He punches Edward in the shoulder and laughs.

"Another favourite is *Karamojo Bell*, ivory hunter from the early 1900s, a soldier, fighter pilot, writer and painter. That's the guy I revere. I'm sure he woke up with more than a few local lovelies. Eh?" Mike punches Edward playfully again.

"I'm just trying to do a job and get back home," said Edward as they bounce along the dark road in the middle of nowhere.

Mike looks over at Edward sadly.

"You know what Edward? You need to cheer up. Here's how I see it; there's different kinds of folks in the world. There is no pleasing some people unfortunately, they don't know what happiness is. They blame all their sorrows on something external to themselves and are always miserable, no matter what. There is no helping those people. Don't waste the effort.

And then there are those folks that realize that where ever they go, whatever they are doing, whatever is going on around them, the one constant is them, and how they perceive it. And they look for the good in it. They find the joy in it. They are happy people, despite any external bullshit. Look at the Africans here.

This is one of the poorest countries on earth. These people are dirt poor Edward, but have you ever seen a happier bunch of folk? Besides buddy in the back seat and a few others of course. You get my drift?"

Edward nods thoughtfully.

"I get so sick of being back in the first world with everyone's first world concerns. Africa is the Wild West my friend. It's the place to be. It scares off all those pedantic assholes that want everything spelled out for them, everything governed by highly defined rules and regulations. First world, there is no thinking for oneself, no risk taking of any kind. It's all cover your ass, follow the procedures. They want everything to be neat and tidy with zero room for interpretation. This here is the place to be yourself, to find yourself. I feel closer to humanity here. I feel more human."

Edward just nods, confused.

"I've made some grave errors Mike, so I'm just down. A little worried about the whole situation."

"Who doesn't make mistakes Eddie? A man makes mistakes, but you move forward. How you react, how you deal with problems when they arise, is what defines you. The more you are challenged, the more you test those waters, the more confidence you have in dealing with whatever may arise. Therein lies what it is to be a man. All these challenges give you confidence, that you'll be able to cope with whatever life throws down."

Edward looks at the floor dejectedly.

"Listen buddy, I know you've had a rough go of it, especially tonight, but you got to get up when you get knocked down."

"Mike, I'm not sure you appreciate our situation. We are driving a stolen Police vehicle with an unconscious cop that hates me in the back seat, and I'm going to be heading home and lord knows what diseases I'm taking with me, and I think my wife is having an affair..." Edward's voice trails off and he starts to cry. Mike doesn't notice.

"Driving a stolen Police vehicle with an unconscious cop in the back, how fucking cool is that?"

Edward shakes his head and his crying turns to laughter.

"That's it mate. I fuck up all the time Eddie. I'm a huge fuck up but I don't give a shit. You do what you do and if it doesn't work out, tough luck. I'll pay the dues I have coming. I know I ain't perfect, but I won't be blaming any of my screw ups on anyone else or the fucking government or the rules or lack of them or anything else. When I screw up, I'll wear it. There ain't no accountability anymore. No one has any balls."

They are high in the hills when the sky lightens and Mike checks his phone.

"Got a signal mate."

"Who are you going to call?"

"I'll call Chet, see if he can swing a maintenance flight at first light, come and get us."

He dials as he drives and puts the phone to his ear.

Edward looks back at their passenger. He doesn't stir, still out like a light. After a few minutes Mike throws the phone onto the seat.

"Yeah, they are already at the airport. They can change the crews out of the Capital airport with a little more fuel. Chet said he can swing a maintenance flight first thing with Tor. They'll meet us at an old grass strip about another half hour up this road."

"And then what?"

"We'll cut numb-nuts loose and leave the windows open so he doesn't bake in the sun, and hopefully we're long gone by the time he wakes up. I told Chet to book you out of the country on the first available flight. This fucker is connected, you best get out while you can."

They arrive at the grass strip as the sun peaks over the horizon. The humidity is high. Mike gets into the back seat and with his pocket knife cuts the tie wraps from Amina's brother's hands and feet. The brother groans and Edward and Mike share a concerned look. Off in the distance there is a familiar buzz, and it steadily grows louder. Mike leaves the doors of the truck open and tosses the keys onto the front seat where Amina's brother can find them. Edward grabs his bag and they walk towards the grass strip. The approaching helicopter grows louder and is soon in sight. They crouch in the grass beside the strip as Chet arrives. The helicopter flares nearby yet far enough away that the downwash doesn't cover them with debris. They watch as the helicopter settles into the long grass. They receive a nod from Chet and note Tor in the co-pilot's seat, so they stand and run towards the helicopter.

Mike opens the door and they both jump in and fasten their seat belts. Mike gives a thumbs up to Chet and the aircraft shudders and lifts into the sky. They climb out as they pass down the grass strip then turn back towards the capital and Edward looks out his window and watches the police SUV grow small.

Chapter 20

Edward sits to the rear of the jetliner squashed between two large and colourfully dressed African ladies, the air thick with their sweet perfume. The engines roar and Edward sinks into his seat as they accelerate down the runway. With his limited view out the small window he watches happily as they climb steeply into the skies over East Africa. He puts his head back and relaxes for the first time in a long while. Next stop Zurich, then home.

His mind drifts back to the phone call with his wife. He had called her that morning to tell her he was coming home early. She sounded relieved but stressed. When he pressed further, she confessed that she had a surprise in store that was incomplete. Eventually she admitted that she was converting her unused sewing room into an office and man-cave for his return. His own brother, the carpenter, was doing the work, and Edward realized that it was his voice he had heard in the background on that fateful phone call. His brother was only there to help. Edward begins to sob. Torn from his remorse by a warm hand on his knee, he turns to face the lady beside him.

Reassured by her smile he collects himself. She pats his knee and leaves him be.

Soon they arrive at cruising altitude and the *fasten seat belt* sign vanishes with a chime. Passengers rise to use the toilet and the stewardesses push their metal trays of drinks past his seat. They rattle and thump down the aisle.

Edward considers the challenges he had faced, and dare he admit, his *adventures*. A sly smile creeps across his face. *Was I brave?* he asks. *I keep finding bravery then losing it again.* He sighs. Bravery was never his forte. Boldness does not run through his veins. But he had come where others would not. He had ventured far beyond himself.

And what does it matter, he asks himself, *if I am brave or if I am not?* Mike doesn't care, doesn't care about any of it. He just is. Mike didn't have time for self-reflection, he was too busy living.

The stewardess eventually makes her way to Edward's row and he requests a drink of water. The lady beside him passes the cup over and spills some on his lap. Edward smiles meekly.

I have faced my demons and survived. Am I a better man for it? he asked himself. He then answered;

Perhaps Edward, and while it's more than most have done, those demons won't stop dancing with you until your dance is over. You will always be who you are, but certainly Edward, you have grown, and isn't that what life is all about?.

His crotch itches.

Synopsis

Far removed from the nine to five existence of normal folk, nomads of the modern age scour the hinterlands and remote corners of our globe in a never-ending quest for resources. Modern day explorers, these hard men endure months away from loved ones, exposed to foreign cultures and exotic dangers, all to scrape out a life, and perhaps find a little adventure.

An established career in the First World grows stagnant, an opportunity presents itself, and a timid man ventures abroad.

In the unforgiving world of offshore oil exploration in a small African village, Edward tentatively drifts beyond his self-imposed boundaries, and finds himself drawn deeper into an existence he cannot escape. This is Edward's struggle with his environment as much as his own nature, and the man he desires to be.

About the Author

Darcy Hoover lives in Nova Scotia, Canada.

Beginning his career as a Canadian bush pilot, Darcy has spent the majority of the past decade kicking around various corners of Africa. Having flown helicopters for thirty plus years in over thirty countries, he is presently flying in Trinidad & Tobago.

"The Helicopter Pilot" is his first novel.

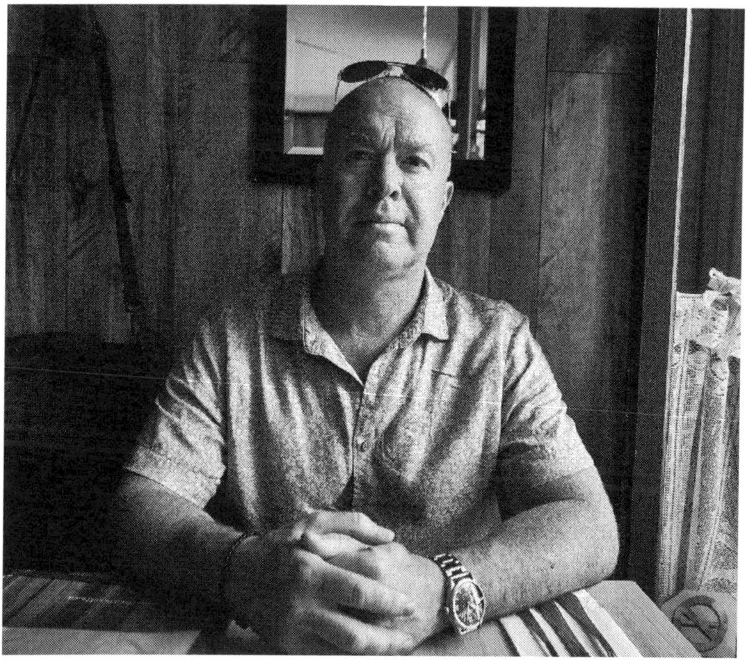

Made in the USA
Middletown, DE
28 March 2019